M000224314

PAINKILLERS

Also by Simon Ings from Gollancz:

Hot Head
Hotwire
City of the Iron Fish
Headlong
Wolves

PAINKILLERS

SIMON INGS

Copyright © Simon Ings 2000
All rights reserved

The right of Simon Ings to be identified as the author
of this work has been asserted by him in accordance with
the Copyright, Designs and Patents Act 1988.

This edition first published in Great Britain in 2014
by Gollancz
An imprint of the Orion Publishing Group
Orion House, 5 Upper St Martin's Lane, London WC2H 9EA
An Hachette UK Company

1 3 5 7 9 10 8 6 4 2

A CIP catalogue record for this book
is available from the British Library

ISBN 978 0 575 13139 2

Typeset by Deltatype Ltd, Birkenhead, Merseyside

Printed in Great Britain by Clays Ltd, St Ives plc

The Orion Publishing Group's policy is to use papers that
are natural, renewable and recyclable products and made
from wood grown in sustainable forests. The logging and
manufacturing processes are expected to conform to the
environmental regulations of the country of origin.

www.simonings.com
www.orionbooks.co.uk
www.gollancz.co.uk

For Anna

HONG KONG
1997

I remember them. Their mouths, and their needles.

There were ten of them, that I recall. Not one of them was out of her twenties, and most were younger. They'd not worked anywhere else, you could tell that. There was nothing usual about them. Nothing used. Armed as they were, they were immune to wear.

I never saw them on the street. Entering the respectable-seeming fabric wholesalers' in whose attic they worked, I cannot remember once passing a girl on her way through to the outside. The godowns and junks, the coconut sellers of the wholesale market, the men sorting clams, the cranes loading trucks parked along the Praya – did they ever see these things? Were they even aware of them? Did they know this was Kennedy Town?

Inside, I never saw them dressed. Perhaps they had no real clothes. I never saw any. I remember sea- and flame-tinted silk; rich brown lace against white skin. That is all. That, and their painted eyes. Their mouths. They never spoke.

They wielded their machines with the cold proficiency of nurses, screwing their needles through your skin as easily as they might puncture the rind of an overripe fruit. Then they would straddle you. Hose scratched your hips, or the buttery heat of flesh slid there, and already it seemed too much to bear. As though, even without the machines, something obscene had taken place inside you: a tumescence of the nerves. So, for a second, you were tempted to pluck out the needles, be done with all of that, and lose yourself instead inside the girl: a comforting, proletarian fuck.

But you never did.

They clipped fine plastic-sheathed wires to the needles they had buried in your stomach, pubis, thighs, and plugged the wires into a box by the side of the bed. Sometimes, as they leaned and twisted, sorting wires, turning dials, you stroked their breasts. You weighed their breasts in your hand as they hung, straining the embroidered cups of a bra or sliding wetly about against a silk slip. You could gently pinch a nipple, or maybe tug a strap free, and the flesh would slip like mercury out of its sheer container and into your sweating hand. You could do that, but it wouldn't make any difference.

Sooner or later, she would turn that dial.

They were merciless.

Eva thought I was having an affair. Someone from work, she thought: a young ambitious business graduate, arcing her taut body so her hips met mine a clear foot above the sheets, and her well-thumbed mobile phone purred rhythmically beneath the damp pillows of our motel bed.

In the day, alone with her imagination, Eva wept. In the

2

evening, when we went out, fashion shades hid the pinkness of her eyes.

She did what she could to keep me solely hers. She went through my pockets while I was in the shower. When I made a phone call from our apartment she would hover behind the door, listening – and she ordered itemised bills that told her nothing she didn't already know.

She dressed up for me. Gucci. Donna Karan. Alexander McQueen. I remember the night I came in pissed from Frank Hamley's birthday party. She stepped out of the bedroom in a new Stella McCartney slip dress and let me take it off her, very slowly.

She did not make love to me. She simply couldn't. The shame had eaten too deep. It had ruined her. She made home instead. She studied *World of Interiors* and *House & Garden*. She hired designers. She bought expensive originals. She browsed for homewares in Seibu and Daimaru. (What would her grand-daddy think, whose head had rolled on Stanley Beach some fifty years before, as he surveyed all this Nipponese extravagance from his frame by the kitchen door?)

She rang me late at the office to ensure I was really there. I always was. Kennedy Town was a very occasional, and strictly daytime, affair: the single release I allowed myself. Anything more ordinary, more human, would have probably finished me off.

Sending Justin to the Higashi school in Tokyo was costing me about £70,000 a year. Then there was the luxury to which Eva was accustomed. Her mother had been swaddling her in Chanel since her fourteenth birthday, and had substituted cash for compassion the moment our son was diagnosed. 'Why can't you treat him properly?' she'd say, and more: unmothering the daughter she had never loved.

To start with, Eva used her allowance to help pay for his

3

therapy. But when at last I threw her mother out the house, the cheques dried up. Justin was still living with us then. He was in the room with us, that evening of the final row, banging his head steadily and with increasing force against the leg of a Franck Evennou chair.

The last I saw of the Kennedy Town girls, they were on TV. I was sitting at the bar in the Big Apple on Luard Road, trying to tune out an early-evening *Mr Bean* rerun, when the picture on the heavy JVC hanging above the optics yawed and span and the TVB Pearl newsroom came up; and after that a shot of Kwai Chung.

The camera was looking inland from the anonymous centre of the container port. Smuggler's Ridge was a grey line above Kwai Chung's brutal grey apartment blocks. In the foreground, police boats were gathering around an antique Saab junk, retrofitted for salvage work. The junk swung about. The gears at the top of the derrick juddered spasmodically.

It was lifting a container from the shallow water: one of those long steel boxes you see being loaded here by their hundreds onto ships bound for Taiwan and Nagasaki. When I looked again they had lowered it onto a concrete jetty. There were no markings on the box's sides; no identifying plates. Trapped sea-water sprayed from the door's seams, drenching the four policemen who were hammering away at the latch. When the door came free the outflow knocked one of them over.

I grinned, ordered another bourbon. Then they opened the door.

Horror isn't dressed up here; it's an ordinary part of life. On Reclamation Street, men chop live turtles to pieces. Calves' heads bleed into the gutters. Later, on the portable TV at a nearby *dai pai dong*, I once saw a policeman slipping the dismembered remains of a shark victim into individual plastic bags. Once, a car had burst into flame on the Eastern Corridor; the tabloid photographer used a telephoto lens to capture the way the driver's hair, caught in the searing updraught, ballooned and sprung away from her crisping scalp.

The way it's all displayed so openly – you never quite get used to it. It wasn't much before eight when the TV displayed the contents of the container.

The police had cordoned off North Street by the time I got there. I stood watching over the heads of a curious crowd of restaurateurs and market traders as the police carried box after box, crate after crate, out of the fabric store. I guessed they were taking away the girls' effects. It couldn't have been anything other than perfume, lipstick, underwear, a little cannabis if they were lucky. Certainly no heroin, no small arms or haul of dirty money. It wasn't that sort of establishment.

I thought about their little black boxes: the dials, the pins and the wires. The scent of rose talcum. I realised I was crying.

Hamley wasn't at home and he'd switched off his mobile. I caught the tram into Central and crawled the bars pretending to look for him until I was good and plastered. I hoped he was safe. If he wasn't, then neither was I. The little black boxes, the women with their shiny, silent mouths. Hamley had introduced me to them, but he knew no more about them than I did. Less. Someone had decided to erase the experiment. Did the erasure extend as far as the punters?

I rang his flat again from a phone box off Citibank Plaza; this time I woke up his girlfriend. I was only making things worse. I crossed Garden Road and waved down a cab.

*

We lived above Magazine Gap, high up the Peak, where the Japanese had erected their Temple of the Divine Wind during the occupation. They never got around to completing it, the British eventually blew it up, and now, from an eighth-floor apartment in nearby Cameron Buildings, Eva's martyred grandfather looked out from his gilt frame on one of the most commanding views in Asia.

I let myself into the apartment as quietly as I could, but I needn't have worried. Eva was out for the count. I swallowed a handful of vitamin B with a glass of tapwater and slipped under the duvet beside her. I lay there, stroking her, stroking her fingers, tracing the elegant curve of her nails, the slight dryness over her knuckles, the hot square of her palm. A little, childlike part of her came alive, just long enough to squeeze my hand. Then I lost her again.

It turned out Hamley had seen the same news report I had. The next day he phoned me at the office, from Macau. He had an onward flight already booked.

'Lisbon?' I said. 'What the hell are you going to do in Lisbon?'

He didn't know. He had no plans. He was just too frightened to stay. 'I mean, Adam, Christ, their *fingers* ... Why the hell would someone do that to their fingers?'

'They did it themselves,' I told him. 'Trying to force the door.'

'You reckon?'

'A school-friend of mine saw it once.' Dimly, it occurred to me that I was making it worse. 'A fire on board a ship he was serving on. The hatches lock automatically. Steam pours in. A rating got trapped in a compartment and tried to claw his way out.'

'I'll call you from Lisbon,' Hamley said. But he never did.

1

LONDON
SPRING, 1998

1

The next time I saw Hamley – the last time – was last spring. Eva and I were back in London by then, running a small café by Southwark Market. If you weren't told about us, you'd never have found us; we were squashed in between on one side a specialist fabric wholesaler who opened maybe one day in the week if the elderly owner could be bothered, and on the other, a glorified garage full of broken barrow wheels and boxes of fluorescent tubing.

Nevertheless, the day had been hectic. A bunch of public relations people from the Tate's Bankside development had adopted us, and someone had put the word around about us at IPC tower, which housed something like a hundred magazine titles. Hannah had to go out twice to buy more bread. I thought we had enough chorizo and pecorino to last us the rest of the week, and we were left with about half a day's supply.

I kicked the last of our customers out around five forty-five. Hannah offered to stay and help clear up but it was her early night so I didn't take advantage. I was stuck here until seven anyway, when Eva arrived with the next week's stock.

I set about sweeping the floorboards clear of crumbs and dropped receipts. In the kitchen, hot water spilled from the tap into a bucket plashed with Dettol, and the antiseptic smell of it was just now cutting under the fug of coffee and burnt sugar and melted cheese. I reached for the handle of the front door so I could sweep the step, when it opened by itself. 'We're closed,' I said – then I registered who it was.

I asked him where he'd been, what he'd been doing with himself, and he said he'd kill for a cup of coffee. The pressure had gone out of the Gaggia but I had a jar of instant in the kitchen. When I got there the bucket was overflowing and a fine skein of spray had fanned the polished plaster behind the sink. The floor tiles were sodden.

Hamley followed me in.

I reached for the mop. 'This won't take a second,' I said.

He closed the door behind him.

It was only now I saw how old he had become – and strange. His shoes, which had that weird, squared-off toe fashionable among the Italians, were scuffed down to the leather. His green wool pleated trousers had lost their crease, and there was a large grease-stain on the right lapel of his nasty brown-pink check sports jacket. A cheap blue-and-white stripe shirt was open at his neck, and white chest hairs poked luxuriously up through the gap. They grew so thickly, I imagined they'd run seamlessly into his beard, if he had one; but his face was so smooth and pink he might have shaved only an hour ago.

He said, 'You'd better pray I'm going to prison.'

'What?'

'The day I come out is the day I'm coming after you. Cunt.' The word sat clumsily in his mouth; he had no practice, saying that sort of thing.

'I don't understand why you're so upset,' I said.

He swallowed, broke eye contact. I thought maybe he was going to leave, as suddenly and inexplicably as he had arrived, but he just stood there, staring off into the middle distance like a bored life model.

He had a face that had lost personality as it aged: his sunken eyes had nothing to say. His cheeks had grown jowly, and taken together with the unremarkable line of his chin, they lent him an air of weakness.

'Frank?'

He reached into his jacket and pulled out a letter for me to read.

It was from Hong Kong. The Top Luck inquiry had sub-poenaed him.

I folded it up and handed it back. I said, 'This hasn't got anything to do with me.'

He said, 'I don't know what it is you think you're running from.'

Not strictly true: in May 1997 an investigation into the murder of senior Hong Kong movie executive James Yau Sau-Lan stumbled across a money laundering operation.

Yau's company, Top Luck Investments, was established in 1989 to finance Cantonese film production in Hong Kong. In 1992 Top Luck floated its film interests on the Hong Kong stock exchange. They even made movies: an output one film critic called 'pre-eminently forgettable, but pure box-office'. So far, so good. The problem came when you looked at the company's annual turnover. 50 million unaccounted-for US dollars passed through Top Luck's books every year.

It wasn't the first time difficult questions had been

asked of Top Luck. As long ago as 1991, an audit report had been ordered on the company at the offices of the Serious Crime Group. The report, which I had compiled and Hamley countersigned, drew only the most ambiguous and tentative conclusions, however, and Top Luck was left free to trade.

The shocking and violent death of its managing director ended Top Luck's run of remarkable – well – *luck*. When it was revealed in court just how gently Hong Kong law enforcement had treated the company over the years, an enquiry was inevitable.

True, it should have been me giving evidence at the inquiry. But nothing in my behaviour since could possibly arouse suspicion. I served out my time, as shabby and undistinguished as countless others. Come the handover of the colony to the People's Republic, I handed in my badge and slogged my way over to Chek Lap Kok with the rest of the apparatchiks.

It was Hamley, my superior, who had fled so suddenly and inexplicably, and several months before his time, and it was hardly surprising that the enquiry's suspicions had fallen first on him.

I tried pointing this out to him, but it didn't do any good. He wasn't much interested in talking. I don't know what he expected to get out of this meeting, and I don't think he knew either, which of course could made him even more frustrated. I don't remember much about what happened next, except that it got physical. In the end I had to throw the Dettol in his face.

I ran water in the sink for him to bathe his eyes, then I went and looked out a towel for him in the cupboard under the stairs. When I got back I found the kitchen empty and the water still sloshing about weakly in the sink. I heard a car pulling away from the kerb. I ran to the door in time to see the reflections of his brake lights gutter and die in the puddles of the opposite pavement. I rubbed my neck. I thought maybe he'd twisted it, but it felt okay now. I went back inside and fished the Wray & Nephew out of the hole in the back of the cupboard under the sink. The bottle was half full. I looked at my watch: I had about half an hour before Eva turned up. So I finished it.

2

By the time she arrived I'd wiped down the tables, mopped the floors, and arranged the packet teas in attractive pyramids in front of the window. But I hadn't even begun to clear the paper liners from out the counter, and I'd clean forgotten to scrub out the juicer. Carrot sediment had dribbled and set on the chrome in dirty orange streaks.

'I can't leave you to do any bloody thing,' she said, scrubbing the sheen off the metal with a scourer.

'Leave it to soak for a couple of minutes, darling.'

She dropped it into the sink, knocked the remaining pieces in after it, and tore off her gloves. Her eyes darted about the kitchen, as she hunted for signs of catastrophe.

She went back to the till. 'Haven't you cashed up yet?'

'I haven't had the chance,' I said, hating the whine in my voice.

She started scooping change out of the till and onto the worktop in short, compulsive jerks. She scraped pennies into her palm, counting them with an expression somewhere between boredom and contempt. I watched her fingers curl and jerk. She wore her nails short now, and even so one of them had torn. The skin on that side of her finger was inflamed.

'Look at me,' I said.

She looked at me. 'What?' she said.

She was my age: twenty-six when we first met. But

nothing that had happened in the years since had changed her the way it had changed me, or Hamley. The crows' feet at the corners of her almond eyes were still the suggestive, bedroomy hints I remembered from our first meeting. Her skin was still sound and white: the proverbial porcelain of Orientalist fantasy. Only her hands had changed, coarsened by her work at the café – but that was nothing a little cream and a return to our old life wouldn't cure.

'What?'

Her mouth was small, her lips full and puckered: when she was younger she used a dark lipstick to make them appear bruised, an eruption of something absurdly sensual at the centre of that perfect sloe-eyed mask.

I said, 'I think the Japs must have put us in a guide. They like our teas.'

She started counting the silver.

'They come here after matinees at the Globe.'

'I'm counting,' she said.

'Twelve,' I said, plucking a number out of the air.

She flapped a hand at me to shut up.

'Six,' I shouted. 'Twenty-four. Plus three.'

'The cakes are in the boot,' she said, not missing a beat. 'Let's not be here all night.'

Our Mazda Xedos was parked opposite. Its silver skin, so striking in the day, reflected back the sodium-lit surfaces of the street like a fly-spotted mirror. I got all the way to the boot before I remembered the keys. Eva had them. Had she watched me, traipsing out here like an idiot? I went back inside. 'I need the keys.'

'Oh—' She pressed a fistful of coins to her forehead, as though the close contact might help her remember what they came to. But it had gone out of her head. She slapped the coins back on the counter with a bang. Several went spinning off and disappeared behind the worktop.

'Sorry,' I said.

She fished in her pocket and threw her keys in my general direction. 'Ta,' I said, for all the good it did.

In the boot there were stacks of flat square boxes: the sturdy, corrugated cardboard ones contained pecan pies and apple tartins and carrot cakes so juicy and fatty you could hardly cut them without the whole thing collapsing into a gooey mess. The thin white ones held rounds of brie. There was a carrier full of large paper packets of coffee beans, and the smell coming out of it was so heady and spicy I stuck my head in the bag for thirty seconds of pleasurable hyperventilation. I slung the carrier round my wrist and carried the brie in on top of a stack of cake boxes.

Eva was bagging up the money at last. I dropped the boxes and the bag on the worktop beside her.

She walked past me and out into the road. I followed her. 'I'm quite happy to unload,' I said.

She hoisted the boxes out of the boot and made for the café. She was holding them away from her as though they were dirty. They wobbled precariously.

'Let me,' I said. I made to take them from her.

She swerved to avoid me, staggering to keep the pile upright.

'Eva?'

'I can manage.'

I glanced into the boot. Something had leaked onto the plastic sheet lining the boot. I ran my finger through the goo and licked it. It was honey.

When I got back inside, I knelt and felt under the sink for the dustpan and brush. They weren't in the usual corner. I reached further in.

Eva stepped towards me, poised for the kill. 'Needing another tipple?' she said.

I backed out the cupboard and looked up at her.

She said, 'I know where you keep it.'

'I'm looking for the dustpan and brush,' I said.

She laughed: it was the closest she ever came to scream-ing. 'Adam, I can smell it on your breath.' I watched her, showing nothing, until she had to look away. She looked up haughtily at the ceiling instead. 'At least have the decency to switch to something tasteless,' she said. 'Vodka. Now isn't that what people usually do?'

Eva turned everything that pained her into social comedy. It made it hard to take her seriously.

Back home, as usual, Boots got under my feet. I sat at the kitchen table with the day's post, kicking him out of the way. He took it well. What a game! Scrabbling for purchase on the terracotta, chewing my shoelaces ...

'Oh for fuck's—'

'Bootsie! Come here.' Eva knelt at the foot of the stairs, arms extended towards him. He ignored her. He growled, terrorising my shoe.

It was all junk mail. I tore it up and threw it in the bin, turned and tripped over the dog.

'Oh for God's sake feed him, can't you see he's hungry?' Eva straightened up. Her hand shook as she gripped the banister. 'I'm going up to change.'

Boots gave her a cursory glance as she climbed the stairs, heels clicking on the unpolished boards.

'Stupid sod,' I told him, when she was gone. 'You're sup-posed to be hers.' Boots wagged his tail. I went over to the fridge and took a half-empty can of shit from the door. He scampered over to his bowl and looked up at me with his big cow eyes, ready for our Big Bonding Experience. I emptied out the can into the bowl. He let go a big grateful fart.

I poured myself a Coke and, hearing Eva ascend the car-peted stairs to our bedroom, spiked it with rum from the

16

bottle on top of the Welsh dresser. I sat back down at the table, drank off half, and tried to put my head back together. Even Boots got bored, I sat there so long, and eventually he hauled his way out of the room.

I watched him go, scratching up the wooden staircase Dad and I had built.

Out in the garage, wrapped in greaseproof paper in the drawer of an old chest, sat the beeswax blocks we had bought, the day we had hammered in the last nail. We figured it would take about a week to rub all that wax into the raw pine, and give Eva the antique effect that she wanted. From where I was sitting, I could see the shiny pool where my dad had started the job.

'Adam?'

I came to with a start. I hadn't heard her come down. I was lost in memories, she had taken off her shoes, and besides, we'd done too good a job, Dad and I – not a board on that staircase that squeaked. I turned and read the clock over the fridge. It was half past midnight.

She came over, took the bottle from the table and screwed the cap on. 'Where does this one live?'

I nodded at the dresser.

Maybe she figured something really was wrong; maybe she was just too tired to fight. She didn't say anything, just put the bottle back where it belonged, then folded up a couple of jumpers that were drying on chairs near the washing machine. She folded them up and dropped them onto the bottom step, ready to take up to the bedroom when she was done here.

'Eva?'

But she was miles away, off in Tidy-up Land. Her own drear little vice. There were some cups on the draining board. She checked they were dry, then she put them away. Boots had finished his shit. She put on rubber gloves, washed his bowl under the hot tap and set it to drain.

'For fuck's sake,' I said.

I'd left the rest of my junk mail and empty envelopes on the table. She sorted through them, choosing what to keep, what to throw away.

I nudged my empty cola glass to the edge of the table. Stuck out a forefinger. Tapped the rim.

The glass shattered at my feet.

Eva, who was far too well bred ever to show a hit, crossed smoothly to the stairs, picked up the jumpers and slapped her way back to the bedroom.

I looked at the glass shards, glinting on the terracotta tiles Dad and I had laid. About an hour later I got around to sweeping them up, and a little after that I turned off the lights.

The bedroom curtains were very thin and I could see well enough to undress without waking Eva. The trouble began when I tried to get Boots off the bed. He was stretched out on my side like he owned the place. 'Piss off.' I nudged him. He woke and wagged his tail.

'Shush.'

He growled happily, paddling the bed like a cat.

'Shut up.'

He lay down again, still on my spot. The room stank of him.

'Jesus.'

I left them to it, got the spare duvet out of the airing cupboard and laid it out on the sofa in the living room. In the bathroom, I sucked water from the tap and swallowed a couple of vitamin B. Closing the cabinet door, I caught sight of myself in the mirror.

There were red marks round my neck, where Hamley had seized me. An unmistakable pattern. By morning they would be bruises.

I sneaked back into the bedroom. They were both asleep again. Boots was laid up against Eva's arse, whimpering softly. Good on you, I thought. Pity you can't like her when she's awake. I dug out a turtle-neck from the cupboard and took it with me into the living room.

That way, in the morning, Eva wouldn't see the marks.

Her knowing was the last thing I needed.

3

When Jimmy Yau Sau-Lan died, no one as much as phoned me. That's how far out of the loop I was. That's how unimportant I had become. I had to find out through the newspaper, and that was only by chance.

Several days after his death – when the news of it was quite stale – the *South China Morning Post* happened to carry a story about the worsening Triad situation in Macau. With pictures. After that, I knew it was only a matter of time before things started falling in on top of me.

What Jimmy Yau was doing in Macau that day no-one seemed to know. But there probably wasn't any mystery in that. It's only a ferry ride away from Victoria Harbour; I used to take day trips there to sample the restaurants.

What is mysterious is how his attacker knew where and when to hide, to catch Jimmy as he drove his hired convertible along the Rua das Lorchas. The grenade fell short, blowing a two-foot-deep hole in the tarmac; it was the shock wave lifted the vehicle over the rail and dumped Jimmy into the Porto Interior. Witnesses said they saw the upturned car plunge in on top of him. The police had divers and dredgers out there all day but they never found his body.

Four days after Hamley's short, sharp visit, Brian and Eddie – Jimmy Yau's sons and heirs – came bounding into the café.

You could tell they were the men of the family now because Eddie had got himself a sensible haircut.

I was in the kitchen, making sandwiches, when I heard the prang and clatter of the table football machine. We'd really only put it in the café for decoration, and it was so near our busiest time, the players must have been treading everyone underfoot as they rushed from handle to handle. I carried in an order of Italian chicken baguettes to the counter. Hannah was spooning froth into the cappuccinos. She placed them one at a time onto a tray. Her hand was shaking.

Then again, her hand was always shaking. People frightened her. The only reason she worked here was her mother arranged it one summer holiday for her and she hadn't the self-confidence to move on. I asked her what was wrong. She nodded at the boys capering about the table. 'Is it all right, Adam?'

I glanced at them, saw who they were, and stretched my mouth into a rictal smile. 'Of course it's all right, Hannah. Can you look after this lot? Table two.' I nudged the tray towards her. Reluctantly, she took it up and headed into the room. She eased uneasily past the brothers. Eddie spun the handles with a flourish and stepped back into her. She dodged out the way – just about. Eddie grinned. Brian scored.

'Fuck me,' said Eddie, surprised.

Brian was faster than his little brother, and more patient. Eddie was smarter. He hunted for an advantage. At a crucial moment he tilted the table by the handles. The legs juddered and scored the floor.

Hannah was still handing out plates and cups to table two, bending from the hips in an unconscious, neurotic display of sexuality. The tourists she were serving – they were so amorphously big, they could have modelled for Gary Larsson – took no notice.

Eddie did. He said something to Brian. Brian studied the backs of her knees. Unable to put it off any longer, I went over. 'Fancy a sandwich?' I said. They turned to me.

Eddie smiled for the both of them. Smiling wasn't in Brian's vocabulary.

'Hey,' said Eddie. He came over and slapped my shoulder. He was wearing a blue and red skinny-rib jumper, rolled up to the elbows. I glimpsed the tangle of scars up his arm, the circular burn-marks from fat cigars. No wonder people weren't eating much. 'Adam, man.'

'Hi, Eddie,' I said.

'Mr Wyatt.'

'Hi, Brian.'

Brian was wearing a black shirt and black jeans. His hair was black. So were the pupils of his eyes; it was like he was frozen in a state of dumbfounded astonishment.

'Are we making a noise here, Adam?'

'It's okay, Eddie.'

'We didn't mean to hurt your table,' said Brian – a truculent child making a rote excuse.

'It's had worse.'

'Hey Brian, it's cool, right?' said Eddie. Jimmy Yau had sent Eddie to study in London, and Eddie had picked up most of his English from parties in Hoxton and raves in posh squats off the M25.

'Yeah,' I said, 'it's cool.'

'Cool.' Brian blinked. It was impossible to say how much Brian understood. It never seemed to make any difference to what he did.

There wasn't anything anyone wanted to say after that, so I went back to the counter.

'Is everything all right?' Hannah squinted across the room, like she was trying to tune out the parts of it that worried her.

'I know them, Hannah. It's fine.' I plucked a handful of slips from the hook by the coffee machine. 'Are these fresh orders?' Without waiting for an answer I returned to the kitchen. If they wanted to say something to me, they were going to have to say it. I didn't have time for their Joe Pesci impressions.

It didn't take them long to start fucking the place about again. When Hannah came in to tell me, she gripped the door-jamb like it was the only thing keeping her upright.

'Get him another coffee,' I told her. 'Sponge him off and calm him down.'

'He wants to complain.'

'So let him.'

'To you.'

I followed her out of the kitchen in time to see a blue Mondeo pull away from the kerb.

'Hey, we're sorry, man,' Eddie said.

The other customers looked like the only reason they were still here was Brian had nailed them to their seats.

'It was an accident, Mr Wyatt,' Brian glowered.

'No problem,' I said.

Hannah meanwhile had fetched a cloth, and she began to mop up the table where Brian had backed into it. Then she knelt and ran the cloth over the floor. Brian had a good long look at her arse.

'That's enough,' I said.

Brian looked at me like I was the one with the problem.

Eddie played diplomat.

'Do you have ten minutes?' he said.

We walked down Stoney Street, past the Clink to the river. The sky was clear, and there were pockets of warmth wherever the sun found a way through to ground level.

Eddie said, 'They listened to Hamley yesterday.'

'Was I mentioned?'

'Oh yes.'

He hadn't wasted any time. I said, 'What's going to happen to me?'

Eddie shrugged. 'Frank knows a little bit. It's nothing Top Luck's lawyers can't chip to shit.'

'He said I knew about the money?'

'He said you turned a blind eye to certain things.'

The road led under Cannon Street railway bridge and slewed right, to meet the embankment. The Thames was still black and gelid, like it had bubbled up from an ice cave. A Japanese family were hesitating outside the Anchor, intimidated by the pub's authentic interior: a warren of gloomy snugs. The pub was set back from the river and I picked us a table in the shadow of the bridge.

I insisted on going in and buying; that way Eddie wouldn't be there to see me pouring one double into another. A thin stream of Coke filed off the pungency of the rum. While Brian and Eddie's lagers were pouring, I drank off a finger's-worth and added some ice.

'Mum wants your help,' said Eddie, when I got back.

'Oh yes?'

Money. Great name, scary woman. I liked her, as much as you can like someone you don't trust.

'She wants you to come round for dinner.'

'I can't see what use I can be to her,' I said.

'Don't worry about that,' said Eddie. 'Think what use she can be to you.'

I thought about Jimmy Yau's promises to me, and I thought about Macau. I thought about Frank Hamley in Hong Kong, telling tales.

'I'll try and make it,' I said. 'Things are busy right now.'

'She's doing eels and bitter melon,' said Eddie. Like this would tempt me.

I wondered if their sister would be there. 'When?' I said.

23

'Next Thursday.'

I shook my head.

'You can make time for it,' Brian said.

'It's Justin's birthday,' I told him.

Brian blinked, like, so what? But Eddie was all heart. 'Hey, man, we didn't know. How old is he, anyway?'

We walked back to the café. I thought they were just going to get back in their car, but Brian whispered something in his brother's ear, and after a short conference, conducted out of my hearing, they followed me in.

There was a queue waiting to pay stretching almost to the glass partition, and Hannah had given the till a nervous breakdown. Eddie and Brian waited patiently while I sorted her out and helped her get through the line. When the counter was free, Eddie and Brian came and leaned there. Eddie with me, Brian with Hannah: he had drills for eyes. Hannah couldn't meet his stare. She turned her back on him and started wiping down the juicer. He watched her backside.

'I'll get Mum to suggest another night, then.'

'Sure,' I told Eddie. 'Right.'

'My name is Brian,' said Brian, startling us both. Eddie watched his brother. 'We're in film,' Brian said.

The object of Brian's affections ducked down out of sight and changed the CD in the machine. And changed it again. It was a good machine – a Nabeshima – and it had lots of buttons ...

Brian knew when he was being snubbed. He shoved his fists in the pockets of his jeans and tried to act casual.

Eddie sighed. 'Good to see you, Adam,' he said.

'Likewise.'

Eddie led his brother out of the café. At the doorway he turned. 'Hey, Adam—' He held up something small and shiny. Oblique sunlight cast strange, intagliated shadows over his scarred arm. 'Catch.' He threw it to me. I snatched at it and missed. It ricocheted painfully off my thumb and bounced across the floor. It was the ball from the football table.

Eddie grinned. 'Too much Coca-Cola, mate,' he said.

4

I was already half-way up Hemingford Road before I remembered that tonight was Eva's dinner party. Angelica Loh and her husband had already arrived, drinking brandy from Eva's best glasses. Them I could cope with; they were the least pretentious of Eva's Hong Kong friends. Loh Han-Wah was a patents lawyer with run-down offices in the City. Angelica had resigned from her stylist's job at *Elle Decoration* to look after their second baby and was well into her second year of domestic contentment. They had left Hong Kong in 1995, eighteen months before we did, and had been good to us when we first arrived. The others, who arrived in dribs and drabs over the following hour, were people I could have lived without – women who spent their lives giving each other dinner parties to help out various fashionable charities.

How they'd rolled up in London I was never too sure; the Handover hadn't triggered the exodus some British newspapers had expected, and most of the colony's smart money had stayed put. Maybe their stockbroker husbands had caught wind of the depression soon to sweep over East Asia. Princesses from mansions overlooking Shek O, they had emigrated en masse to Little Venice and the King's Road, acquiring, after a couple of British winters, the lost and ludicrous aspect of exotic birds shivering their lives away in a municipal zoo.

This evening Eva – ever ready to bind herself to the rack of social disappointment – had invited them over for supper in our tiny, petit-bourgeois kitchen.

While Eva poured brandy in the living room for David Kwok, the art dealer, and Flora Chau and Brenda Lai, Loh Han-Wah followed me downstairs to the kitchen and helped me set the table. His eyes twinkled behind round wire-framed spectacles as we worked. 'What's for dinner, Adam?'

'I've no idea,' I admitted, my mind still occupied with the day's disastrous trade at the café. 'Here, we'll need an extra spoon, apparently.'

'Ah,' he said. He liked me, but my reputation made him uneasy. He always seemed to be about to make some devastating witticism, but he never did.

'Business going well?' I asked. A client of his was contesting rights to a minidisc format. His firm and the suits from Nabeshima had been head-to-head for months.

'I think we're ready to settle.'

'Shall we come down?' This from Eva, peering at us from over the banister.

Loh smiled vaguely at her. His glasses, reflecting the hob light, hid his eyes.

'Sure,' I said.

'Darling, you're always *so* enterprising,' said David Kwok. Kwok ran an off-Bond Street gallery of antique oriental fabrics, prints, and what the decoration magazines call 'artefacts'. It was all unbelievably nasty stuff. Since shifting operations from Hong Kong's Hollywood Road to London's West End he had begun to fancy himself as a connoisseur, which for him meant adding a nought to everything and screaming abuse at the poor sods at Phillips whenever a piece didn't make its reserve. 'And how long has it been open?' He tented his fingers in front of his mouth, waiting for the response. His hands, smooth and plump as a child's, always unnerved me.

'Eighteen months,' Eva told us. 'The returns are excellent, especially with all the work that's going on in Greenwich.'

The trouble with Eva was, she had to talk everything up. She had to compete. Our café wasn't anywhere near Greenwich – the Millennium Dome was two whole bends in the river further east – it was in Southwark.

But oh no, Eva had to compete. 'It's a bit of fun,' she said, with a casualness any fool could have seen through. 'Just while Adam gets started again.'

I stared at her. Brenda and Flora exchanged glances. Loh fixed me with his speculative smile.

'That's *so* good,' his wife, Angelica, enthused. She laid her perfectly manicured hand on Eva's wrist. 'It's a *great* idea.' She was a dreadful Pollyanna, but she knew how to keep potentially acid evenings like this bright and bubbling; I was grateful.

'Red, anyone?' I said – my own attempt at social lubrication. Very suave. Very urbane. Everyone here knew I'd not be 'starting again' any time soon. How could I, given the cloud surrounding my departure?

Against all evidence, I had given Top Luck a clean bill of health. If now the enquiry did not think I was culpable, it was only because my subsequent performance provided me with a dismal kind of alibi. I spent a lot of time between '92 and '97 on sick leave. Dreadful, shrieking stomach pains, like talons, shredding my insides, had me in and out of clinics for months. The doctors couldn't find anything. And the rum smell in my skin and hair, the long lunch-hour, the tie askew and the three day-old shirt gave personnel more straightforward reasons for my poor results.

'And how are *you*, Adam?' said Angelica, treating me like an invalid as usual. 'How are *we*?' I'd half-expected her to say

– though I saw her difficulty. The codsup I had made of Hong Kong was hardly for the dinner-table. If it hadn't been for the Handover, I wouldn't have lasted the year. As for another appointment – well, word travels fast in this business.

Easier, then, to make out that I'd suffered a misfortune, a breakdown, ME – something for which I could not be held culpable. 'Oh, keeping busy,' I said, in my best duffer-pottering-about-the-garden manner. 'Eva keeps me in trim.'

David Kwok laughed a dirty laugh. Eva coloured up.

'And you, David,' I said, feeling the heat of the second bottle of merlot rise in my throat. 'Flogged any treasures recently?'

Nobody else missed my tone – Loh's spectacles were flashing like there were LEDs built into the rims – but David Kwok was too fat and too happy with himself ever to notice a hit from me. 'You must come,' he went on, explaining about his latest venture, a fine arts gallery in Dering Street. 'It's next to Anthony D'Offay.'

He had new pieces arriving from mainland China every couple of months. How he got away with it I could never figure. Most of it belonged in a museum, which is probably where it originated. David Kwok was going up in the world. The first time I met him he was churning out fake Alexander McQueen for Stanley Market.

The phone rang. I stood up. David, bless him, decided he still wasn't getting enough attention, and got to the phone before me. '*Wai*?'

I took the receiver off him. He winced and shook his hand, like I'd hurt him. As if.

'Adam?'

'Yes.'

'It's Money.'

I swallowed. 'Uh-huh.' I couldn't have been put more off my stride if she'd turned up at the door.

'Did Eddie behave himself today?'

I glanced round at the dining table. Everyone was looking at me. 'Yes,' I said.

'You know how those two are.' She made them sound like a couple of feisty dogs.

'Yes,' I said.

'I forgot it was Justin's birthday, I'm so sorry.'

'That's fine,' I said, as neutrally as I could.

She twigged at last that something was wrong. 'Have I caught you at an awkward moment?'

'We've got some friends round.'

'Who is it?' said Eva.

'It's a *woman*, Eva!' said David Kwok. As though women were an exotic breed of deer. 'A well-spoken *woman*!' He turned to look at me over his shoulder, all coquettish. I half expected him to flutter his eyelashes. 'Very mysterious.'

'Would you like me to call back?' said Money.

'No, no. Let me take it upstairs. Stay on the line, yes?'

Eva wanted me to tell her who it was, but David was prancing around like a fairy, distracting us all. '*So* sorry,' he was saying, 'I hear a bell, I answer it – just like Pavlov's dog.'

I ran up to the living room, where Boots was flopped disconsolately on the sofa. He stood up and shook himself, expecting some attention. I ignored him, and took the stairs to the bedroom two at a time. But Boots was too fast for me: as I opened the bedroom door he muscled in past me and jumped onto the bed. I had to tussle with him to get to the phone. I snapped up the aerial. 'Mrs Yau?' I sat down on the edge of the bed and held Boots at bay by his flea collar. He licked my hand.

'Eddie tells me you have a lovely café,' Money said.

God knows where that came from. I could hardly imagine Eddie saying, 'Guess what, Mother, Adam Wyatt and his wife run this lovely café ...'

29

'Thank you,' I said.

'Look, Adam, I realise you're busy but we really ought to meet up. I haven't seen you since Jimmy ... How does next Friday suit you?'

'I'll have to ask Eva,' I said.

'I'm not inviting Eva.'

This was more the woman I remembered; I almost smiled.

'Frankly, I don't think she'd be too delighted to know I was seeing you.'

'Do you have to tell your wife everything?'

I stayed silent – the telephonic equivalent of a shrug.

'I don't suppose for a second you've told her about Frank Hamley.'

Boots leapt on the bed and nuzzled the phone. I clouted him and he fell off the mattress.

'Adam?'

'I'm here.'

'Friday, then,' she said.

'Friday I work at the café.'

'Wednesday?'

'I don't think so.'

'You might want to have a read of today's *Post* before you put me off altogether.'

I swallowed.

'Adam?'

'What's happened?'

'Frank was knocked down by a hit-and-run crossing Queensway.'

I felt as though I were falling.

'He was due to give further evidence. They don't think he'll regain consciousness.'

'What are you saying?'

'The inquiry is going to be looking for a new witness.'

'You know I wouldn't cooperate.'

'I know,' Money said. 'But I'm not the one who ran over Frank's head.'

5

I got downstairs again to find things warming up pleasantly. Angelica and Loh Han-Wah were holding hands, listening to a funny story of Eva's. David Kwok had drunk himself silent and Brenda and Flora were bullying him into making a liberal gesture for some charity or other. Hardly anyone noticed when I took my seat.

'But you *must*,' Flora insisted. David blinked. 'It'll bring so many interesting people to your new gallery—'

Loh's laughter drowned out Flora's third-degree. Eva, pleased with her story, leaned over to me. 'Who was it?' she said.

'Some old friends,' I said, off the top of my head.

'Who?'

'Mike and Ylwa,' I said. They were old acquaintances of mine from Hong Kong. Still there, for all I knew.

'Really?' Eva looked like she wanted all sorts of gossip, so I set about clearing the table of empty bottles. 'More wine, anyone?'

Flora and Brenda wanted David Kwok to auction something for a regional opera company they fancied. 'Something small,' Flora suggested. 'Something jade.'

They all left early, off to mansions in Barnes and mill-houses in quaint little villages served by the M4. Eva washed up. I dried.

'Even when you grill it, it just falls apart,' Eva complained. 'Let's not do it again.'

She had cooked a favourite of hers this evening – talapia

with a peach salsa. She'd lifted it from a copy of *House & Garden*.

'It was delicious,' I said, and meant it.

'It looked like we'd scraped it off the grill.'

'Nobody cares about that.'

But Eva cared. Nothing, apparently, had been quite right. 'We should just have plonked a bowl of fruit on the table,' she said, demolishing each stage of her perfectly nice meal in turn.

'You like tirami su.'

'It was too wet,' she said.

I let it go. It wasn't the food was upsetting her, it was the people, and the games they played.

There was a third of a bottle of red still on the table, but I resisted and screwed the cork in.

Eva snapped off her rubber gloves. 'Let's leave this.'

'I'll finish.'

'No. Come to bed.'

I followed her up.

In the bedroom, she took off her earrings and heeled her way out of her shoes. Boots bounded up the stairs. Eva swung the door shut on him and after a couple of minutes whining and scrabbling, he got the message and thumped back down the stairs.

I watched her undress. It had been a long while since we had been this intimate with each other. Her body surprised me. The way it had thickened. Was her period due? I had no idea. She slipped into bed.

I finished undressing and got in beside her. The sheets smelled of dog.

She reached for me. Her hands touched my hands. Fumbling, I took hold of her. She rolled onto her front, moving closer. I laid my hand like a dead thing on her back.

The knobs of her spine made a ridged line against my palm.

'Thanks for tonight,' she said.

'I'm sorry I got a bit pissed.'

'Did you?'

I yawned. I couldn't help it.

'What did they have to say?'

'Who?'

'Mike and Ylwa.'

I'd had time, by now, to get my story straight. 'It was a social call,' I said. They're coming to London in about a month.'

'It was nice of them to look us up.' She smiled, the way she used to. 'Don't you think it's nice?'

'Yeah,' I said, resisting another yawn.

She touched my cheek. 'Sleep tight.'

I closed my eyes. Relief flooded me. I couldn't lie to her any more – not tonight.

I lay there a minute, forcing my shoulders to untense. I thought she was going to turn off the light, but nothing happened. I opened my eyes. She was looking at me. 'What are those marks on your neck?'

I rubbed at them, hiding them; I turned the other way. 'Just muck, I suppose. I should have had a shower when I came in.'

She believed me. Because I was a good liar. Because it was easier.

She turned out the light.

6

Money Yau lived in one of those huge Georgian piles over-looking Blackheath. I had the taxi drop me at the bottom of Eliot Hill, and walked the last half mile from Lewisham. The streetlights fell away at the edge of the scrubland, and the roads that criss-crossed the darkness were barely wide enough for the BMWs and Volvos that frequented them. In place of road markings were lines of fussy white stakes, everywhere chipped and scraped after one too many private parties at the V&A, one too many bottles of rioja at Zinc.

Jimmy Yau bought the place, thinking to retire here come the Handover. He never lived to enjoy it. He'd have been the only householder on Wat Tyler Road who didn't belong to the Chelsea Arts Club. What he had seen in the place I had no idea, unless it was an ancestral preference for high ground. I imagined him, in furs and leather helmet, defending his hilltop palisade. It was the only picture I had of him that ever seemed to sum him up.

The gate was open when I arrived. I caught a glimpse of white walls, elegant high windows, honeysuckle – the security light flashed on the moment I stepped on the gravel. I stumbled through a halogen glare and took shelter in the porch. They must have noticed the light go on inside because the front door was already ajar.

'Adam.'

I was still dazzled, and the light from the hall was streaming out past the girl who stood there. All I could see was her silhouette.

'Remember me?' she said. There was an edge to her voice; she had expected more from me than this rabbit-in-the-headlights gawp.

'Zoe,' I said, stupidly.

She was at least as tall as her father. Much taller than Brian and Eddie. I wondered if they envied her that – her physical similarity to their father.

'Come on in.'

'I hoped you'd be here,' I said, stepping past her. Her hair smelled sweet and androgynous. I watched as she shut the door.

She was wearing a georgette slip dress sheer enough that I could follow her long, too-slender legs past the beaded hem. Her Miu-Miu sandals were wafer-thin, the straps wire-tight.

'Mother's in the kitchen still. Would you like a drink?' The pearl studs in her ears picked up and accentuated her eerie, blind-seeming grey eyes. Her teenage gawkiness was gone, but she had filled out hardly at all. Her breasts were tiny, pointed nubs against the grey silk. She looked more than ever like a half-starved Siamese.

I followed her into the living room.

'Do you still drink rum?' she said; she was watching me in the mirror above the drinks cabinet.

'White, if you have it.'

'Bacardi?'

My mate Ron. 'Why not?'

Her eyes didn't leave me once.

I sat down uninvited on the sofa and stared into the fire. 'I noticed there's a film on tonight. One of Brian and Eddie's.' The fire was one of those gas contraptions, the flames too blue at their heart to be convincing. 'I think I remember it. What's it called?'

'Full Auto Angel,' she said.

She sat on the seat next to mine, sipping from a glass that was clear and ice-filled, like mine. How old was she now? Twenty. Twenty-one. Her arms were smooth and unblemished. I thought about Brian and Eddie. I wondered where her scars were.

'How's Eva?' she said.

'Fine.'

'Eddie said your café's nice.' She drew her nails through her hair, drawing it from her ear, showing off her smooth, freshly shaved arm-pit.

I looked away. 'I guess it's what I need right now,' I said, and strained the rum out of the ice. As soon as I swallowed

I knew it was a mistake. Everything went rubber: my neck, my gut. I closed my eyes, fighting a sudden nausea. Deep inside, the aliens flexed, multiple elbows drumming at my chest wall as they sucked the clear hot goodness from my intestines.

'And Justin?'

'Justin's well,' I said, when I could.

'Where is he now?'

'A school in Kent.'

I tried breathing, and decided it was good.

'Knox Lodge,' I said. 'It's a special school. New.'

'I missed you at the service.'

'I wasn't invited.'

'Would you have come?'

Jimmy Yau was always getting in the way of Zoe and me. Death itself had not stopped him.

'Dad liked you a lot,' she said. She looked at the fire. She drank her drink. 'Do you miss him?'

I didn't know what to say.

She put her glass down with a thunk on the coffee table. 'Nobody else does,' she said.

'I'm sure that's not true.'

'Mother's angry with him.'

'That's not so unusual—'

'Granddad's lost his mind. Brian and Eddie, well, they wouldn't show feeling if you chopped them into little pieces in front of each other.'

I dared a small smile.

Zoe watched me. As usual, she was hungry for something.

'I miss him,' I said. 'In some ways I'm not sorry about what happened. I took a lot of damage, knowing him.'

'Adam?'

I turned in my seat. Drops of split rum chilled my thigh.

'I hope you set your video.' Money Yau had aged a lot in

the two years since we'd last met. The whiteness of her hair I had expected; but not the way her face had sunken in. 'I'm so glad we've done this at last,' she said.

'Money.' I stood up. 'It's good to see you.'

Her eyes, which had always seemed so mild and reticent, alone still held the spark of life. And her voice – that too remained poised and youthful. The overall effect was of a vital and indomitable woman looking and speaking through a grotesque paper mask. 'Come through to the dining room,' she said. 'Everything's set.'

Eddie and Brian were carrying dishes in from the kitchen. Eddie grinned his not-quite-friendly grin and asked me how I was doing. Brian, distracted by my arrival, lost the plot and began orbiting the table, anxiously sniffing the food on each plate. Obviously this meal was something he found profoundly unconvincing – a charade he might yet penetrate, given brains enough and time.

Either Eddie had been having a little joke with me, or Money had changed her mind about serving eels. Crispy duck was followed by red mullet in a hot ginger sauce, a dish of bitter melon, and a salad of cucumber and beansprouts and about half a ton of salt. I'd forgotten how much of a taste I'd acquired for the Hong Kong style: I ate so fast I hardly spoke. Plus, I was trying to soak up Zoe's too-generous glass of rum. My insides were okay but my head still felt like it was bobbing about near the ceiling rose. When I swallowed it lashed about at the end of my rubber umbilical neck.

'It's quite an early film,' Money said. 'Isn't it, Eddie?'

'Yeah,' said Eddie, poking experimentally at his mobile phone.

'My husband did the choreography.'

It had always puzzled me, the simple pride Money took in talking up her sons' films. As though she didn't know full well where they came from, or what they had involved. I wondered what the commissioning editor at Channel 4 would think – some silk-tie innocent, scoffing posh school dinners in the Union – were he suddenly to be confronted by Eddie's smile, Brian's drowned eyes, their arms, their burned and shredded backs.

I tried to get her to talk about Jimmy, I suppose to show Zoe I cared.

'Privacy came naturally to Jimmy,' Money said. 'It's very hard, now that he's gone, to know what to do for the best.'

'Zoe tells me his father doesn't understand what happened.'

'Zhenshu's senile,' she said, flatly, refusing my easy sympathy. There were other things on her mind.

'Most of these are businesses I've never heard of. I'm beginning to think some of these so-called managers are taking me for a ride.'

I nodded and grunted, my mouth full of rice scented with lotus flowers. I felt awkward, listening to Money's business problems when her children were in the room. Not that Brian or Eddie were paying any attention. Some communication was taking place between them, some wordless, piquant traffic. They seemed to stir and turn their heads and move their hands in unison, as though this unlooked-for and unprecedented screening had triggered old routines in them.

'The tax office sent me another reminder.'

I dragged my attention back to Money. She was still on about her financial worries.

'I know they're going to fine me but it's the interest they charge that frightens me.'

A whole case of rum couldn't have made that evening any more surreal than it already was. Each year organised crime launders about twenty billion US dollars through Hong

Kong; not a little of it passed through Jimmy Yau's hands at one time or another. And here was his widow, worrying over her annual tax return.

The first, stylophoned bars of 'Für Elise' burst from Eddie's jean-jacket. He took out his mobile and thumbed it. 'Hello?'

'Edward, turn that thing off.'

'Seb? Right—'

'Ed—'

'Cool.'

'Edward, we're eating.'

Smoothly, Eddie got up from the table and walked to the window, phone still pressed to his ear. 'Eleven thirty, mate. Yeah. Kickin'. Rice grains fell from the lap of his linen trousers.

Everything was 'cool' with him. 'Big', or, even 'wicked'. Things were 'happening' with him. His laughter was clipped, anxious, and coke-fuelled. Brian, meanwhile, sat watching his younger, smarter brother – the grub who had usurped him – with eyes flat and impenetrable as steel plate.

'It takes me the whole of every morning, just replying to official enquiries about the estate,' Money complained.

I couldn't work out what she wanted from me. She wasn't so naïve: her anxiety over such routine matters had to be part of some strategy. But what was she angling for? I gave her the calm-down speech I'd used on tax evasion suspects: your tax man is your friend and your confessor, with good will all can be redeemed, and so on.

Brian meanwhile had turned his attention back on his food. He prised a chopstick into the poached eye of his fish and used it to snap the bony plate over the gill.

'Brian. Stop it.'

Brian stared his mother down.

'So, Adam,' she said, fingers fluttering at her throat.

Brian unnerved her – there was too much of his father in that dead stare of his. 'How long can an appeal like that drag on?'

Eddie laughed. 'Yes, mate. Yes. Hell, mate, yes. Hell, yes. YES! Yes mate.'

The skull came to pieces under Brian's chopstick. He mushed the cream inside fish's tiny brain pan.

'Thirty, forty minutes, mate,' said Eddie. 'Yes. Yes.' He thumbed off his mobile. 'Fucker,' he said.

He came back to the table and clapped Brian on the shoulder. Brian stood up and followed his brother out of the room.

Money said nothing, just let them go. Was she intimidated, or just fed up? Her face was too loose and sunken to read.

The front door banged shut.

'Well,' she sighed, 'let's all have a drink.' She said it as though she'd just put two toddlers to bed. Not intimidated, then – and I had the sense that her flighty-and-no-good-with-numbers routine hadn't been meant for me at all, but for them.

7

She led us back into the living room. 'What'll you have, Adam?'

I'd eaten well, so I risked a whisky and soda. Zoe went to the sideboard and made three.

'I was hoping you could come visit me sometimes,' said Money, 'and help me with all this.'

'It would be worth investing in some professional advice,' I said. Zoe handed me a glass. I sipped. It was practically neat. 'I can't see that I'd be much use.'

Zoe sat on the sofa beside her mother and set down their

glasses. The liquid inside them was pale, the soda water fizzing furiously. I sipped again from mine. There was barely a hint of gas. Was Zoe trying to get me drunk?

'Of course,' said Money, 'Zoe does what she can to help.'

Zoe shrugged.

'You know she deferred a year at college? To help me.' Money smiled at her daughter. 'But I was never a good listener, was I?'

Zoe returned her mother's secret smile. Had they had a row? Were they making up?

'Like I said, professional help will be cheaper in the long run.'

'But complicated.'

'How so?'

'Adam,' said Money. 'I want you to do me a favour. I want you to deal with Jimmy's affairs.'

I stared at her.

'Zoe stayed home to help, but I'd sooner she used the year to relax. It's been a difficult time for us all, and she deserves the time for herself.'

'I don't think—'

'I want her to travel, to enjoy herself.'

'Another drink?' Zoe said. I looked at my glass. It was empty.

'Jimmy's affairs weren't always very clear,' Money admitted. 'I don't want her getting into trouble.'

She'd rather I did. Well, I could hardly blame her for that. I wouldn't want my child associated with Jimmy Yau's 'unclear' affairs, either.

'What about Eddie?' I said, angling for an easy out.

Money snorted. 'I need help, not stunts.' Her contempt for her son was appalling. She had a crudeness that had been bred out of Eva's friends, though they all came from the same stock.

41

'I'm sure he could do a good job,' I said, 'given the chance.'

Zoe set down my glass. There wasn't the faintest hint of soda in it. She knew my weakness. She wanted her mother to know it, too, for some reason.

Still, it was my out, so I took it; I drained the glass in one. The aliens in my chest spasmed and thrashed. 'I can't help you,' I said. 'For one thing, I've already got a job.'

Money laughed. 'You surely don't mean the café.'

'Eva's relying on me,' I said.

For another thing, I was breathing fire into her face. Sweat had broken on my forehead, that had nothing to do with the gas fire. Even I could smell it. Whisky, Wray & Nephew, last night's wine and God knows what else. She really should have taken the hint.

'Would you like another?' said Zoe, reinforcing the obvious point.

'Leave him alone,' Money said.

None of us said very much for a while. We had moved into new territory. Black water. The deep dead sea where deals rise like foam off the tip of an oar – and last about as long. There is nothing so evanescent as organised crime.

'I want you to tidy up Jimmy's affairs,' Money said. 'Turn as much as you can into legitimate interests. Liquidate the rest.'

The enormity of it misfooted me. I struggled not to laugh.

'Is that so unreasonable a request?'

I turned to Zoe. The kid who thought she could show me up with a couple of shots of Glenlivet. 'Is this what you've been up to, Zoe?' It was too absurd. 'Taking apart a triad?'

She sighed. 'We control fifty money-changers in the Hong Kong-Kowloon region. Four money transmitters, a securities broker, two remittance corporations. Dad shut down Miami operations in '95, once FinCEN got wind of our Mexican giro house investments, and converted them to roubles.

Thirty billion, all ready to plough into St Petersburg, only the Florence DIA arrested dad's co-investor. He managed to divert about half our moneys into arranging exports of Kazakhstani mercury. The money we get now from the mining companies in Brazil we trade for cocaine in Columbia and change that for Italian gold in Slovakia.'

I stared at her.

'We are not a fucking *triad*.' She refilled my glass.

I looked at Money. She was serious. I looked at Zoe – her hungry eyes.

They were monsters.

'You want to demolish all that?'

'Top Luck's just the weakest, the first to go,' Money sighed. 'But without Jimmy, everything else will come apart in time.'

Zoe explained. 'When we launder money from Shenzhen, we take eighty per cent. The market rate is only sixty, so why do our clients keep coming back to us? Last year we exported a consignment of caesium to Korea, and they insisted on paying us for red mercury. That's triple our expected profit and we—'

'I don't want to know this,' I said.

They tried again.

I stood up. 'I don't want to know.'

'We're sitting on a time bomb, Adam—'

'It had nothing to do with me.'

'No,' Money agreed, coldly. 'But Top Luck has.'

Slowly, clumsily, I sat down. My hand was shaking so much, Zoe had to take the glass off me before she could fill it.

Money cocked her head on one side, examining me. 'How did you think you were keeping the enquiry at bay? Personal charm?'

'Jimmy said—'

'Jimmy protected Frank Hamley, too.'

I tried picking up my drink. The rug was old but fuck it, I thought, whisky won't stain it. I wiped my chin.

'I'm the one protecting you now,' Money said. 'I'm all that's standing between you and the inquiry. For the moment, you're safe. But it's only a matter of time before my bluff is called. Look at Hamley.'

I looked at Zoe instead. She was studying the ice in the bottom of her glass. It had been Money's idea to get me drunk. That's why Zoe was still here. Money was using her daughter to soften me up.

I thought about what would happen if I said yes to them. The work they would have me do. The lies I would have to tell Eva. The double life I would lead. Zoe's thin arms, her blind, hungry doll eyes. The androgynous scent of her skin, like a perfume.

I thought about what would happen if I said no. About Hong Kong, about testifying at the inquiry, about what I would say. I thought about Jimmy's colleagues, clinging to the wreckage of their fractured empire, watching me from the gallery, watching me on TV, reading about me in the papers and on the internet, waiting for the moment when the gweilo starts to squeal.

Or rather, not waiting. What load does it take to crack open a skull? Does the speed of the car make a difference? The pressure in the tyre?

'Which is it to be?' Money said.

I told her no.

Never, but never, make a grand exit. Be quiet, dignified, melt into the background, fade gently away – then if something goes wrong you won't make a prat of yourself.

They rang me a taxi but I didn't want to linger there a moment more than I had to. I said I'd wait outside and get some air before the ride; I said a few other things as well, and I don't think they were sorry to see me go.

They swung the door on me and I headed down the gravel drive between rhododendrons and untidy ornamental firs. It was a clear night, and cold, and the air hit the back of my throat like menthol.

The moon, a fat crescent, lit my way to the gate. A partial eclipse had taken a bite out of its bottom corner; it hung there, precise and asymmetrical, like a carefully turned engine part.

I cast my mind back, trying to recall when I had last seen the stars. A summer night beside the Cam, in my first summer vacation. Sleeping under a net on a small game reserve in Zimbabwe. The night the electricity failed in the resort town of Buzios, during my six-month affair with KPMG Rio ...

I'd got as far as the open gates when the security light from Hell came on again to light my way. Even reflected off the gateposts, the glare was unbearable. I winced, shielding my dark-adapted eyes, and tripped on something hard and unyielding.

I threw my hands out to break my fall and crashed like a tree. Something big and sharp razored my palm. I sat up, dragged in a burning breath, and held my hand up to the moonlight. There was a glass shard there, a big one, sticking up out of a rising pool of blood. Black blood filled the basin of my palm and dribbled off.

Shock made me stupid: I pulled the shard out. I must have screamed, but no one came to the door.

I got up and saw what had tripped me. A metal plate: the gates locked into it when they were shut. I catted. Saliva ran down my chin. I wiped it away with my good hand. It smelled of spirits and fish and soy sauce. Blinking against the harsh light, I staggered back to the house.

I rang the bell and waited, studying the wound in the light from the glass-panelled door. Bits of shattered glass were still buried there. I could see them glittering – bright flecks. Or was it bone?

The door opened. 'Adam,' Zoe said, then, 'Jesus.'

'I fell,' I said.

'Let me look,' said Zoe. She sighed, and led me down the hall.

There were voices coming from the kitchen. Music and screaming. *Full Auto Angel* through a cheap speaker.

The kitchen wasn't a bit like the rest of the house. The red floor tiles were lifting. The table was topped with sickly yellow Formica.

'All I need is a tissue,' I said. 'I'll take the cab to casualty.'

Money was clearing up after our meal. There were garlic skins and fish-guts all over the chopping block.

'Don't be silly,' she said. 'Zoe, get me the first-aid box.'

The TV sat on the top of the fridge.

Brian was tied to a table. A girl in a bikini and RayBans was whipping him with a car aerial. The scene was cut to look like a special effect.

In a moment the door would burst in under a hail of shotgun pellets. Cantonese extras in Versace jeans and blue sweatbands identifying them as members of the secret Order of the Paper Chrysanthemum would steal in like ghosts, silence the girl with a touch, and pass through.

Brian would not appear again until the third reel, posing as a wheelchair-bound cripple. Taken apart and reassembled, the wheelchair would in Brian's hands make a primitive but impressively loud heavy machine gun, in a scene praised by cult film critic Kim Newman for its 'exuberant post-Besson pastiche', and later analysed shot by shot in a long behind-the-scenes exclusive in *Fangoria* magazine.

Zoe came back in with a Tupperware cake-box and a bottle of medicinal alcohol.

Money dipped the bottle over a cotton swab and cleaned the cut, then used a pair of eyebrow tweezers to pull the bits out. I told her not to probe so deep, to let me go and get the cut seen to properly, but she wasn't listening. I winced and tugged away. She leaned her wrist into mine, pinning my hand against the table, and probed still deeper.

'Fuck! Shit!'

'Oh, grow up,' she muttered, peering myopically into the tear.

Eddie was taunting his pursuers, knocking one after the other off the top of the HSBC building in ever more gymnastic and unlikely ways. It was like watching music. Like jazz. Like the dialogue you get between guitars. Eddie was much fitter then.

She rummaged about in the cake box and came out with paper sachet. She tore it open and withdrew a bright, scythe-shaped needle. Now I was really in trouble. 'I'd rather—'

'Oh Adam,' she said, losing patience with me, 'I do this all the time for the boys.'

The girl in the bikini had revived and was being comforted by her faithful, somewhat boyish female companion.

I thought about Brian and Eddie – their scarred arms.

'The scraps they get into, if I hadn't learned how by now we'd never be out of Casualty.'

'But my palm—'

'Put your hand on the table.'

'Cab's here,' said Zoe, leaning in.

'Tell him we'll be a few minutes.'

'I can—'

'Oh for God's sake, Adam keep still.'

I swallowed. 'Is that proper surgical thread?'

'For heaven's sake,' she sighed. She pressed the needle in.

47

'Christ!'

'What now?'

'You can't just poke it in like that.'

'Why not?'

'Because it *hurts*, you stupid bitch. It hurts, damn it.'

She blinked at me. 'Brian and Eddie don't carry on like this,' she said.

'Here,' said Zoe, coming in again. She handed me a glass. It was so full the rum dribbled off my fingers.

'What?' she said, meeting my eyes with her hungry, Siamese smile.

'Now. Adam,' said Money, '*hold still.*'

Zoe hunkered down beside me and slid her arm round my shoulders. I looked away, at her hand. The long bones of her fingers, her delicate wrist, the blue tracery under her skin. I smelled her again.

Money's needle went in, and out, and in.

8

The letter came lunchtime the following day, franked Hong Kong, with a government stamp. Eva saw.

'Aren't you going to open it?' she said.

It was thin – a single sheet. A friendly one-liner from a former colleague? A formal summons on ICAC letterhead? Would it make any difference, which it was? I crammed it unopened into the inside pocket of my jacket, drew the jacket off the chair and slipped it on, one-handed. 'Let's get going,' I said.

'You can't drive in that state.' Eva pulled the plug out of the sink and snapped free of her rubber gloves. We'd just eaten a late lunch, and planned to get to Knox Lodge by four thirty. 'Why won't you listen? We'll have an accident.'

'Tell you what,' I said, kicking the kitchen door open.

The warped wood grated sickeningly on the stone step. 'You keep rehearsing that idea – see if you can make it happen.'

There was a narrow leaf-sodden path connecting the basement area to the garage. She followed me out in her slippers.

'Adam, I am really not that interested in your fragile ego, I am—'

'I'm driving,' I said. I unlocked the garage door and pulled it up on its rollers with my good hand. I glanced at her, ready for the next round, but she had gone back inside.

The garage was on the same level as the kitchen, which was to say seven foot below the road. The drive was absurdly steep – there were steps set into one side because you couldn't walk the slope without them. In winter sometimes the whole thing became an ice-ramp. When we were visiting Justin once, the AA had to winch us onto the road.

The Xedos needed cleaning – I tried not to rub against it as I sidled towards the driver's door. I took a moment to fuss about with the controls, adjusting wing mirrors and the seat position so I could drive comfortably one-armed. Eva had insisted we buy an automatic and for once I was grateful. I reversed up the steep drive and onto the street. Eva was already waiting on the pavement, arms folded over her Karen Millen suit. I unclipped the door. She started to get in when I remembered Justin's birthday present.

'I thought you had it,' she said.

'Of course I don't,' I said.

'Okay,' she said. 'I'll go and get it. Jesus.' I watched her back to the front door, noticing the stiffness in her shoulders, the mincing steps she took in her new boots. She let the door stand open while she went inside.

All this damage from one sly little visit to Money. I was a nervous wreck. My hand was stiffened and useless. Eva had dressed it that morning and in the light of day the stitches looked frighteningly professional. 'Where did you go?' she asked me. 'Did you have to wait long?'

'Did it hurt?'

'Did they give you any antibiotics?'

Drizzle spattered the windscreen. I thumbed the stick down one notch to turn on the wipers, and stretched the stitches in my palm. I winced.

The pain became a warmth, then, as it eased, a buzzing shape – a thick crescent, with an edge taken out of one corner. It felt as if the shard was still there, and it reminded me of something.

Eva was back already, struggling with the PlayStation box. She had wrapped it in shiny gold paper. I leaned over and opened the door for her. She clambered in part way and dropped the box over her seat into the rear of the car.

I waited till she'd strapped herself in. 'Eva?' I wanted to say I was sorry.

'Can we go now?' she said, tightly.

I put the car into gear. There's a button on the stick you have to press to take it out of reverse, and another bolt of heat shot through my palm. This time I recognised the shape.

'There was a lunar eclipse last night,' I said.

'I wish you'd let me drive.'

'It was very pretty.'

'I'm only trying to be nice,' she said.

We took the A13 to the Dartford Crossing. The M25 was so unnaturally quiet, I even got to play with the cruise control. Since it was clear by then that I wasn't going to run us off the road, Eva cut back on the anxious glances and sharp intakes of breath. She wasn't any more relaxed – but there were different reasons for that.

Knox Lodge lies just outside Staplehurst, about forty

minutes off the M20. It started life as a country house, but it's been institutionalised for so long, accreting prefabs and benches and extra toilet blocks, today it resembles any mediocre private school.

Injured pilots were treated here during the second world war; the Ministry of Defence used it as a sort of workhouse-cum-retirement home for fifty aged pen-pushers when they restructured Porton Down; in the Seventies, young offenders went there as an alternative to Borstal. The district health authority rattled about in it until '92.

The rumour was it was going to be Britain's first Higashi school, especially since local authorities were refusing to help out parents paying for their kids to go to the one in Boston.

The principal, Guy Criville, was a convert – he had a photograph of himself with Dr Kitahara on the wall behind his desk – but whatever his professional allegiances, his school hadn't the money to run his mentor's full programme. A lot of people found Criville's pint-sized version pretty disappointing, but Justin had already been through Kitahara's Daily Life Therapy in Tokyo and it was pretty obvious by the end that he simply wasn't up to the full programme.

If you're autistic, the world is meaningless.

Literally. Meaningless. The parts of your brain that give meanings to things don't work properly, or at all. That's why, in extreme cases, you never really acquire language. All you have, at best, is a series of bird calls – noises that conform roughly to words, which you rote-learn to use in specific situations. Calls for food, calls for the toilet, calls for Give-me-that and for Take-this-away.

Because nothing in the world makes any sense, you can't spot the obvious patterns. Sunset, bedtime; breakfast, bathtime – to you it's just one damn thing after another. You never know what's going to happen next, and of course it's only a tiny step from that to thinking that the next thing that'll happen could be *very bad indeed*.

The best you can hope for is a little control. A routine you can rehearse, repeat and comprehend. Lunch at 12.05:00pm and not, under any circumstances, 12.06:35pm, because that opens a window for the chaos to get in. A tea of bread and butter cut always into isosceles triangles of exactly the same size, because a square piece once choked you, and you daren't risk it happening again.

And then, just when you think you've got the lid on things – this is where the irony becomes really delicious – there are other people.

We're all born with a message inside our heads: a piece of information so incredible, it has to be coded in our genes – because we'd never work it out on our own. It says to each of us – if you can believe this – that there are other people, like us, waiting to make contact. Think about it: *other people*. It even tells us what they look like!

If you're autistic, you can't hear the message. Without it, there is only one reasonable conclusion left for you to draw: you are alone. (The animated furniture around you wants you to join in with their unpredictable games – and sometimes you do – but nothing on earth will convince you that that you are one of *them*.)

It was just before four thirty in the afternoon when three hat-stands entered Justin's room. They stood there a moment, flailing and hooting, and then they started interfering with him.

Justin's favourite carer, Francis, came and led us to his room. School was over for the day and the kids here were left to themselves until tea at 5 p.m. Justin was bouncing up and down on the bed when we came in. He was very beautiful. Eva's breath caught in her throat.

There was his face, of course, but we were used to that. It's that expression of theirs: calm, untouched, transcendent. If you let yourself, you can end up believing it's not a lack of something but – on the contrary – a surfeit, that makes them act the way they do. Popes have canonised such holy fools; there are saints whose lives read like case studies in pervasive developmental disorder.

These days, no-one's fooled for long. The real world's the only radio show in town: dare to tune out and you're nowhere but gone.

Francis crossed the room and extended his hand. 'Justin,' he said, easily, 'come over here.'

Justin stopped bouncing. His hair, which had grown almost to his shoulders, descended in a fan around him. He shook his head, clearing it out his eyes.

It was his hair made the difference, I decided. A dark halo for a fallen angel. (Parents are entitled to their metaphors, however trite.)

'Justin?'

He turned and looked at Francis with eerie beneficence.

Francis extended his hand. 'Take my hand.'

Justin gripped his forearm.

Gently, Francis brought the hand into his.

'Remember? It's your birthday. Remember the story? Your birthday.'

He didn't remember a thing, so we sat down and read it all through with him again, only this time with Eva there too.

The front of the scrap-book read 'My Birthday Book'. Inside there was a photographic mock-up of the afternoon as we hoped it would go.

There were Polaroid snaps of the PlayStation game, and its modified handset with outsize buttons. There were pictures of Eva and I; a picture of a birthday cake. Beside each picture there was a sticker with a clock-face printed on it. Francis and I had drawn in the hands ourselves with a gold pen, so Justin could rehearse what was going to happen and when.

In Justin's world there was no such thing as a pleasant surprise. The previous year we took him to Camber Sands, but it had never occurred to us to tell him that we were only going out for the day. As far as he knew he was going to be stranded in this sandy wasteland for ever, never to see his home again. He spent the day screaming his head off, unable to tell us why he was so afraid.

Eva, feeling excluded, got up and walked round the room. The walls were painted a muted orange – a warm, restful colour. Justin's latest pictures were blu-tacked above the bed. A tree, a house, and a picture of Francis. You could tell it was Francis because the head was dark brown. The face was a blank: tiny white dots for eyes, another dot for the mouth, no nose. Faces meant nothing to him, and besides, being autistic means you look more at the edges of objects than at their surfaces – the same, they say, is true of cats.

Mobiles hung from the ceiling: planes, clowns, five-pointed stars, and some dough decorations we had brought him last Christmas. The more glittery ones were hung low enough for him to stir with an upraised hand.

Eva rarely visited Justin. It was her fear of him that had put him in residential care in the first place. Now that he was older – now that he wasn't smashing light bulbs or poking his finger in and out of his anus – a more complex feeling was holding her back. Embarrassment, and an uneasy and mistaken idea that, in her absence, Justin and I had formed an exclusive bond.

Justin loved Eva's gold wrapping paper. While I assembled the machine he tore the sheet into confetti and threw hand-fuls into the air. I plugged the lead into the aerial socket of the TV and left Francis to sort out the tuning. I sat on the floor and gathered the scraps up. Eva came and joined me. Justin held out his hands. Eva poured the rubbish into his palms. He threw it straight away into the air. Eva laughed, shaking it out of her hair.

Francis turned the PlayStation on. Sony's fanfare blasted across the room. Justin stuffed his fingers into his ears and screamed.

'Nice one, Francis.'

'Fuck. *Shit*.' Francis fumbled with the remote and killed the sound.

Justin rocked back and forward – an old stereotype.

'Oh dear,' Eva sighed, deflated by the sight. Justin did outgrow things, but so slowly, it was hard sometimes to believe in his progress.

'Hey, Justin,' said Francis, 'show Daddy and Mummy your present?'

Justin blinked at him.

'Your other present?'

He still had his fingers in his ears.

Francis extended his hand. Justin gripped his forearm and stood up. They walked round the far side of the bed together.

'We got another present,' Francis explained, as Justin disappeared under the bed.

'A present?' said Eva. 'From whom?'

'I can't read the card.'

'Your present!' Justin shouted. He turned to Eva. 'Your birthday! Your present!' He waved a thick red plastic cylinder over his head. There were diamond patterns transferred onto the barrel: white and blue and green.

'It came this morning,' said Francis, ushering Justin back into the centre of the room. 'Show mummy your present.'

Justin hoofed the carpet, a temperamental foal. 'I'll get you Jews!'

'Do you want a drink?' said Francis.

'I'll get you Jews!'

'Show mummy your present. I'll get you a juice from the fridge.'

I touched the cylinder in Justin's hand. He whipped it away from me.

'Was there a card?' Eva asked.

Francis had it in his back pocket to show us. He handed it to Eva on his way out to the fridge.

'I'll get you Jews!' Justin chanted, waving the cylinder in the air.

'Soon, Jessie, soon,' I soothed – not that 'soon' meant anything to him, any more than the niceties of 'you' and 'I'.

Justin thrust the cylinder at my face. I took it. Justin stood back and watched.

It was a kaleidoscope. I held it up to my eye.

Justin clapped his hands, laughing.

'It's from Money,' said Eva. She crumpled the card in her fist.

I let the kaleidoscope drop from my eye. Justin pushed it back in my face; it cracked against my cheekbone. '*Fuck.*'

'There.' She threw the card at me. 'Look.'

I laid the kaleidoscope on the floor and flattened out the card. 'Now you are SEVEN,' it said. I opened it. Underneath the doggerel, Money had written a message in Cantonese. 'What does it say?'

'Oh, it's terribly *nice*,' Eva spat – but whatever sting hung off the tail of that remark, it was interrupted by Francis's return.

9

At tea-time Francis led Justin off to eat with the other children. Normally Eva and I would have eaten with Guy

Criville and his staff, who made a point of their hospitality towards parents; but Criville was at an NAS conference in Birmingham, and when Justin's language therapist met us in the corridor, Eva was full of excuses about how we'd just eaten.

'We can't just ignore them,' I complained, as she led me across the lawn at the back of the main building. 'Don't you want to hear how he is?'

'Don't you dare play the guilt card with me!'

I made a good show of being exasperated. Six brick stairs led us down to the sports field, and beyond it − where I remembered fields, a couple of years ago − a housing estate. 'What are we doing out here, anyway?'

'You think I don't know what she's like?' Eva snapped. 'you think I don't know what she *married into*?'

It didn't take a genius to work out what this was all about.

I thought of him, Eva's luckless grandfather, looking out from his frame on our living room wall, flushed by the light flooding in from Magazine Gap.

Come the Japanese occupation, it was said, Eva's grand-dad worked with Hong Kong's rag-tag resistance, spying for Britain through a cabal of canny pro-Allied fishing concerns. That, anyway, was the excuse the Kempeitei had made for beheading him.

Why Jimmy's father Zhenshu should have been the one to betray Eva's grandfather, no-one could ever tell me. There were no personal or business ties to speak of between them. Eva's granddad owned a fishing fleet; Zhenshu, one of a meagre handful of Chinese lecturers, taught electrical engineering at the University of Hong Kong. But Zhenshu's friendship with the senior officers of the Kempeitei had already made him a notorious figure long before any blood was spilled, and perhaps he was simply their spy.

Whatever − by the time the war was over, the rumour of

Zhenshu's treachery was rife enough that living any longer in Hong Kong was clearly impossible. Zhenshu met his wife the day he arrived in Tokyo, penniless and brandishing questionable papers. A wealthy woman by all accounts, she died in childbirth, less than a year after they met. Where her fortune went to wasn't clear, though as I later discovered while looking through his papers, Zhenshu's life was a long and confusing catalogue of legal wranglings and Quixotic projects, and might easily have consumed a dozen such personal fortunes.

Little Jimmy grew up with his father in the Japanese whaling port of Abashiri. He told me about it once. The boats. The smell. His dad, living from hand to mouth, fixing short-wave radios.

Yes, I knew what Money had married into. I also knew, better than most, the price she had paid. 'She's living in a foreign country,' I said, 'and she's just lost her husband. Cut her some slack, love, please.'

'You wouldn't know a threat if it grabbed you by the neck and shook you.'

'Really,' I said, conscious of the faint yellow marks under my chin.

'She knows where Justin lives.'

'So?'

'Adam, *think!* How could she know that? She's been spying on us.'

'Oh, really ...' Money wasn't spying on us. She didn't have to. She knew where Justin was, because I had told her daughter, only the night before. 'She's got no reason at all to threaten us, Eva. None. She's just a lonely old woman.'

We got back to find Justin kneeling on the bed, the kaleidoscope glued to his eye, and Francis hogging the PlayStation.

'Yes, he should be able to manage that,' Francis said,

quickly dropping the outsize, brightly-coloured control box. 'Justin? Come here, your daddy wants to show you something.'

Eva, sidelined again, shot him a hurt look.

'Justin,' I said, 'come look at this.'

Justin climbed off the bed.

'Mummy?' I said, 'are you going to see, too?'

Eva sat down cross-legged between me and Francis.

'Justin!'

Justin came over to our friendly triangle, collided with Eva and, unable to distinguish her from the furniture, clambered right over her into the centre.

'Oh. But – Christ,' said Eva, fending off Justin's random, scything movements.

'Are you okay?'

'Oh, it's terribly *nice*.' It was so close to her intonation – a perfect playback – I thought at first it was Eva had spoken. But it was Justin.

'Justin,' said Francis, 'come here.' He got him sat facing the screen and gave him the control box. Justin turned it over and over under his nose, sniffing it.

When he was done, Francis guided his fingers over the buttons, into the first level of *Return of the Jedi*. 'No, Justin, move it like *this*.'

Justin dropped the control box and started flapping his hands.

Something was disturbing him. The sound from the TV was low enough, it shouldn't be distressing him. Was it the screen – something in the repeat-rate of the frames? Or had the break to his usual schedule unnerved him at last, in spite of all our rehearsals?

Eva tried stroking his hair. He slapped down her hands.

'Such hair,' she cooed, 'why's it so long?'

Francis caught my eye before I forgot and gave the game

away. Justin's terror of having his hair cut was a quite usual obsession at his stage of development. The last time the school barber was round his tantrum lasted well into the night. I'd tried a couple of times, but I was expecting trouble, and maybe some of my nervousness had transmitted itself to him. Justin was hypersensitive to other people's anxiety.

Saying nothing, Francis left the room a moment and returned with scissors and a comb. He offered them to Eva.

'Oh—' Eva crooned. 'But it's such a pity to cut your beautiful hair, isn't it?' Justin flapped at her to be still. I saw how, as she stroked him, the sleeve of her dress was rubbing back and forth across his arm, just below the hem of his T-shirt. Eva's dress wasn't a harsh material, but to Justin – it must feel like sandpaper to him.

'Maybe this isn't the best time,' I said, as lightly and casually as I could manage.

Francis shot me a look to be quiet.

Eva blinked puzzled, from Francis to me. 'What is it?' she said.

'Try cutting his hair,' said Francis.

Eva smiled. 'Okay.'

Francis reached over to hand Eva the scissors.

Justin looked up as they passed overhead.

He threw the control box at the screen.

'Justin!'

He came upright suddenly, as though jerked on the end of a wire, and started prancing and hopping all over Eva's legs.

'Calm down,' Francis urged, trying to steer him away.

Justin gave a yelp of fear and batted Francis's arm out the way. Seeing a gap open up between Eva and Francis, he bolted for freedom and flung himself on his bed.

From the TV came a muffled explosion. Justin wheeled round and looked up at the screen. It was full of flame and spinning wreckage. Justin started banging the back of his head against the headboard. It boomed, rebounding off the wall.

'Justin, stop that!' said Eva.

Justin looked at her, his mouth a perfect O, and screamed.

Eva, brooking no nonsense, went over to him, grabbed him by the arm and pulled him off the bed.

What happened then was so predictable, I could only stand there and watch it happen, as in a bad dream. Eva recoiled, blood streaming from her nose. Justin lashed out again and again. He caught her in the chest, again in the face.

I launched myself at him, snaring him, pinning his arms at his sides. He screamed and bit my hair. I yelped as it tore from my scalp. I squeezed as hard as I could. He kept struggling. I turned us both round and saw Eva with her face buried in her hands, blood streamed between her fingers. She bent over, her head between her knees, the way she used to when morning sickness hit her unawares.

Justin, exhausted at last, gave himself to my bear hug, and broke into a new fit of more melodic screaming. I squeezed harder. My bad hand was on fire, the moon-shaped cut opening round the stitches, and I could feel blood sticking my hand to Justin's towelling shirt.

Eva took her hands away from her face and stumbled out the room and down the hall. If she wanted the bathroom she was going the wrong way.

Francis, defeated and embarrassed, picked up the scissors and comb from the floor, and started straightening the room. He bent down at the foot of the bed and picked up the kaleidoscope.

He tipped it upright. Shards of brightly coloured plastic fell onto the carpet.

*

We must have made a picture, driving back from the school. Eva's nose wouldn't stop bleeding, which meant she couldn't drive. Not unless she wanted to be snorting and spitting blood out the window the whole way: hardly her style. My hand was so stiff and sore, meanwhile, I had to slow to a 10mph crawl and steady the wheel with my forearm whenever I made a sharp turn.

The driveway was a particular challenge.

'For God's sake watch what you're doing,' Eva cried, as the gatepost loomed up out of the darkness towards her window.

I braked hard, to be spiteful.

I watched Eva to the door. She let herself in and switched on the hall light. Her round-shouldered, mincing turn as she swung the front door shut reminded me, in a way her words could not, how much damage she was taking.

I put the car into first gear, with the little button they give you for that purpose, and slid the wheel around. This time I got the angle.

I pushed the car into Park, got out and walked round the front of the car, rummaging through my trouser pockets for the garage keys. Standing there, knowing that the Xedos, at the flick of a button, could roll down and emboss me on the garage door, gave me the usual cheap thrill.

I unlocked the door and swung it up on its weights.

The stench of dog shit assaulted me immediately. My first thought was, I must have locked Boots inside. But there was no sound. The door trundled and clanged to a stop. I stood aside, removing my shadow, letting the car's headlamps light up the interior.

It took me a moment to make sense of it.

Boots was nailed to the wall.

10

They had crucified him St Andrew-style. His legs, splayed and stretched, made a rough X. His chest was impossibly expanded, the two halves stretched apart by the unnatural extension of his forepaws. The skin over the ribs was tight like a drum. The belly, its contents drawn up under the ribcage, was tiny and concave, like the pictures I had seen of starvation victims.

The left eye was tight shut, the eye muscles puckered and creased. The lip on that side was drawn up in a snarl so extreme, it looked as though his cheek had been cut away. Flecks of blood on the teeth sparkled in the headlights.

The top two bolts were driven between the bones of Boots's forelegs, just below the paws. The paws hung limp, at right angles; it looked, comically, as though Boots was waving. Congealed blood hid the bolt heads.

His back legs had been more difficult to fix. The bolts were only part-way into the wall, and the tissue through which they'd been shot was broken and shapeless.

I got back in the car. I shifted into neutral and feathered the brake, edging into the garage. Once I was parked I engaged the handbrake, turned off the headlights, and pressed the lever that unlocked the bonnet. I left the engine idling, so the exhaust would cover the smell.

I had left a crawl-space of a couple of feet between the front bumper and the rear wall, where Boots was fastened. I edged along it and felt under the bonnet for the bonnet release. I got the bonnet up and manoeuvred the rod into place to hold it upright.

I kept a tool chest in the corner of the garage. I emptied it out one-handed and found the tyre-iron – absurdly small, it was more like a tin-opener – fishing about in the bottom. I edged back to where Boots was hanging and wedged the iron under the first bolt. But I was one-handed and clumsy and the lip slid off the head. A bone cracked.

The kitchen door grated open.

I dropped the tyre iron and came out from behind the bonnet.

Eva poked her head around the garage door. 'Have you seen Boots?' she called, over the purr of the engine.

'No.'

'He's not in the house.'

'He must be,' I said.

'He's not.'

'Well, he's not in here.'

She hesitated at the door, all little-girl-lost. 'What are you doing?' She wrinkled her nose. 'Trying to gas yourself?'

'Well don't stand over the exhaust pipe,' I said.

She stepped round the side of the car.

'No.'

'What?'

'The car's filthy, you'll get your dress messed up.'

'What are you doing anyway?'

'I think a spark plug needs replacing.'

'What's the matter with the light?'

She reached for the switch.

'I don't need it,' I snapped.

'Oh well, break your neck in the dark then,' she said. 'Miserable sod.'

I waited until I heard the kitchen door slam shut.

Boots's leg was shattered, splinters of bone sticking through the skin. I bent the leg away from the wall: it made a wet, clicking sound. If I wasn't careful I'd prise the leg away and leave the paw bolted to the wall.

With my good hand I fixed the tyre iron under the bolt again and worked it more gently. It began grinding in its socket. Another minute and the thread disintegrated. After that I managed to jiggle the bolt out by hand. I looked for somewhere to wipe the blood off my fingers. There was an old pair of jeans I used for painting in a bag behind the toolbox. I was just fishing them out when the kitchen door opened again.

'Bootsie?'

I heard Eva scuffing about in the basement area, and a rustling as she pulled aside the undergrowth of overgrown budleia and honeysuckle. 'Oh Boots.'

The other bolts were loose. They'd used too powerful a gun, because the cement had pulverised around the metal. Once that first, difficult bolt was free, Boots was pretty much just hooked there.

I got him down, clumsily enough, trying to keep his blood off my clothes. When he fell his muzzle came open and a black pool ran out of his mouth. I knelt down and felt inside.

His tongue was missing.

The message was pretty much unmistakable. How many more of these, I wondered, before they ran over my head?

I cast around for the tongue in the dark. Maybe it was somewhere in that puddle of brown slurry at my feet. Either that or we were going to find it under the pillow come bedtime. Or floating in the milk carton at breakfast.

I slid into the driver's seat and turned off the engine. I took the keys with me as I climbed out. I went round the back of the car and opened the boot. I lifted out the plastic liner Eva had laid there to catch crumbs and spillages. Flakes of dried icing dusted my trousers.

I carried the liner round to the front of the car, laid it out and rolled Boots onto it. I wrapped him up and dragged him round to the boot. I needed both hands to get him into the car. I tried not to rub the liner across my stitched palm, got my arms round him at last, and manhandled him into the boot.

'Are you going to help me or not?'

I slammed the boot shut so hard the car bounced.

'He's not in the house,' she said.

'Did we leave a door unlocked?'

'No.'

I put my hands in my pockets in case she saw bloodstains. I stood side on to her, and glanced down my shirt front. It was too dark to see anything. 'Then how can he have gone?'

I followed her back into the house along the leaf-sodden path to the kitchen door. In the light from the kitchen window I saw my shirt was clean.

In the house, there was nothing out of place. No sign, beyond the missing dog, that they had been here. I couldn't resist looking under the pillows in the bedroom – God knows what Eva made of that – but there was nothing there.

I wondered how I was going to explain the holes in the garage wall.

I said, 'Did you see him when you went back for the present, this afternoon?'

'I left him in the kitchen.'

'Did you *see* him?'

She thought about it. 'No.'

'But you left the door open when you went back.'

'No I didn't.'

'You did. I saw you.'

'Did I?'

'Yes.'

She thought about it. 'I went upstairs for the PlayStation. It was still in the bedroom.'

'Well,' I said, 'there you are, then.'

'Well wouldn't you have seen him?'

'I don't know,' I said.

She swallowed. 'Oh, Adam ...' She reached out to touch my arm. I stepped away, conscious suddenly of the smell sticking to me; something gluey between the second and third fingers of my left hand. I shoved my hands back in my pockets. 'I'd better get moving,' I said, and headed down the stairs to the kitchen.

She followed me down. 'Where are you off to?'

'Well if he's not in the house I'd better go look for him, hadn't I?'

'I'll come with you.'

'Wait in the house. He hasn't been fed – he'll probably be back before I am.'

'Where are you going to go?'

'I'll just drive around a while, see if I can see him.'

It needed two hands to open the kitchen door.

'Adam,' she said, 'wait.'

'What?'

'Your hand's bleeding again.'

'It doesn't matter,' I said. I gave the bottom of the door a kick and it came open.

'Let me drive.'

'For God's sake,' I shouted, 'let me do something.'

Her smile was so gentle, something dropped inside me. 'Thanks,' she said, softly. 'If you're sure.'

I smiled back at her, because it was what she wanted, and went back to the car.

11

My hand felt like there was a wasps' nest under my skin. It was so swollen, the palm so blackened, I couldn't bear to look at it. I drove one-handed down Hemingford Road, then swung a left and tried heading south, but the traffic was so heavy I lost my temper and turned again too early, losing myself in the mews and plazas that fill the junction of Liverpool Road and Upper Street. When at last I found a way through, I found myself on Islington Green, heading towards the Angel. I remembered the canal and braked sharply for the left turn down Duncan Street. The driver behind nearly rear-ended me. As he overtook, we wound down our windows and he called me a cunt. 'Leather interior,' I sneered back. It was nice not having Eva in the car.

The Grand Union Canal runs underground through Islington, directly beneath the road I was driving down. At the end of the street, where the tunnel ends, a small copse of mature trees hides the emerging water. I dog-legged right and drove slowly, trying to see into the cutting. There were lights down there – houseboats, moored along the towpath from the mouth of the tunnel all the way down to the next bridge. So that was out. After that the road veered right, away from the water. There wasn't any other traffic just then so I whipped as fast as I could through a four-point turn and drove back the other way, and over the canal. I took the first right turn, hoping this road would follow the line of the water. The Georgian facades moving past me were smart enough but the road might have been a dirt track, the way it felt under my wheels, all patched and pitted, with speed bumps every few yards. I gritted my teeth, kept to a steady 25mph, and tried not to hear Boots thumping about in the back.

I reached the junction, looked right, and there was a pub, the Narrowboat, built on the corner of the bridge and the cutting. So that was out.

I dog-legged left again and then I really lost it: every street I tried turned out to be a dead end until I reached Rheidol Terrace, by which time it felt like I was miles off course. I drove down it anyway until it suddenly opened out, roads leading off every place, and a church rose up ahead of me, and I finally admitted defeat. I turned immediately right, more out of panic than anything else, and found myself in the middle of a council estate. The road disappeared into the darkness, straight and uniform as a scene from an arcade game. Every few yards it narrowed into pedestrian crossings, but the only people I saw were gathered around a phone-box on one of those paved dead spaces the designers call squares.

I should have turned around, but I was mesmerised by the road and the simple shapes of the buildings. There were climbing frames and swings in front of each block; and lawns, if you could call them that. Someone had gone mad on the landscaping: there wasn't a flat foot of grass anywhere.

The darkness ahead of me grew. The estate ended. I couldn't make out what lay beyond. Belatedly, it dawned on me: that unlit strip, where the road finished, could only be the canal.

The kerbs branched off here and there like cilia into parking bays. The ground rose slightly and the road ended at last in a small turning circle. I found an empty bay and parked.

The road, barred to vehicles by metal posts, ended here. But the pavements met and continued over the canal on a concrete footbridge. About eight feet upstream, a square metal duct carried power cables over the water on a separate bridge, topped by a cruel metal railing. The gap between the footbridge and the duct was in shadow: neither the lights from the factory opposite nor the estate's streetlights penetrated that strip of water. I looked around, wondering how easily I would be observed.

The kids were still lingering near the telephone box, lit brutally by the fluorescent light coming from the all-night store on one side of the square: they were too far away to matter.

I opened the boot. The in-built light came on. The plastic was smeared brown in places where Boots had shifted about in his wrapper, but nothing had leaked. I gathered him up, cast around quickly and, unobserved, carried him onto the bridge.

I balanced him on the rail a moment as I tried to get my bad hand out the way, but he tipped off anyway. He plummeted into the water, leaving behind, as his epitaph, the scent of honey.

The wrapper came undone immediately. It unwrapped, a grey, shapeless bloom. Trapped air kept it bobbing on the surface as, caught by the small, sluggish current of the water, it disappeared under the footbridge.

I should have tied him up.

I crossed the bridge and waited for Boots to emerge. The wrapper came first, the old plastic glistening, smeared by streetlights. Then Boots. His legs were sticking up out of the water.

I should have weighted him down.

The left front paw hung at a drunken angle, where I'd broken it with the tyre iron. His head was bent back under the water, and the collar looked like a strangler's cord around his neck.

The collar.

I'd forgotten the collar.

All this cloak-and-dagger business and I'd forgotten the one thing that really mattered – the collar had a brass disc clipped to it, and engraved on the disc, the word BOOTS. And our phone number.

I had to remove the collar. I had to get Boots back.

Downstream there was a large play area, landscaped into terraces. A winding path connected the bays – one for swings, one for a Wendy house, one for a frame; others I couldn't make out. There were no lights, and I couldn't see the steps. They were so shallow and needless, I couldn't predict where they'd be. Twice I stumbled.

The fence separating the playground from the towpath was only just above waist-height. There were trees growing near the fence so scaling it wasn't a problem.

Boots wasn't much further downstream than when I'd left him, but he'd moved further into the middle.

I cast round for something – a stick, anything – to pull him into the bank. I tried breaking a branch off a tree. The bark cracked easily enough, but the green wood within tore wetly and wouldn't give. I tried twisting the branch and got a mouthful of leaves. It was too heavy to twist with one hand anyway – in my hurry I'd snapped off about a third of the tree.

The striking of a match brought me back to reality.

There was a boy on the footbridge. He was sitting astride a mountain bike, lighting a cigarette. He took in a lungful of smoke, and blew it over the match. The flame guttered and died. He flicked the dead match idly into the water.

He didn't take his eyes off me once.

I dropped the branch. The leaves, hitting the gravel, made a sound like rain.

The boy tapped ash over the rail.

I walked along the canal towards him. Silhouetted by streetlight, his face was unreadable. I avoided his eyes and kept walking, under the bridge and out the other side. I heard the rhythmic clicking of his back wheel as he rocked back and forth on the bike. As I came out from under the bridge I looked up, nervously, expecting to see him there, but he wasn't. The towpath opened out for a strip of grass and some benches, some trees: the ground was white with blackthorn blossom. I looked back again.

The bridge was empty.

The Narrowboat was barely five minutes' walk upstream. I looked for a way up to street level, but it turned out I didn't need one: the pub had a narrow yard which gave onto the towpath; the door was open and spiral stairs led up to a veranda with a view of Wenlock Basin.

Inside, blackboards offered 'good food', board games, and After Noah playing live on Friday night. I ordered a large Lamb's and used the wallphone by the bar. I lost my only small change straight off because I didn't realise it was one of those phones you pay only when the other party answers. Which meant getting more change from the barman and another double.

I said, 'Is he back yet?'

'No. Where the hell are you?'

'I've been round everywhere. You sure he's not in the garden or something?'

'Adam, I don't understand this. I'm sure he didn't get out while I was upstairs. You'd have seen.'

'Maybe I didn't.'

The jukebox kicked in.

'What's that music?'

'*The Champions*, I think.'

'What?'

'It had William Gaunt in it. Look, I'm coming home. I can't drive much more with this hand.'

'Is that a jukebox?'

'I'll see you in a few minutes.'

'You're in a pub!'

'Well of course I'm in a bloody pub,' I said, 'It's got a bloody phone, hasn't it?'

She slammed the phone down on me.

I got a third large one, stared down the barman, and looked for somewhere quiet to sit. The back room was carpeted and done out like a barge, with wooden sloping walls and a wooden ceiling. There were old prints of canals on the walls, and a photographic blow-up of a rustic lock-gate on the back wall. Most of the tables were free: a group of students, a middle-aged couple in pebble glasses, contemplating their drinks in silence.

I nursed my rum, working up the courage to open that morning's letter. It had been burning a hole in my pocket all day. Finally I got it open.

It was official enough. On ICAC letterhead, no less. They were even offering to pay my air fare. They had a contact number for me to ring in London 'at your earliest convenience'. Underneath there was a PS.

Call me first – DW.

Daniel White: typical of him, still keeping things so friendly so long after the event. I missed him.

I screwed the letter up and dropped it in the ashtray.

Which left me with my only other alternative.

I got my wallet out and counted through my small change.

Directory Enquiries had no number listed under Money or Jimmy Yau.

'Try Yau Wai-hing,' I said, and spelled it out, stretching the operator's patience. Yau Wai-hing – Money's Cantonese name.

'Here's your number,' she said.

I let the number repeat, so I had it. I took a deep breath – and I dialled.

HONG KONG
1989

12

When I first arrived in Hong Kong, in March 1989, it was with the idea that I'd be lecturing on management culture or business ethics or some such thing – a junket, basically.

It was a view my boss, Frank Hamley, seemed happy to encourage. He wasn't a policeman – he had no law enforcement background at all – but had joined the Serious Crime Group straight from a stint pen-pushing for Legco. When I arrived, Hamley's unlikely empire consisted of a handful of underpaid, overworked pen-pushers in an annex off the old Serious Crime Group building.

Massive expansion in the Far Eastern exchanges had snapped the old lines of corporate accountability; nobody, inside or out of these vastly distended companies, knew how to maintain effective control of them.

'We're the ones with our fingers in the dike,' Hamley

told me proudly, over deep-fried oysters on the terrace of a restaurant in Lau Fau Shan. 'We're the ones at the sharp end,' he added – he had an unhappy knack of mixing his metaphors.

The job excited him. You could see it was a game with him. He didn't have to work. Hamley had money – he was born into it. With that came certain social expectations, which he seemed determined to foil. Still, joining the Serious Crime Group hadn't seemed to spoil his social life any. Had he joined an outfit more obviously targeted at the Establishment – the Independent Commission Against Corruption, say – reactions would have been quite different.

Hamley did a lot of entertaining, those first few weeks of my stay, and he was never slow to show me around. I shook hands with Chris Patten and talked dogs with his wife Lavender. A minor Jardine invited me to Bermuda. At a piano recital in the China Club Hamley, staggeringly drunk, insisted to David Bonavia that I was the man he had to talk to for his latest volume of punditry.

Everyone wanted the novelty of knowing him. Even minor royalty like Victor Pang.

'I met him at Jardine's,' Hamley told me. He had a way of talking about his business contacts as though he'd stumbled across them at a cocktail party. 'Miserable old sod. Mind, his daughter's good for one.'

Victor Pang Ka-Shing was an anomaly. Born in Hong Kong during the Japanese occupation, he was brought up by his mother in Shanghai. A fervent and romantic Maoist in his teens, he joined the PLA straight from school, and it was only during the Cultural Revolution that he fled to Hong Kong. A self-made man, he proved himself as much of a workaholic as any of his peers. But he broke the mould early on, using his money to create a private world far away from their influence.

They despised him for that. In the Lusitano Club he had become a 'character', for which crime his wife had never forgiven him. But that wouldn't stop the Lusitano Club – nor his wife, come to that – driving here tonight and eating his food and drinking his brandy.

While we ate, the sun mellowed into late afternoon over the Chinese mainland. On the shoreline, a hundred metres off, the waves spat and rattled, sculpting dunes from the town's beach of a billion discarded oyster shells.

'So what went wrong in Rio?' Hamley said.

Rio was my last job – a consultancy post with KPMG. I enjoyed the city more than my job, but Hamley's question mystified me. 'Nothing went wrong,' I said, pursuing an oyster round my plate.

I looked up at him. He'd gone back to his food. A drop of sauce ran down his slightly receding chin – he wiped it off with his hand. He leaned back into the late sunlight. Tiny crumbs of golden batter clung to the chest hairs poking luxuriantly out of his open-necked shirt. 'You left pretty suddenly, they said.'

'My contract expired.'

'Our friend Harold said you're an adventurer.'

Harold was my old boss. It was his reference had got me my posting.

'A bit of a buccaneer, he said.' He shovelled rice into his mouth and swallowed it without chewing. 'Only you don't know it yet.'

I pushed my plate away. 'Very Harold,' I said.

'Really?'

'Dramatic. He spends his weekends writing screenplay proposals.'

'I didn't know that,' Hamley admitted.

'They don't sell,' I said.

*

76

Essentially, the Serious Crime Group were an anti-Triad office, fielding two hundred detectives – many of them in deep cover – all over the New Territories. They had few establishment connections, and no background in finance. So how had they managed to recruit Hamley, a leading market consultant?

Today, the arrangement seems quite natural, because we're much more used to the idea of crime as an industry. The south-east Asian crash of '97–'98, for example, is directly related to a global criminal recession: between ten and thirty per cent of all Japanese non-performing bank loans are gang debts.

Back in '89, though, the arrangement was unprecedented, and not a little spacy. Somewhere – working undercover in a hong, ransacking secret data cores – an SCG detective (this is what I fantasised) had stumbled across something. A hint of what was to come. I imagined it: a laundering network so big, the markets themselves were at risk!

I ironed my shirts very diligently in those days, and trawled Golden Arcade for the most fuck-off counterfeit RayBans I could find.

'The Rolex too?'

Coyly, I flashed my fifty-dollar timepiece in the sun.

Hamley shook his head. 'I can never keep my focus in those places. The last time I went in for a watch I came out with a Shrap Elsmate calculator and a five-CD set of Anita Mui.'

Before sunset, we drove on. Hamley wrestled the Saab through eddies of traffic bound for Un Long and Sheung Shui. It was turning seven when we turned left onto a gravel road and wound round a hill bright with suburban overspill and night-time construction. Another turn-off took us onto an older road, once metalled, now pitted and rough. The Saab's cultivated suspension wallowed and pinged in distress.

I pulled the shade down against the setting sun. We were driving straight into it now, away from the suburbs of Yuen Long and into a region of market gardens.

The windscreen was tinted, browning out the sunset, and mellowing the raw electric lights of the villages. The road dipped sharply. We rounded a bend, and the sea came back into view. It burned like blood in the dying light.

'A pretty place, don't you think?'

I nodded.

'Make the most of it. Most of our clients have land deals round here. Here and Shenzhen.'

'Pang actually lives around here?'

'Why not?'

'It's a way out of town,' I said. I'd expected an exclusive retreat; I was disappointed.

'He got fed up of Shek O,' Hamley said. 'or maybe he got fed up of his wife. She lives there, anyway, doing the Shek O thing.'

About half way down the hill we joined the queue of big cars pulling into sandy lots along the beach. Flames leapt from iron drums, screwed into the shingle every twenty metres.

Hamley led me up the bank, hands shoved casually in his trouser pockets, and down again towards the party. Old oil drums gave way to bespoke iron braziers, camp fires to barbecues. The coconut matting laid over the beach must have run to a couple of acres. Paper lanterns, swinging in the sea breeze, lit the way from pavilion to pavilion, barbecue to barbecue. Tibetan prayer-flags fluttered against bamboo poles, marking the tide line.

We passed a servant in whites carrying a silver tray. Hamley picked up a couple of glasses and handed me one. I drank, and snorted, as the champagne went up my nose.

'Victor?'

Victor Pang stood sentinel at the head of the path, absurdly formal in a black linen suit and a shirt so flat and shiny it might have been made out of plastic. He had one of those childlike, despotic faces you find leering through the fog in old Sherlock Holmes serials. Hamley introduced me. Pang squeezed the blood from my hand.

Hamley and Pang caught up while Pang greeted the new arrivals. They came from private islands off Lantau, from casinos in Macau and car dealerships in Shenzhen and private galleries in Central. They'd acquired their wives the way you acquire expensive sports cars – late in life and with a degree of embarrassment. Their wives, like their cars, had a skittish look about them, as though at a sharp bend they would cheerfully tramline and send you flying over the crash barriers.

'Come on,' said Pang, already bored of his role as host, 'Let's eat.'

The first fire we came to stank of burnt feathers. Foetal chickens lay in neat rows, charring over white charcoal.

'Try it,' Pang insisted. 'Go on.'

I glanced at Hamley but he wasn't going to help me.

I capitulated. A soft baby skull burst its sweetness over my tongue.

'Come on, Frank,' said Pang.

'You must be kidding,' Hamley laughed. We followed Pang to the next barbecue. Hamley took me by the arm and whispered in my ear. 'Don't try and compete with this monster. You'll end up eating cat.'

Pang heard. 'Cat? That peasant crap?' A boy in whites handed him a plate of spare ribs. He offered it round. 'Monkey, Adam?'

I looked at him.

'He's only joking,' Hamley said.

'Come on,' said Pang, 'meet the vultures.'

I hovered at a discreet distance, fascinated by the women, picking their way uncomfortably across the shingle. They were dressed to impress, their simple, sleek clothes sculpting mere wayward flesh into forms out of *Vogue* and *Tatler*. Their ungainly approach I found disarming, though I wondered if the beach setting – the raw smoke and the uncertain ground – were not some subtle misogynistic joke on Pang's part. The men talked to me, found my salary wanting, smiled and moved on; their wives, wise to me from a glance, struck a pose.

I kept trying to withdraw but Pang, presumably because I'd arrived with Hamley, had taken a shine to me.

'You're going to have to come up with a job title,' he said. 'You're frightening everyone off.'

I should have found it patronising, being talked to like this. Maybe Pang's irony was seductive; maybe I was just intimidated.

'But I don't have a job description.'

'You can't keep saying you're a consultant. Nobody will ever trust you.'

'What do you suggest?'

'How about "spy"?'

'That'll make people trust me?'

'Oh Adam, we're all spies or thieves here. You should read your le Carré.'

A guttural croaking interrupted us. It was supposed to be laughter. 'Talking of the honourable schoolboy, where's Patten?'

The voice came from behind and above us. I turned round. Pang winced as though someone had drawn their fingernails down a blackboard.

The stranger was Chinese, but not of any caste that I had seen. He was taller than me. His teeth were jagged, grey and shiny like steel. Unusually, he was bald: what hair was left to him was shaved close to his skull. His ears were too small: delicate pink shells. He picked at one with a thick, dark workman's finger.

'Adam Wyatt.' I held my hand out to shake.

His calluses scraped my palm.

Pang, making no effort to keep the sigh out of his voice, introduced us. 'James Yau Sau-Lan,' he announced, deadly formal.

'Call me Jimmy,' said Jimmy Yau, cutting Pang out. 'Have you been in Hong Kong long?'

'Just a couple of weeks.'

'One of Rob's boys, eh? Fresh from SIMEX?'

'SCG,' Pang told him, stiffly. 'He's a police spy.'

Jimmy Yau didn't bat an eye – maybe Pang was right. 'London, then,' he said, brightly. There was such strength and certainty in his face, I didn't like to contradict him.

I looked to Pang for help, but he was glowering into the middle distance. I said, 'Do you know Frank Hamley?'

'Frank? Sure.'

Pang barked, humourlessly. 'Oh Jimmy's great friends with Frank,' he spat. He was still facing deliberately away from us. 'Aren't you, Jimmy?'

Jimmy Yau shot Pang an amused, supercilious glance, like a small dog had just yapped at him. 'Been to Shenzhen?' he asked me.

'This winter,' I said, too eagerly.

'Carry a gun,' he said.

Pang wandered off. Jimmy Yau watched him go, and smiled.

'So how come you know Frank?' I said.

'Just business.'

'So—'

'I'm in import,' he said.

'For?'

'Have you been out to Lantau?'

'Not yet,' I said.

'We specialise in land reclamation. Pumping equipment and pipework.'

'Uh-huh.' I wondered what possible business he had with the Serious Crime Group.

Jimmy Yau yawned. 'Want a drink?'

Pebbles crunched dully beneath the matting as we walked. He was a big nasty man, in a big nasty suit, and I felt dwarfed and child-like beside him. Fireflies and moths as big as my palm dive-bombed the linen curtain. Jimmy Yau pulled it back for me and we went inside. A bar ran the full length of the tent. Chandeliers hung from the roof, filling the space with creamy light. Below the buzz of conversation came the purr of a petrol-driven generator. A string quartet was assembling itself out of a pile of cases and music stands in the far corner.

'Brandy?'

'Whisky.'

'When in Rome—'

'I'm afraid brandy makes me sick.'

Jimmy Yau shrugged and got me a Glenlivet.

He was so tall, he must have come from the North – from Shanxi or Manchuria, where the mildest clerk cracks his knuckles sometimes, and dreams of rape and wild horse-craft, the sun setting on a Mongol camp. 'So you know Shenzhen well?' I said.

Things could only get more asinine after that, but it was hard to get away. Pang was deep in conference with Lavender Patten and he was hardly going to come over and rescue me; I hadn't seen Hamley since we'd arrived.

Saved in the end by my bladder, I made my excuses and left the tent. The toilets were little pavilions, arranged in a horseshoe facing the sea. They might have been changing rooms in an upmarket Edwardian resort. When I was done and pulled the braided curtain aside, it was like I was stepping out onto a flame-lit stage. Everything was theatrical here: a fancy-dress party where everybody had come as more vivid versions of themselves.

The barbecued chicks had done for my appetite and I was too nervous to drink any more. Overpowered, I headed towards the sea. The matting stopped just out of the circle cast by the last brazier. My feet sank unsteadily into the shingle. I moved slowly, finding my feet, while my eyes adjusted to the dark.

I wasn't alone. People were walking back and forth along the tide-line, where the shingle gave way to sand. Most were in couples: men in Sam's dinner jackets, women glimmering in dresses from Sogo and Matsuzakaya, shoes hanging from their hands like necklaces. Against the stars, against a sea bright with reflections, they moved, poised and slow as ghosts.

But inland, it was clouding over: the sky had turned orange beyond the hill-line, reflecting the streetlights of Shenzhen. I imagined that dead glow, sweeping over us. It was only a matter of time before the developers got here, too, sank marinas into the sand and blurred the sky with sodium.

Back out to sea, a ghost woman passed, all soft cream curves, barefoot, carrying a flame in her hand. She brought it to her lips and drew in, lighting a cigarette.

'Have you got a spare?' I said.

She turned to me, taken aback. A real princess. 'Of course,' she said. She opened her purse.

Her shoes were slung round her wrist by their straps. They sparkled like glass when she lit her lighter for me.

I looked into her face. Her mouth was red like a wound. She crinkled up her eyes against the light of the flame. She looked so vulnerable.

I took a deep drag from the cigarette and my head reeled.

'Are you all right?'

'A bit strong,' I said.

'It's only Silk Cut.' She smiled. The flame was gone, I couldn't see her properly – only the dark, provoking crescent of her mouth. God had slapped and beaten her into shape, puffing up her lips in bee-stings, bruising her eyes into bedroomy slits.

'I'm Adam,' I said, bumbling and bearish.

'Eva.' Her hand was cold and smooth.

'I'm new here,' I said.

'I'll show you around.'

'Please don't.'

'The governor's here.'

'I met him.'

We didn't have anything to say.

'Adam, is it?'

I threw the stub into the waves.

'What do you do?'

Land reclamation. Import–export. Futures. I work for a Saab dealership.

'You're not a *merchant banker*, are you?'

'I'm a police spy.'

'Oh,' she said.

'Apparently.'

'Is it exciting?'

'Yes,' I said. 'No. I don't know.' I looked out to sea. 'I only started this week,' I said.

I was surprised when she didn't laugh. 'I'm sure it must be,' she said.

'What do you do, Eva?'

'Me?' She laughed. 'Oh, I don't do anything. I lunch.'

'Oh.'

She studied me in the light coming off the sea. She wrinkled her nose. 'That's sweet.'

'What?'

'You're intimidated,' she said. 'Most *gweilos* just take the piss.' Her hand found mine in the dark. 'Take me for a walk,' she said.

It was about three when I got back to the car. Hamley had picked up a couple of accountants from somewhere. The girl, a blonde in a pencil skirt that did little to hide her generous backside, had her face pressed to the boy's chest and her hand down the front of his pants. The boy had beefy, blown, ruggerish looks – the sort that deteriorate as soon as schooldays end. He fixed me with a wild, blind blue eye. I didn't engage. When Hamley saw me he unlocked the rear door and poured them into the back. They entered the vehicle like a single defective animal, arms and legs flailing. I went round to the passenger's side and strapped myself in.

Hamley put the car into Drive. 'Enjoy yourself?'

'Some.'

Behind me, a zipper whined open.

I caught Hamley's eye and gestured with my thumb to the couple in the back. He just shrugged.

He gunned the car and we wallowed out onto the track, trailing distant tail-lights over the hill and deep into the darkness of Lau Fau Shan.

'Saw you with Jimmy Yau,' said Hamley.

'"Call me Jimmy".'

'Fucker.'

'How so?'

Hamley shook his head.

'Is he a friend of yours?'

'Jimmy Yau doesn't have friends.'

A knee dug into the back of my seat.

Hamley adjusted the rear-view so he could watch.

'Pang left me with him,' I said.

'As lizards leave their tails behind.'

'There's no love lost between them, I noticed.'

'Jimmy's dad got Victor's dad executed by the Japs.'

'You're kidding.'

'It's the way Victor tells it. You seemed to make an impression.'

'On whom?'

'Victor.'

'I hardly spoke to him,' I said.

'You were all over his daughter.'

'Eva?'

A belt-buckle rattled. The girl in the back started making 'Mmm' noises.

Hamley let go the wheel. 'Hold this a sec.' He loosened his tie.

I seized the wheel in a panic and held it steady against the rightwards pull of the camber.

I was just thinking that maybe we'd get away with it, when the road slid suddenly to the left. A single concrete post marked the turn. Behind it, the hillside fell away.

I yanked the wheel. I practically fell in Hamley's lap to make the full turn. Hamley hit the brake and the safety-belt snatched my throat like a hand. 'Jesus Christ.'

Hamley shot out his thumb and gave the wheel a life-saving nudge. He went back to his tie, pulling it off and away in a single gesture. He took back the wheel and checked his mirrors. 'Ugh.' He reached up and knocked the rear-view askew. I glimpsed skin; maybe it was upholstery.

'In the glove compartment.'

'What?'

Hamley undid his collar button. 'In there. In there.'

I opened it.

'Oh shit.'

Was that the boy or the girl?

'Oh *shit* ...'

'Go on!'

The bottle was still cold; there was sweat on the glass. I tore off the foil and unwound the wire. The cork ricocheted off the edge of the sunroof and into the night. Foam ran down my hand.

'Go on, then.'

I didn't want it, but I took a swig anyway. Bubbles shot up my nose.

'Not you,' said Hamley, exasperated. '*Them!*'

I looked back.

'Cool those little fuckers off!'

13

Any ideas I had about becoming a latter-day Harry Palmer were quickly scotched, those first few weeks in the office. It was modern enough for its time I suppose, its workspaces arranged in little islands, its coffee point a comfortable if smoke-laden lounge where all the real work went on. But if at first this all seemed very Silicon Valley, very Bill Gates, I soon learned there was a good reason for it: for we were as severely desk-bound as any code-monkey rattling the bars at Microsoft, and our work was as far away from 'police work', as it's popularly imagined, as it is possible to get.

There are three stages or levels of laundering. First, there's the messy business of actually finding somewhere secure to hide your ill-gotten loot. Second there's what's euphemistically called 'layering', which is a middle-class way of saying 'burying'. The more layers of mind-numbingly complex transactions you make with your dirty money, the cleaner it seems, if only because anyone who tries to follow the paper trail quickly ends up on Prozac. Then there's integration: now your dirty money is indistinguishable from clean, you can feed it back into the economy: legitimate money making more legitimate money, the way Adam Smith and Margaret Thatcher intended.

At the dirty end of the business there's a vibrant and well-lubricated social scene. A criminal mastermind (at least by his own estimation) meets a sharp broker (ditto) at some cocktail party or other – usually in Happy Valley – and gets him good and plastered. The next day the broker, all pie-eyed, is buying hair-of-the-dog for all his office pals on account of he just pulled this really great new client at last night's shindig. And it's only weeks or even months later, when his instructions get all muddled up – full of last minute changes, investments in unrelated third parties, purchased outside a regular custodial system, cancelled early, refunded to third-party accounts, or what you will – that your credulous broker starts getting a nasty taste in his mouth.

At the other end of the business – the end we had most to do with – is the slew of strategies, practices, legal obligations and compliances that are supposed to prevent this kind of scenario from ever happening. If companies don't put safety procedures in place, or more usually if they fail to comply with their own safety procedures, then they're breaking the law. And the only way you find out about that is by chasing paper. Lots of paper. Mountains of bloody paper.

Maybe my old boss in Rio had a point about my buccaneering instinct, because soon my disappointment and frustration began to show in my work.

'You can't go pulling people around in bars. You haven't the authority.'

'For God's sake, Frank,' I said – and sank uninvited into the chair opposite him – 'he knew when they approached him that the deal wasn't straight. What kind of investments were they suggesting anyway? Two-per cent. Who the hell invests clean funds at such a shitty rate of return? If we can only—'

'You're not a policeman and you're not empowered to question witnesses.'

'Frank, the paper trail's cold, like I said. Haven't you read my report?'

There was a moment's impasse and then, quite unexpectedly, Frank Hamley grinned. 'You're a little monkey, Adam.'

'Oh?'

'Don't take it as a compliment. Right now you're my office's biggest liability.'

'Because I met someone in a bar?'

'Because you scared the life out of him.'

'Well—'

'Tipping off a suspect carries a jail term, Adam.' He left that hanging over me for a good long while. It soaked in well enough. At last he relented: 'I can't use you in here,' he said.

I stared at him. I'd never been sacked in my life.

'Oh don't look so gobsmacked,' Hamley complained, waving away my astonishment. 'It's not like we're going to stick your head on a pike.'

My dad was delighted when I told him I was moving desks. I tried playing it down, but it didn't do any good. 'It's not a promotion, Dad. It's a *secondment*.'

'Do you get more money?'

'No, Dad.'

Hamley had been very friendly, very avuncular. He promised to smooth things over at work about what he dubbed my 'over-zealous approach'. And, since I was not 'a natural team player', perhaps it would be best, he said, if he gave me 'more of a roving brief.'

This wasn't unusual. With few resources of its own, Hamley's Serious Crime Group team regularly provided expert assistance to other Hong Kong agencies. 'ICAC would really benefit from your perspective,' he said.

'I don't know anything about them.'

'Four legs and a tail: what's the difficulty?' Victor Pang took a final slurped spoonful of bird's nest soup and leaned back in his wing chair, weather-eyeing the monitors strung above the restaurant bar.

For now he was laughing at me, but if I didn't place a bet soon he'd think I didn't know how to enjoy myself. I tried to make sense of the odds spooling across the distant screen. I wished Hamley were here. 'How about Fool's Money?'

'An accumulator would be safer.'

'A what?'

Victor Pang hid his frustration behind his brandy glass.

Spoiled by Hamley's toting me around everywhere, I'd expected this evening to be spent, if not in a private humidor fug high above the track's vast public video screen, then at least buoyed up by champagne in the Lusitano Club's private quarter. (I knew Pang was well established there; he had inherited Portuguese connections from his bereaved mother's remarriage in the late Forties, and maintained several business interests in Macau.)

But Pang took his gambling seriously, the way his wife and her American cronies could not. Once the races started and they all started jumping up and down like game show contestants, he'd shot them a look of contempt worthy of the surliest Gerrard Street waiter, and led me by the arm out of the club and into a public restaurant barely one level from the public stands, 'where we can concentrate'. Where he could concentrate, and I could look like a lemon.

Now, it seemed, I'd failed the restaurant test. 'Come on.'

90

He stood up, left an insultingly large tip, and led the way from the terrace restaurant straight down to the members' enclosure. So much for waiter service and highballs under the stars.

I'd expected an hour, maybe less, in Pang's company: the usual glancing social contact. Not an entire evening of painful misconnection. I couldn't see why he was bothering with me in the first place, unless it had to do with work. But he had friends more powerful than I to lean on, hadn't he?

Hadn't he?

I'd never been to a race before, and obviously this was the place to start. At Happy Valley, even the horses have private swimming pools. As I watched the gates spring open on the huge public video screen in the centre of the track, I thought maybe all this gloss and brilliance and high-tech was missing the point of the place, but then Pang elbowed us a path to the rail and I got my first real taste of occasion.

The riders appeared, rounding a bend in the track: a terrifying, hectic blur of limbs and leather. The ground shook. I didn't know to expect that. The horses thundered past, and the sound of them rose through my feet, and something fluid and free stirred inside me.

Maybe that's why I asked him.

'God, no,' he laughed, 'it wasn't my idea.' Like he wouldn't be so dumb as to invite me. He glanced around. 'Where is she, anyway?'

I knew straight away who he meant. If it wasn't him had invited me here, there was only one woman in his circle it could be. Adolescent paranoia swept over me: *My God, what if she's*—?

The ground trembled – a simple, regular rhythm this time. I turned to look. A single, laggard horse, so far behind the pack it might have been running a different race, scrambled past.

Pang squinted. 'Isn't that Fool's Money?'

I crumpled up my card.

'Don't take it too hard, Mr Wyatt.'

'Get back on the bloody horse, is that it?' I meant it to come out ironic. Funny, even. It didn't. I smirked like a prat to cover my embarrassment and went inside to place yet another blind wager.

Eva was waiting for me, just inside the glass doors. She was experimenting with Laura Ashley, and it wasn't working. She kissed me on the cheek and came with me to the line for the teller. It was hard for us to say what we had to say.

'He prefers wet ground,' she warned me, as my pen descended uncertainly toward Secret Service.

'It pissed down this morning,' I said.

About four people ahead of us, the teller was explaining complex accumulators to a pair of befuddled Australian tourists.

'The track's synthetic,' she warned me, but I bet anyway.

I lost again, and just to rub the pain in it started to spot with rain. 'Told you,' she sighed, leading the way from the rail into shelter.

'Yes, you did.'

'Don't be down.'

'I'm no gambler,' I said.

'You wouldn't have come here if you weren't.' Typically Eva: so aphoristic.

'I was invited,' I said. 'You invited me.'

Her smile was shy and adult and I felt as though I was falling into it. 'I'm talking about Hong Kong,' she said.

The rain came to nothing, so we went back to the rail. It was deserted now. Unlit. We were alone. She said, 'We're always wandering off into the dark.'

'It does seem that way.'

Her hand was tiny and strong. Not a child's hand at all.

'One more race,' she said.

'Not again.'

'Forget your plastic?' The rain glistened in her hair.

'I like it here,' I said.

'In the dark?'

'With you,' I said. 'I thought I wasn't going to see you again.'

She glanced around. Her father was standing behind us, in a pool of light, yards away. Rainwater drizzled from the balconies. It was like a curtain, cutting him off. I made to raise a hand but Eva stopped me with a touch. He hadn't seen us. We turned back towards the track.

She said, 'I wasn't pregnant, incidentally, if that's what you're thinking.'

I shrugged.

'Sorry. That was a rotten thing to say.'

'No it wasn't.'

She leaned against the wet rail, her hands clasped, very earnest. She said, 'I wouldn't have minded.'

'What?'

'You can fuck me as much as you want. I love you. I've been a cow.'

'What was that about'

'I want to be your girl,' she said.

I glanced round, nervous as hell. Pang was still standing there, still looking in the wrong direction. It couldn't last. 'Can't we do this somewhere else?'

She led me into the shadow of the stewards' social club, and down a covered alley, out of the rain. It was very dark. I had to touch her just to figure out where she was. There was a sweet refuse smell coming from somewhere. Above us, cheap cigarette smoke and muffled Cantonese wafted from a kitchen window.

'I'm going to tell them,' she said. 'Everybody. Friends, parents. I want you to come to lots of parties with me. I want to show you off. I don't know why I was so afraid. It wasn't you, it was me—'

I shut her up with a kiss. Big lower-middle-class brute that I was.

'Your dad'll think I've buggered off,' I said, when we were done.

'Don't be so nervous of him.'

An unpleasant thought struck me. 'God, you don't want me to ask him for permission or anything, do you?'

She laughed and kissed my nose.

'He thinks I'm a wuss as it is.'

'Let me choose you a winner then.' Out in the middle of the track, the big video monitor was screening odds for the next race. She tried to read them over my shoulder. 'Get your hand out my knickers – there.' She bobbed up on tiptoe and squinted. 'Who do you fancy?'

'I daren't look.'

'It's only a race.' She led me out of the alley and back into the Jockey Club building. 'Pride of Asia?'

'Sounds like a fruit company.'

'Lucky Jim?'

'No …'

'Hmm?'

I picked blindly.

'Oh Adam,' she cried, despairing of me, 'It's forty to one.'

'Double Happiness or nothing.'

'Adam, *why*?' Victor Pang cried, drawing level with us in the queue. I practically had a heart attack.

Pang, on the other hand, seemed quite unsurprised, finding Eva and I with our arms round each other. She must have told him about us. Or had he seen her unhappy these past weeks, and set this up himself?

I thought about Pang's notoriously snobbish wife, Eva's mother – how he had arranged it so that she was still blithely ensconced with her Vanderbildt/Stepford mob ...

'Yes, Adam,' Eva chipped in, 'why?'

The worst chip shop in the world is the Double Happiness in Mile End – I was hardly going to tell her that.

'Okay,' Eva sighed, admitting defeat. She reached into her purse and pulled out her plastic. Dad contained himself – just. 'I'll match you,' she said.

It was a big wedding; even the *Hong Kong Tatler* said so. Our winnings barely paid for the reception.

ICAC's choice of offices – above a fortress-like multi-storey car park on Garden Road – might indeed have been invented by John le Carré. High in their forbidding concrete eyrie, Hong Kong's Independent Commission Against Corruption answered to no-one. No-one had even bothered to tell them how long they could entertain their suspects without trial – an oversight that caused more than one Hong Kong broker to glance up nervously as he crossed Statue Square of a Friday night.

'Adam?'

I turned from the window.

His suit was reddish brown; a metallic thread ran through it, lending the material a strange, hectic bloom. 'Daniel White,' he said. 'How're you doing?' I came and shook his hand.

He was your typical FinCEN yuppy, fresh from some Tony Robbins-style leadership course in Key West. They were all bastards. I hadn't met one yet who didn't own a video of *Wall Street*.

He leaned his head to one side, squinting at me from

under thin, gingerish eyebrows. His eyes were the blue of oxidised egg yolk. 'You want to see him now?'

'Sure,' I said.

ICAC needed bodies to beef up its investigation into Top Luck, a local film investment company. Hamley had recommended me, for his own reasons; I impressed at interview, and I was in.

It turned out that Daniel White, my immediate superior, was on secondment, too, though he'd been working at ICAC full-time for a couple of years now. I followed him through an open-plan office and past a line of rooms, none of them occupied. I watched my reflection bounce back off every glass panel. White saw. 'Why do office doors these days all have to have windows?' he complained. 'What do they think we'd do in there? Mainline?'

I smiled a beatific smile.

He cracked, eventually: 'You don't say much, do you?'

'I have my moments,' I said. I was only obeying orders. Back then, British officials were required to feel a lot of animosity towards their US counterparts. All through the Cold War the CIA had thought it was running the government, and no sooner was that over then these FinCEN yuppies turned up thinking they were policing our economy.

We entered a conference room, startling its sole occupant: a young man with a cheeky, freckled face.

'John Pollard, this is my colleague Adam Wyatt.'

There were huge bags under his eyes, and when he reached out to shake, his hand trembled. Imagine Richmal Crompton's William once he's discovered masturbation. His palm was so damp, as soon as he wasn't looking I wiped my hand on my trousers.

He unpacked his squash bag onto the big central table: files and notebooks and a handful of computer disks. By the look of him, he hadn't used the bag for its intended purpose since arriving in the colony. When he bent over the bag, his gut folded itself over the table.

Three extremely scary Chinese women from ICAC followed us in. We only ever addressed them by their family names because their first names were all Suzy. Privately, ICAC staff had nicknamed them the Weird Sisters.

Pollard must have been made stupid by the intimidating surroundings because it took him half the interview to realise White and I were mere observers, and it was up to the women whether this belated whistle-blowing of his was enough to keep him from prison.

'And as far as you've been able to ascertain,' the first Sister began – a shark could not have smiled an uglier smile – 'your firm has had no previous dealings with Top Luck?'

'No, Ma'am,' he panted, his eyes flicking back and forth as he tried to keep all three predators in his field of view.

It took us the best part of two hours to assemble an order of events from the records Pollard had copied for us, and they made unedifying reading. No wonder he was blushing as we returned to run it through with him.

'When were you first approached?'

'Five months ago.'

'Where?'

'A wrap party in Chatham Square.'

'"Wrap party"?' The third Sister made it sound like a pyjama party, or worse.

'Yes, a film party,' Pollard explained, and added, unwisely, '*Double-barrelled Vengeance*, I think.'

The Sisters sneered collectively.

'Who approached you?'

'One of the directors. Yau Sau-Lan.'

Call me Jimmy I remembered, and a cold thrill went down my spine.

Sau-Lan was his Chinese name. Jimmy was the name he went by. Jimmy. Jimmy Yau.

'And Mr Pollard, did you know that Chatham Square is notorious as the headquarters of Sun Yee On triad?'

Pollard swallowed. He looked to me like I could help him. Like I wanted to.

Pollard had agreed to do business for Top Luck Investments after only the most cursory of verifications. A lot of it was his company's fault: their compliance systems were culpably shoddy and this wasn't the first time they'd failed in their legal obligations.

Nevertheless, Pollard only had himself to blame for what followed. Soon he was receiving instructions to redirect funds to random-seeming accounts in Switzerland and the Caymans, sometimes as little as half an hour before those transactions were due to process. No-one Pollard spoke to at Top Luck ever showed the slightest interest in the relatively poor rate of return they were getting from their investments. So at last – this was his story – the penny dropped. Poor sod. His only available defence was that he was a complete idiot.

It was a straightforward case on the surface, and the amounts involved were positively trifling. If it wasn't for the bizarre personal connection – Jimmy Yau's dad getting my girlfriend's granddad slain on Stanley beach – I wouldn't have been that excited. 'And besides,' I asked White, when we were done, 'what's a straightforward compliance failure got to do with the ICAC?'

White hit the button for the third floor. He looked at me, enquiringly.

'Same,' I said.

The lift slid shut and jerked into life.

'Maybe Pollard's paranoid,' White admitted, as we rode down. 'ICAC's the only body he says he trusts.'

'Yes, but this is hardly ICAC's scale: you'd think with an ordinary case like this ICAC would refer him down to the SCG,' I said.

White fixed me with his discoloured eyes. He smiled. 'They did,' he said.

The doors opened.

He said, 'Frank Hamley's had this on his books for two months now.'

I was so surprised, I nearly got stuck in the doors.

'So when you run your paperchase,' said White, as I caught up with him, 'on Top Luck and these brokers, you might keep a weather-eye open for Frank Hamley. See how he reacts to what you're doing. Yes?'

I felt dizzy.

White stopped. 'This is mine.' He pushed the remote button on his car key, and a nearby white Porsche 911 blinked and serenaded him.

I found my voice, somehow. Maybe it wasn't my voice. Maybe it was someone else's. It sounded very odd. 'Are you accusing Frank of obstructing an investigation?'

'Whatever,' White said, losing interest in me. He crossed to his car.

A bolt of anger shot up my throat. 'I don't answer to you,' I said. 'I don't have to tell you what my boss does or doesn't do.'

'Well, of course you don't.' He looked at me like I was stupid. 'You got seconded to the Weird Sisters, didn't you? I'm just the errand boy. It's them you have to tell.'

'Well, why the bloody hell would they think Frank's obstructing?' I pleaded.

'How the fuck would I know?' He shed his suit jacket. Its metallic thread caught the lights. It glittered, like it was wet. He opened the driver's door and threw the jacket over onto the passenger seat. 'It's you that works for him,' he said.

2

LONDON
SUMMER, 1998

14

Boots never turned up. Eventually Eva gave up puzzling over his disappearance. Did she accept that he'd run out, in the couple of seconds the door had stood open that day? Or had she consigned the puzzle to whatever part of her couldn't see the bruises on my neck, or hear the Wray and Nephew bottles clinking about in the trash? I didn't know, and I didn't care to know. I was still waiting for Boots's mummified tongue to turn up one day, mulching a flower-bed or blocking a drain.

There were no more little warnings. I tried not to think about it too much. The work, incidentally, was as Money had promised: clerical, easy, almost legitimate.

When Jimmy Yau vanished under the waves, he left behind a hotel in Mauritius, fifty-one per cent of the shares in a Salt Lake City bottling plant, and interests in tea plantations in Kenya, titanium sands in Malawi, container shipping in Nagasaki and oil from the Gulf. These were the major businesses, and at a first glance they seemed legitimate. Big enough, anyway, to employ a real workforce and keep up at least a pretence of normal trading.

The scary part of the animal was its soft accretion of dormant, shell and holding companies. Funds passed through them all – including the dormants, which was far from sensible – but where from and why and to whom these funds were eventually to go, it was next to impossible to find out.

Jimmy Yau had functionaries in the usual places: Hong Kong and Macau, Belgium and Amsterdam, Toronto and even Miami; their names kept coming up as directors, treasurers, company secretaries and so on. They were courteous enough on the phone, because why wouldn't they be? They were getting their take from the cash flow; in return, it was their names on the paperwork and it was they would be carrying the can should the authorities trip over whatever it was they were doing.

Money wanted me to set about liquidating any company that couldn't show a legitimate yearly trading record. 'Import–export,' she sneered, reading off my scratch-pad, 'is that all you could elicit?'

'He owns the company, Money,' I said. It was 11 a.m. – too, too early to have my balls broken. 'As far as he's concerned I'm just some curious gweilo at the wrong end of a phone line. If I tell him to pack up and he calls my bluff, what am I supposed to say? Either we find what it is Jimmy had on these people or we let them get on with it and look suitably blank when they implode.'

I glanced down my crib sheet. That 'import–export' business had no warehousing and had paid nothing to manufacturers since 1978. 'And that's only the start of it,' I said. 'Once we get control of bastards like this, once we start laying off staff ...'

'Staff?' Money barked, incredulously. 'This company *employs* people?'

'That's my point,' I said, gently. 'The paperwork says yes. Instinct says no – it says that this is simply a laundering outfit. But if its paperwork has created the illusion of employees, we have to maintain that illusion. We have to make these paper employees redundant. We may even have to *pay* them. All so the tax records tally. Believe me, if this outfit is a laundry – if its import-export business is entirely fictitious – closing it down is going to be like defusing a bomb.'

'And how many companies like this are there?'

'Altogether, or the ones that make no sense?' I didn't want her to panic. If she did she might be tempted to throw in the towel and give evidence at the enquiry. If she did that, she wasn't going to be able to protect herself, let alone me.

Besides, the more she bought into the dream of legitimising her dead husband's concerns, the longer – and better – I got paid. So far she'd been more generous than I had expected. She'd even arranged me an alibi for the time I spent working for her. I was now the proud manager of a long-dormant software publisher in Holborn.

'The ones that are obvious trouble,' said Money. 'How many companies?'

'One hundred and forty-seven,' I said.

Eva was impressed when she saw my job offer, the letter-headed paper, the address. 'Darling, you're back in the City.'

'It's hardly that,' I said. The aliens in my chest squirmed with embarrassment. They scrabbled at my chest wall, desperate to bail out.

'How did you find out about this?'

'I rang Mike,' I lied. 'He's just back from Hong Kong. He

said that time he phoned he might put some business my way.'

'Well?'

'Well what?'

'So come on,' she insisted, eagerly, 'tell me.'

Luckily for me, I'd spent that afternoon reading the company's scrapbooks.

'Telex verification,' I told her. And, 'Their platform-independent financial software ran on the Arpanet.' All true. I hazed and hazed, and meanwhile the taste in my mouth got worse and worse.

At least Eva was pleased, more pleased than she'd been in a very long time – and the sheets didn't smell of dog any more.

Afterwards she said, 'Are we going to ask Mike and Ylwa over for dinner?'

15

I started work most mornings at 6.30 a.m., which meant I could ride into work with Eva. But the main reason for the dawn start was Hong Kong's punishing time difference. Nobody takes you seriously out there after lunch, and they're five hours ahead of GMT. I worked best in the mornings, fuelling my way through a solids-free business day with take-out cappuccinos laced with Wray and Nephew. I was drinking a whole lot less now I wasn't having to keep the bottle in a hole in the wall.

Money agreed I should have my own office, and paid the deposit for a room above a sandwich shop opposite Southwark Cathedral. A spot of brinkmanship, that – a little touch of the old Hong Kong gambling ethic – my working so near Eva's café. It wasn't long before I began to enjoy my double life. Fooling Eva wasn't something I felt good about, but it sure as hell helped me nail the lid shut on the emasculated duffer I had been. After a year pouring wine for Kwok and Flora and the rest of Eva's Hong Kong cronies, like Max in Sunset Boulevard, I deserved a break or two.

There's great pleasure, I discovered, in propping your feet on your forty-quid office-surplus steel desk, leaning back in your broken-down swivel chair with foam busting out of the arm-rests, and telling a silk-suited poacher on the other side of the world not to bother shipping his container of oh-so-innocent leather goods this month, or next month, or – come to that – ever again.

Money had learned most of her management techniques from her husband: more often than not, it was I who had to go visit her. Brian and Eddie stomped around madly as soon as I crossed the threshold. The moment my calf-skin bag hit the living-room table, Eddie would do this yuppie riff with his mobile – running through stored number after stored number until he found someone he could say 'Hell, mate, yes,' to – and then they'd take off, Eddie and his talented animal assistant Brian, tearing the gravel drive to shit in their 4 × 4.

'Little farts.'

'Zoe.'

'Sorry, Mum.'

Dinners were tense affairs. Money and I had nothing in common. Zoe said little; her blind grey eyes paralysed me.

'And how is Justin?' Money asked, every time. If my wife could have seen her flat expression as she trotted this line out, time after time, it would have allayed all her fears.

'Oh,' I said, 'much the same.' Once or twice I had launched into an account of life at the school – hygiene lessons, singing games, group outings, gym-work – on and on, until you could have cracked the glaze on her eyes with a teaspoon. It never made any difference. Every time it was the same.

The same.

'Oh, much the same,' I said, with my brave little smile.

She never quite knew what to say next. Week after week, the formula she sought eluded her. 'Oh good,' she'd say, and then qualify it immediately, realising she should have said, 'Oh dear,' and then she'd qualify the qualification, figuring that, as there was no hope for him, it was rude of her to be rubbing it in.

It wasn't how it once was between Eva and I. The smart young shark in his suit and his cellular phone; his adoring young wife reading *Hong Kong Tatler* at home: we could never be that way again, thank God. What we had now was new and uncertain.

Eva had sensed the change in me, and liking it, gave it a chance to grow. Relieved of the need to beat up on me, able somehow to trust me again, her own pain receded, and something youthful and bright returned to her crinkled, bedroomy eyes.

We didn't know how to behave with each other. We floundered happily, shaping out the new space we were making together. At night, we grappled with each other, drowning and saving each other at once. They were nights when the sex got us so high, I really didn't care very much whether I was getting away with whatever it was I was doing. Afterward, of course, my heart was in my throat.

Awaiting judgment, I kicked the duvet off the bed and tried to pry ropes of twisted sheet out from under my back. Eva was moving about the en-suite bathroom in a shambling, beat-up sort of way. 'Jesus Christ.'

'What?'

'My face.'

'What's the matter?'

She came in and posed for me, red cheek turned, eyes shining. Proud. 'Vicious sod.'

'Let's see your arse.'

It was very red. I stroked her buttocks with the backs of my fingers; let them ride down the backs of her legs; drew a circle in the small of her back, round and round. She crumpled onto the bed.

She couldn't keep her tongue out of my mouth. It was like the first times. No it wasn't. It was tougher than that, raw and scary and honest. More violent in its demands than any play-rape.

'Christ you're impossibly hard.'

We didn't know what to do with it. She was too sore; I was scared of her teeth.

'Don't worry about it,' I said.

'But I love it.'

'I know you do.'

'I do.'

'It knows.'

She wrapped her legs around me. I moved, touching her cunt with the tip of my cock, withdrawing, touching. Her hair prickled me. She pulled me close and laughed into my ear, until after a while the laughter grew regular and desperate, and I knew she was crying.

I kissed my way across her neck to her chin, her cheeks, her eyes.

Ironic, that the dreadful threats we'd lived through should have given us this: a new start, after all. Strange, that by my deceiving her, we could be more properly ourselves.

She had waited for me for so long. So long, she had waited for me to come back to her. Did what she could to keep me whole. Failed, yes: but failed while meaning well. I felt no gratitude towards her: nothing so cold as that. No guilt, either, for turning out the way I had – the bottles hidden in the wall. All that mattered in the end was that she had waited and I had weathered, and now we were here, together, and her tears had stopped and I was still licking her face and it was starting to get ticklish and awful and she was laughing and trying to push me away -

'Ugh! Get off!'

I pinned her hands to the bed and gave her mouth a wet lick.

'Drink!' she squealed, threshing about under me.

'What?'

'I thought that'd stop you.'

I tried to lick her again. She fended me off. 'Drink! Drink! I want to get pissed!' She crawled off the bed. 'I'll be back in a sec.'

'Love you,' I sighed, as she went out the door.

'Love you too.'

'I Love *you*.'

It was a long way down to the kitchen.

'*LOVE YOU!*'

Clink. Smash.

'Oh *fuck* …'

'Are you okay?' I shouted. I sat up. 'Zoe?'

The aliens flexed and tittered.

'Yeah.'

Zoe …

Had she heard?

The aliens flexed and tittered.

She hadn't heard. She hadn't, hadn't.

'Here I come! she cried'

I strained for breath. The aliens were still laughing, they were sucking up all my oxygen. She stood in the doorway, her arms full of bottles, lovely green bottles. I gasped it out.

'I love you, Eva.'

Eva smiled a melting smile. 'I love you too, Adam,' she said.

16.

The next day, Money phoned me to say that her father-in-law had just died.

'I'm sorry to hear that, Money,' I said.

It was early in the afternoon, twenty-five degrees in the shade, and outside it sounded like the world was ending. Builders from Rattee & Kett were taking down their scaffolding from round the newly restored Southwark Cathedral. An ambulance had got log-jammed on London Bridge and was trying to blast a path clear with its siren. Two doors down, a bunch of boorish suits had strayed across the river for a boozy lunch outside the Mug House wine bar. Normally around now I'd have cooled off with a walk by the river, but only yesterday at this time I had seen Hannah walking towards me down Park Street, laden with bags from Neal's Yard Dairy, and I'd barely time to get out of sight. I didn't dare take a risk like that again.

'I was wondering,' said Money, 'whether you'd feel able to go and take care of his things for me.'

I balked slightly at that. 'Well, I'm not sure I'm really the person—'

The sun beat in through the dust-bleared sash window. The back of my neck was burning. The air in the office was unbearably close now, but the heat had warped the window shut and besides, there were too many wasps in the room as it was. While I watched, one crept drowsily in through the ventilator grille in the ceiling.

'I don't know the family—'

'It's simply impossible for me to get away at the moment, Adam. I really need you to take care of this for me.'

The wasp swung drunkenly towards the window. I levered myself out the way. The office chair dropped an inch or two under me as I rose.

'Adam?'

Yau Zhenshu. I wondered how on earth I was going to explain this one to Eva.

Physicist; informant; traitor; radio engineer; spy. Over the years, provoked by Eva's framed photograph of her grandfather, I had collected snippets about the man they said had caused his death. Zhenshu's life – pieced together out of scraps and hints from Jimmy, Money, Hamley, Victor and the Hong Kong grapevine – belonged to the darker, Dashiel Hammett end of a Thirties serial.

'His affairs may take some time to sort out,' Money warned me. 'He has property in Hong Kong.'

I was curious. Money was unwittingly pressing all the police-paperchaser buttons in me. There would not come another opportunity like this, to test Zhenshu's heinous reputation against reality.

I said, 'You won't want to sell anything.' Property prices there had fallen to a third of their Handover levels.

'I'm always very grateful for your advice, Adam.'

I thought about it some more. 'Where did he live?' I asked.

'Wye, in Kent.'

It was just about commutable. Maybe I wouldn't have to say anything to Eva.

The wasp, frustrated, turned and dive-bombed my head. I dodged, tugging the phone across the desk on a toboggan of loose papers.

'There's no immediate family. I can give you the number of his carer—'

The wasp landed on the armrest of the broken-down chair and caught its leg in the burst foam. It wrestled and fizzed, uselessly. If I had to spend another day in here I would surely melt into the lino.

I took a biro from out my shirt pocket. 'Sure,' I said. 'Go ahead.'

Outside, a scaffolding pipe struck the pavement. It rang like a bell.

If you have to lie, lie in detail. The last time I visited Money I told Eva that Richard Kitney had invited me to Imperial College's new medical school for a demonstration of Dicom 3.

Today, I told Eva I was attending a symposium on emotional interfacing chaired by Kevin Leicester at Reading University. Eva was so impressed she offered me the car. The mileage discrepancy between Reading and Wye was too great, so I chose the train instead, and was punished for my deceit by getting trapped in a window seat on the sunny side of a carriage that had probably carried my grandfather to the Great War. By the time I arrived my skin was rendered to glue. I tried straightening my shirt and the back of it was soaking.

The town was far too small for taxis: I was walking up the street to where the shops seemed to be – antiques, antiques, and, yes, no doubt about it, antiques – when a silver MX5 flew round the bend and slid to a halt, impossibly fast, against the opposite pavement.

Of course, I could guess who it was.

'Hop in.'

'You should have got a 5-series,' I told her. 'Then you could kill yourself in real comfort.' I strapped myself in. It felt like I was sitting on the road.

Zoe sniffed and reached down to scratch her ankle. She was barefoot. 'You know who buys *them*?'

'Who?'

She gunned the engine, paddled the wheel, and car leapt round like a cat to face the way it had come. '*Restaurateurs*.'

'What the fuck are you doing here, Zoe?'

She took my mood in her stride. 'Mother sent me.'

'Yeah, sure.'

'She figured I'd know who to invite to the cremation.'

'For that you needed to come all this way?'

'It didn't take long.'

She slewed the car around a couple of back streets to show me how little time it would have taken her.

'Christ's sakes.'

She laughed. She was nowhere near as good as she thought she was. 'Nearly there.' She turned down a narrow lane between old high walls and hit the brakes so hard, I could feel my guts being strained out through the seat-belt webbing.

I looked around, dazed. Zoe had teleported us out of town entirely. I could see nothing but trees. A dirt driveway led left.

'Down there?'

'Peaceful, isn't it?'

Suddenly we were doing barely ten miles an hour, over the dirt and onto a poorly-maintained drive. Zoe wanted to show the place off to me. The avenue was old, untended for years, and the chestnut trees had bust up the tarmac; roots rippled the surface. The MX5's rock-hard suspension jounced us about as we approached the house.

It was old, rebuilt and refitted so many times, it had lost all memory of itself.

Zoe shod herself and climbed out of the car. She didn't bother with the door. The heel of her Miu Miu sandal left an oval dent in the seat leather. Her outfit today was by her standards pretty restrained: a kitsch floral summer dress, probably Sogo. She picked her way across the crazed tarmac.

She was so small, so childishly thin – the girl in the *Hello Kitty* comic strip.

She fanned through the keys Zhenshu's nurse had given us, looking for a Yale among the heavy, eccentric shapes. I sat waiting on the low brick wall which framed the portico. The gardens were all overgrown. Roses, long-since outgrowing their pyramidal frames, threw off a faint perfume from scant, sickly flower heads. The dominant scent was of loam and damp.

'Here we are.'

'I thought Zhenshu was supposed to be the money-man of the family,' I said, following her into the front room. The furniture was cheap and old-fashioned, unworthy of these high-ceilinged rooms with their painted dado rails and elegant ceiling roses. Zhenshu hadn't so much lived here as camped out.

'He didn't want much for himself.'

In the kitchen, the fridge and the cooker were old models – an Electrolux, a Belling – kept spotlessly clean. The table was a nasty wood-effect laminate effort that folded up against the wall when not in use. There were net curtains over the windows, and nasty china figurines gathering dust on the window-sills.

It reminded me of Arnos Grove, and of the house where I grew up when mother was still alive, dusting every day.

Upstairs, the rooms smelled of glue. Out in the hall, damp had got into the plaster, and a corner of the ceiling had fallen in.

'Nice to see he was being looked after properly.' I toed through the pile of plaster and Artex beneath the hole.

'He never used the rooms upstairs.'

I looked up into the hole, where the attic had to be: a wire crate had fallen onto the unsupported part of the ceiling and cracked it open. There were papers poking through the mesh of the crate. I stood on tiptoe and pulled one free.

'Adam! You'll have it down on top of you.'

I stepped smartly away: my Indiana Jones moment. Nothing happened.

'I'm hungry,' said Zoe, already bored with this.

'We can go grab some lunch in a minute.' The letter was full of technical details: an argument about tolerances, too involved to make any immediate sense. 'If you like.' It carried the Nabeshima letterhead. I showed it to her.

'Oh,' she said, unsurprised, 'yes, there'll be tons of that here.'

I looked at her, blank. 'I thought he was a teacher.'

'He worked at the University of Hong Kong, but he invented stuff, didn't you know?'

'No.'

'That's what caused all the nastiness in Hong Kong. He was forced to work for Nabeshima during the occupation. That's when the rumours got started about him being a traitor.'

I looked at the letter again. 'This is dated '55.'

'He rejoined the company when he moved to Japan.'

'Your dad told me they lived on the bread-line in Abashiri.'

'Oh, that was only to start with.'

I remember thinking, just how complicated were Zhenshu's affairs going to be? I wondered how many more crates were waiting for us in the loft.

We drove to Dover for lunch. Zoe wanted to rediscover a tea shop she remembered from when she was little – a pig-tailed, six-year-old tourist armed with a Nikon camera Jimmy had bought her for her birthday. 'It was a proper camera, lenses and everything. It weighed a ton.'

'A strange sort of present for a little girl,' I said.

'You know that's how he was with me,' she said, without rancour. I felt petty.

We were walking along the top of the sea wall. The sun was so bright, the sea was full of shattered mirrors. I thought about Jimmy, the Praya, the car swerving and falling. 'How were you two getting along? Before he died?'

'He gave me money for my car.'

I looked at her. She shrugged.

Poor Jimmy: the third time around, he finally got a child worthy of him, and it was a girl. She had nowhere he could make his scars.

'No,' she said, 'things were fine. I thought maybe when I went to study in London it might have got easier between us, but whenever I answered the phone all he ever said was, "Can I talk to your mother?"'

'That's not Jimmy,' I said, 'that's men, period.'

'Really?'

'Well, my dad—'

I stopped myself.

'Were you often here as a child?'

'Only once,' she said. 'Zhenshu took me to the Isle of Wight.' She swung her sandals in her hand. I had forgotten that about her: how she was always dancing. 'There's a castle there, and a lighthouse. It was open, and the lighthouse keeper showed me round. I don't suppose he was real – aren't they all operated by machine now?'

'I suppose' I said, watching her dance.

'I ate sugared almonds,' she said. It was strange, hearing her account of these ordinary places; even now, they had a kind of foreign glamour for her. 'I remember he took me sailing once,' she said. 'It was very rough. You wouldn't think it, would you? It's such a pretty stretch of water.'

'Yes.' I was thinking about my father: his collections of

117

things; his tiny, meticulous handwriting. The formal gestures he used with people to hide his fear.

The concrete had weathered and crumbled here, and there was a big puddle in front of us. I jumped across it and offered Zoe my hands. 'Jump,' I said.

She jumped, and snatched my hands. I overbalanced and stumbled into the puddle. She leaned into me, struggling to regain her balance. Her hair smelled of salt water and seaweed. Her breasts brushed me. She looked up at me; her eyes were blind eyes, the pupils pin-point small in grey irises. They expressed nothing.

I tried to smile. My mouth gave way. 'I—'

She laughed. 'I'm *soaking*!'

Water glistened on her ankles.

17

My feet were wet through and my socks were balling around my toes as we wandered from street to street in search of Zoe's café. Every road seemed to lead us further away from the sea-front, into closes lined with four-wheel drive cars and ornamental conifer hedges and ruched blinds in every window.

'There's nothing here,' she said, turning a full circle as she walked. 'What do people do? Where do they shop? It's like an episode of *Sliders*.'

'They all have cars,' I said. 'It's like this everywhere now.'

We went back to the coast road and entered a greasy spoon we had passed earlier. It wanted to be a Fifties diner, with American number plates screwed to the walls and Jimmy Dean on the front of every plasticated menu.

'Egg and chips.'

If Money could have heard us, she would have approved. Zoe, missing her studies at the LSE, wanted me to recall my days with KPMG. I gave her the usual milk-round pep talk about pension funds, ethical investments, and the rest. It was strange, seeing her on the threshold of that world, taking it all on board, drinking it in.

She said, 'I did an ethics paper last year on affinity cards.'

It was a strange conversation.

I can't remember at what point I started not to believe in it. It just snuck up on me somehow: the anger, the desire to confront whatever it was I thought was really going on behind these niceties.

'Why did Money kill my dog?'

'What?'

'I guess it was Brian and Eddie got their hands dirty. It seems their style.'

'What dog?'

'You mean they're working through a list?'

'Adam—'

'Eva's dog.'

Her fork was loaded with ham. She let it fall back on her plate. 'What are you talking about?' She knew it was something bad. Her face had paled already. But it was too late now. 'Eva's dog was crucified against our garage wall.'

Zoe swallowed.

'It was the day after the meal. It was the day I called your mum and said I'd work for you, after all.'

'You didn't say anything about a dog.'

I shrugged. 'Never show a hit,' I said.

'You know,' I said, 'she didn't have to do that. It's fucking crude, apart from anything else. Jimmy would never have done anything like that.'

'She didn't do it!' It was almost a shout.

'Come on, Zoe …'

'She didn't.' There were tears in her eyes.

It was no good. I couldn't stop. 'She has Hamley killed,

119

because he was dumb enough to let the inquiry catch up with him. And when it looked to her like I might get out of line—'

'It's not true.'

I smiled. She had so much to learn. 'Eat your chips,' I said.

She was crying openly now. 'It's not,' she kept saying.

'She more or less told me, Zoe. She's been waving Hamley's accident in my face every time we've spoken.'

'She told you she didn't do it.'

I wiped a scrap of bread round my plate.

'I was there when she phoned to invite you round. She said, "I wasn't the one who ran – who ran over –".' Her jaw trembled.

'She felt she had to force me into working for her.'

'Stop it.'

'I suppose she didn't have anyone else she could threaten.'

Zoe stirred her coffee with a spoon. She wiped her eyes. She waited.

There isn't much you can do with a blanket denial, especially when there's no other evidence to hand. Besides, there's only so long you can feel good about making a pretty girl cry. So though the paranoia was still there inside me I packed it back into its box and put it away and began the long climb down.

'I'm sorry,' I said.

'You can't blame me for being on edge,' I said. 'Friends?'

'Please, Zoe,' I said.

She shook her head. 'It doesn't matter whether we're friends or not,' she said.

'It matters to me.'

'I mean it's not the point.' She looked at me. Anyone else, it would have been what they call a 'significant' look. But her blind grey eyes were useless for that – they conveyed nothing. 'Did you mean it about your dog?'

'I had to get rid of him before Eva saw.'

'Then it's like Mum said, isn't it? Someone somewhere is calling her bluff.'

It had never occurred to me that Boots's death might be intended as a warning, not for me, but for my protectors the Yaus. 'Well, who would want to do that?' I protested.

Zoe tasted her coffee, grimaced, and pushed the cup away. 'How am I supposed to know?' she said. 'You're the spy.'

I'd wanted to clear the air, but all I'd done was stir up more dust. So I did my best to crow-bar the conversation back onto its original track. Zoe joined in. But nothing either of us said after that had much to do with what we were really thinking.

'I'd like to go back to Hong Kong one day,' she said. 'Start my own business there. If the bust bottoms out.'

It startled me, how quick she was to forgive my accusations. I wanted to thank her but I didn't know how so I followed her lead and pretended nothing had happened. 'More than half China's trade spills through Hong Kong,' I said. 'Sure the bust'll end.'

'Just so long as I can lose our heinous family reputation.'

Well, I thought, I guess I deserve that. 'If we do our job well,' I said, 'you won't owe anybody anything.'

'God,' she said, pushing her plate away, still half-full, 'they certainly give you enough.'

We walked back along the main road and through a public marina to the car park. The wind was damp and feverish, and lines tinked against their masts, setting my nerves on edge.

'The thing is to keep Brian and Eddie out of it,' she said, picking between the puddles and flotsam. My trainers and socks were soon so sodden through, it didn't make any difference, and I slopped along untidily beside her. 'They wouldn't have a clue.'

'They seem pretty entrepreneurial,' I said, ineffectually polite. Only five minutes before I'd been calling them dog-killers. 'Especially Eddie,' I offered – a limp olive-branch.

'Eddie imports snowboards,' she said.

'There you are.' My feet were so wet, I felt blisters forming.

'He stuffs them with dope.'

I didn't know what to say.

'He has a sculptor from Central St Martin's hollow them out for him with a plaster saw. Meanwhile he sends Brian over on the Dieppe Ferry in a Ford van with a clapped-out gas heater in the back. When he returns it's crammed to the gills with beer. No-one ever notices the Calor canister's stuffed with cocaine.'

'Does Money know?'

'Mum's not good at asking the right questions. They keep the empties in her garage.'

'Have you talked to them about it?'

She shook her head. 'I dropped Eddie's mobile phone into the toilet once.'

I laughed. 'That must have given him pause.'

'He's going to land Mum in trouble.'

'And you,' I said.

She said, 'They've got this idea Hong Kong's hassle-free, "catch-as-catch-can, mate".' Her impersonation of Eddie was merciless. 'They want to become film producers. The new Heung brothers. They'll be eaten alive.'

There was nothing to say. Brian and Eddie worshipped their father. If they wanted to follow in his footsteps, there wasn't much anyone could do except try and contain the damage.

*

Back at Zhenshu's house, I shed my shoes and washed my feet in the shower. There wasn't a towel, so I made do with a flannel I found, folded up, clean and fresh, on the shelf by the sink.

When I came out I found Zoe struggling with a step-ladder she had brought in from the garage. 'For the attic,' she explained.

I put that off as long as I could, but Zhenshu had been very organised, and it didn't take long to gather the papers in the ground floor rooms. His insurance and pension certificates were arranged in alphabetical order in a series of concertina files. Even his cheque stubs were kept in a box labelled 'Stubs'.

'Shall we have a look in the loft now?'

It was all a big game to her. She was irresistible.

I went first up the stepladder. The stairs were warm under my bare feet. There was no lock, and the panel lifted easily enough. I slid it out of the way.

'Can you see anything?'

'There's a pull-cord here.' I reached up and tugged. Nothing happened. 'The electricity's off,' I said, feeling foolish.

'No.' Zoe went and flicked the hall light on and off, proving her point.

'Well the bulb's gone.'

Zoe found a torch and a spare bulb under the sink and handed them up. The socket was live when I pushed the bulb home. 'Fuck.'

'What is it?'

'I hate doing that.' I looked around. The boxes were stacked so close together, there wasn't even space to walk between the stacks. 'Bloody hell.'

'What?'

They were Viking archive boxes. I pulled the lid off the

nearest. Inside lay a stack of neatly typed technical speci-
fications; a laminated Nabeshima company brochure from
the mid-Fifties; a dot-matrix printout in hexadecimal.

I looked for a way through the stacks.

'Can I come up?'

'Let me make some room.'

An MDF floor had been laid over the joists. I started
making a path and found that the stack was only two boxes
deep. Beyond, narrow paths of chipboard off-cuts made
meandering paths from beam to beam, over fungal, bulbous
pools of old insulating felt.

'How's it look?'

'Manageable. Come on up.' There was an old tricycle
under a drop-leaf table. 'I thought he didn't have kids,' I
said.

'What have you found?' Zoe's voice was bright and
excited. She came up the ladder. I made room for her.

'He kept it!' she said. She rushed over to examine it,
jumping from board to board. I winced: they weren't even
nailed down. She ran her hands over the handlebars. Her
fingers almost fitted the brakes, still. I felt something melt
inside me, leaving me hollow inside.

Leather trunks and plastic bags, rolls of carpet, a wardrobe rack on casters, jam-packed, the clothes hidden behind
dry cleaning bags. I said, 'I don't think he ever threw anything away.'

Behind the table were three tea chests. The first was full of
technical drawings, rolled neatly into cardboard cylinders.
Zoe helped me unwrap a couple: blueprints for radios, or
what looked like radios.

The next chest was covered with a blanket. There was no
lid. I looked in. It was as if Zhenshu had taken a bunch of
old radios to pieces and thrown the bits in here.

I stirred around in the junk; it meant nothing to me.

'You think all those boxes of letters and print-outs are about this?'

Zoe came over to look. 'God,' she said, 'what a depressing idea.'

The third chest contained crockery.

In an old leather trunk we found notebooks written in Cantonese interspersed with mathematical equations, amended, scribbled over and crossed through again and again in angry black ink until surely even Zhenshu couldn't have made any sense of them. There were hardback diaries, used as scribbling pads, and a pile of school exercise books tied with string. When we opened them we found a journal, again in Cantonese, interleaved with photographs, most so faded and blotched we couldn't make out the images.

Old ornaments. Prints. A box full of Goss china. A school-room globe minus its stand, wrapped in newspaper. The map petals were lifting off the ball. We smoothed them down and read off forgotten names. Rhodesia. Sudetenland.

Zoe found a pile of 78s wrapped in brown paper, but we couldn't find a player. I opened a Lloyd Loom laundry basket and it was full of silk *cheongsams*. I held one out for her.

She held it against her. 'It's lovely,' she said.

I said, 'Put it on.'

'What?'

'Put it on.' I had completely lost control of my mouth. 'It looks the right size.'

At the bottom of the basket was a Huntley and Palmer's biscuit tin full of her grandmother's jewellery. She laid the pieces out in the silk nest we'd made beside the laundry basket. Jade and silver. Gold bracelets. Rings that might have been diamond, and probably were. A velvet choker with a ruby sewn into the front.

'I never knew her,' said Zoe, sadly, telling me what I already knew: 'She died giving birth to Dad.'

'There's probably a photograph of her somewhere,' I said. But we couldn't find one.

'Jesus, what a mess.'

We surveyed the damage – the pile of old clothes, the papers scattered everywhere, the globe, perched precariously on top of the pile of 78s. 'It was a mess anyway,' she said. 'Only now it looks like a mess.'

'We'd better put it straight.' I said.

But Zoe had noticed something in the junk filling the middle tea chest.

'What is it?'

She was having trouble untangling its wires. 'I'll show you if I can only – there.'

It looked like a Walkman – a bakelite Walkman, with half a dozen cloth-sheathed wires dangling from one end. Each ended in a crocodile clip.

I swallowed. I knew what it was.

How could I forget?

She misread my expression totally; she smiled, and handed the box over to me. 'Now this would be worth suing over,' she said.

The aliens inside me backed away frantically, bumping against my spine.

There was a brass switch on the side of the box, like an old-fashioned light-switch, and a metal knob with numbered settings up to ten.

'My dad had one. It's a stress-relief thing.'

I didn't dare meet her eyes. *Stress?*

'You know. Biofeedback.'

Maybe I was wrong. Maybe it wasn't what I thought it was. Maybe it was all one big jolly coincidence.

Maybe I was panicking.

'Zhenshu made this?'

'Yes,' she said. 'The family story goes Nabeshima wanted

126

it but Zhenshu would never agree to a deal.' She laughed a dry laugh. 'Not very likely, is it?'

'I don't know.' I weighed the box in my hand. It was very light. '"Biofeedback"? Zoe, the word wasn't even invented until the Sixties.'

'Maybe that's why he could never strike a deal. His work was ahead of its time.'

'How does it work?'

'You pinch the clips to your skin.'

I looked at her.

'It doesn't hurt. Dad's version has acupuncture needles, so be grateful.'

She slid off the backing plate. 'No batteries,' she said, disappointed, and put the box back together again.

I turned away and stuffed newspaper back around the globe. I had to hide my face somehow. 'Let's get on.'

I threw Zhenshu's journals into the trunk. I rolled up the blueprints. I worked steadily. When I turned round, Zoe had gone.

Downstairs, I heard a toilet flush.

Zoe had thrown the box back into the trunk. Maybe it meant nothing to her, after all. Even if it was what I thought it was, it was probably the first, an early prototype: probably it couldn't do what the models I had known could do.

I ran my hand across my eyes, trying to wipe away the images. Their needles and their eyes. Their mouths, their centres, the taste of them.

The aliens rattled my spine, shaking me awake.

I picked up Zhenshu's little bakelite box and pushed open the backing plate. The case was made to hold size-3 batteries. I crossed to the hatch and picked up the torch. I took out the batteries. I slipped them into place inside Zhenshu's box. I must have put the battery cover down someplace stupid because I couldn't find it.

I examined the casing for a light, but there was nothing to indicate that the machine was working.

I dabbed my finger against a dangling alligator clip. Nothing. I threw the switch on the side of the box. The heavy spring snapped the contacts together with a satisfying clack. I touched the clip again.

The tiniest charge sprang off my finger, like static off a TV screen.

'Adam?'

She had changed into a *cheongsam*. It was gold, painted with flowers. She'd had to pull it up above her knees to climb the stairs and the material was still rucked up. She stooped and pulled it down around her ankles, smoothing the silk over her calves. Her breasts moved against the front of her dress. She stood up. Her belly was flat and hard. Her hip-bones jutting sharply against the narrow cut of the dress – two bright points, sheened by the naked electric light. 'What do you think?' Her grandmother's ruby glittered at her throat.

'I think you're beautiful,' I said.

'Yes?'

'You know what I think.'

She saw the machine in my hand. She came over and sat at my feet. As she sank to her knees, the long slit at the side of her dress opened to show me her thigh. She took the box from me. She saw the batteries there, and smiled.

'What?'

'Put your hand out,' she said. She clipped the wires to my skin: one on the web of my forefinger and thumb, two to the skin below my wrist, another two to the loose skin over my knuckles. She got me to squeeze the last one between my third and fourth fingers. The clips were only weakly sprung. They didn't hurt at all – just a slight tingle as they first touched my skin.

She knew what she was doing.

'Zoe?'

There was an old trunk lying next to us. She had me lay my hand, palm down, on the worn leather surface.

'Zoe, please—'

'Do you remember Hong Kong?' she said, and turned the dial.

My hand swelled.

I felt it. It grew and grew. It became heavy. It tugged at my wrist. Pints of blood welled in my fingers. I felt the tips of my fingers filling like balloons, stretching, about to burst. My wrist twisted sickeningly. The sinew and linkage inside puffed and knotted, struggling to bear the heavy hand.

The clips were expanding too. No matter how big my hand got, the clips grew at the same rate. Great metal jaws dragged at skin grown leathery and thick, like whale hide, and I could feel the way each layer of dermis tugged and clung, resisting the pull of the teeth.

I steeled myself, and glanced at my hand.

I knew what to expect, though I still couldn't really believe it. It was lying on the trunk, attached by wires to Zoe's machine. It was exactly as it had been. It wasn't swollen at all.

I swallowed. I tried lifting my forefinger off the table.

I felt the muscles knot inside my hand, and let out a ragged breath as the tendon slid slickly along its carpal tunnel. At last the great bloody bag of my fingertip tore free of its sticky fingerprint and rose from the trunk.

'I—' I said.

Zoe held her hand over mine.

I felt her electricity before she ever touched me. The aura of her flesh. The static hum. The hairs along the back of my hand stood erect for her. Her hand came closer and closer.

I swallowed and closed my eyes.

The weight of her crushed my hand into the trunk. Bone bulged through tissue. Nerves sparked.

She clenched her hand round mine. Her flesh was soft and insistent. It throbbed against me to an alien rhythm, her rhythm, and I could feel the pulse of her heart through her bones.

I blinked away tears. She drew my hand towards her.

'Feel what it can do,' she said – and took my thumb inside her mouth.

HONG KONG
1992

18.

All Eva had ever wanted was love. All her life she had thirsted for it. Her mother had never returned it. The first year of our marriage, I had plotted with an awful fascination the dark void it had left inside her, and, because I loved her, filled it up as best I could. But sex and words can't fill that gaping need, and so we'd had a child, both wanting it, both needing it, and both so happy when it came, we never noticed anything was wrong till well into Justin's third year. We thought for a while it was a hearing problem.

Then the results came back from the DSM-IV diagnostic interview: it was like the flame inside her guttered.

One day in early 1992, on the fourth floor of City Hall Library in Hong Kong, I came across a two-year-old paper by Chung,

Luk and Lee in the *Journal of Autism*. Autistic children, they wrote, do unusually well in the colony, supported and encouraged by a close-knit network of relatives and friends. The trouble with Eva and I was, I had just that week cut us out of that supportive family loop – and I still had her mother's scratches to prove it.

'He's gone backwards,' Eva sobbed, that evening, 'Just listen to him!'

Alone, in the dark, Justin whirled around his room. His bare toes hoofed the carpet. He had smashed the ceiling light so often, we had stopped replacing the bulb. Besides, he hardly ever bumped into things. He looked at everything out the corner of his eye, and as any amateur astronomer or night fisherman will tell you, peripheral vision works better at night. The orange glow of night-time Hong Kong was more than enough for him to see by.

'I'm not doing him any good, Adam.'

I had known this was coming. I had seen it in Eva's face: the self-doubt, the guilt. Her own mother had spat the seeds in through her ear one Saturday when she came round to baby-sit.

'If you only treated him normally, Eva, all this would go away.'

All I could do was sit there, open-mouthed, gravy dripping off my fork. If she'd leaned over the dining table and plunged her steak knife through my wife's heart, I couldn't have been more dumbfounded or more useless.

Eva's mother was incapable of love. Justin, lucky animal, had no need of it. Needless to say Eva's mother handled her grandson better than she had ever handled her own daughter. Around him, and only around him, could she feel whole.

She blamed Eva for Justin's condition. Justin was a lovely little boy, she insisted, the night I threw her out. 'Why can't you two treat him properly?'

She withdrew the knife in time, but not without a hefty twist.

'All I know is, anyone could have done this. Anyone. I don't know a single mother who hasn't felt this in themselves.'

Not Mummy's pearls of wisdom, this time, but those of a Gestalt counsellor she got Eva to see every Thursday afternoon.

And after that I saw it fed, that useless guilt eating my wife, in fits and spurts, by every phone-call Mummy made, and every trip to psychotherapy.

Autistic children cannot show love because they do not know what it is. For a long time it was assumed that autistic children were so cold because their parents – their mothers especially – were cold to them. Autism, it was once thought, was just a symptom of emotional neglect.

Which is crap, of course. Neglected children may exhibit some autistic behaviours at first but put them in a more stimulating environment – put them *together*, even – and they will begin to recover very quickly. The improvements are blindingly obvious after about twenty-four hours.

But there was no point trying to explain this to Eva's mother, or argue rationally at all, come to that. She was bent on her daughter's destruction.

It was up to me then, to tear Eva's guilt up by the root. The trouble was, that 'refrigerator mother' bullshit, however dreadful it was, had at least provided Eva with a kind of explanation for why Justin was the way he was. All I could offer in exchange were scraps and snatches: a threadbare and – thanks to my own ignorance and aspirin-popping upbringing – a largely pharmaceutical hope.

For a little while, Justin had responded well to the dietary supplement DMG. I got our supplies from an outfit calling itself Cognitional – basically a worn, gangly, engaging neurologist called Michael Yildiz.

His offices were not immediately reassuring. On the coffee table in the reception there was a copy of *Caduceus* among the *Hong Kong Tatlers*. 'Healing into Wholeness', it said on the front. 'Trees for life,' it said.

'Our Ancient Guardians.'

'Can dolphins heal?'

I was just reaching for the lift when Yildiz buzzed the desk. 'You can go through,' the receptionist said, without looking at me, like it was beyond her why I should want to.

Quite what Damascene conversion had drawn Dr Yildiz into the woolly world of complementary medicine, I never found out. One minute he was performing the Wada test on bike crash victims in Bangkok, the next he was knocking down the doors of venture capitalists, buttonholing them about a crazy vision he had for a new kind of medical care – something he called 'integrated natural healing technologies'.

What this meant for Eva and Justin and I was reliable information about casein- and gluten-free diets, a video made by parents of autistic children in San Diego about the effects of taurine intake, and near-cost supplies of DMG from a Stateside health-food store.

In his pine-panelled office – it might have been a sauna in a former life – Yildiz handed me some foil strips stamped DMG. 'This stuff's been around since 1965,' he yawned, handing me a copy of Allan Cott's original paper. 'He came across it in Moscow, in the form of pangamic acid. It's not specific to autism: Blumena and Belyakova saw improvement in the speech of twelve out of fifteen mentally handicapped kids.'

I searched his face for clues. He couldn't have changed his razor in months because his neck was one big bloody rash. His clothes were expensive but ill-kempt. His off-hand manner suggested a certain professional assurance, but I was new to all this, and distrustful.

'Has this stuff been tested?' I asked him.

Yildiz smiled. 'There have been plenty of non-autism studies which show it's safe. I'm afraid no-one's going to spend quarter of a million dollars sponsoring a double-blind study for its effects on autistic children.'

'Why not?'

'Because no-one owns exclusive rights to manufacture it. It's a health-food, not a pharmaceutical.'

He was telling the truth, and he was ahead of the game. Eva and Justin and I were already out the other side of the DMG roller-coaster when the hype about it hit the press. A Los Angeles mother crashes her car when her five-year-old autistic mute son shouts 'No! No baby-sitter!' At a Moscow funeral, a mentally retarded girl asks her younger brother why he is crying.

It's officially a food, not a drug, you can't overdose on it, and no-one owns exclusive manufacturing rights, so it's as cheap as spit. It works, too, just like the stories say – for a while, at least.

If researching my son's condition was consuming all my free time and draining my already much-beleaguered bank balance, at least ICAC provided a certain amount of light relief.

'Spying' on Frank Hamley meant little more than accepting his invitations. A bar here. A strip club there. It was never my style, and it was refreshing, to have Hamley draw me out of myself this way. I tried claiming my evenings on expenses but White wasn't having any.

'I'm not doing this for fun, you know.'

'You could just try paperchasing him, Adam. We want a report, not a tabloid exclusive.'

It got silly. He used to set me up with cocktail waitresses. I wasn't very interested, but the attention was flattering. We used to go eat where the lap-dancers got intimate with the desert trolley. He was a Virgil of bad taste, leading his Home-Counties Dante from one unedifying venue to another, abandoning him whenever the mood took him. He used to get me drunk and I'd wake about three in the morning to find myself being carried out of some porno theatre by weary bouncers.

Around about this time, Eva's mother found out that Eva was spending her allowance on Justin, and stopped it.

I shrugged the news off and gave Eva a cheque of my own, like it was nothing, someone else's tantrum, nothing to do with us, something we could easily cover.

It was half my monthly salary.

It was time to sober up, to close down the hatches, to tighten the belt.

I told Hamley I was going on the wagon for a while, I borrowed a cheap laptop from work, and did my researches into Justin's illness from the living-room table.

'Come to bed, love.'

'In a minute. It's a really good site.'

'Adam, please—'

'Have we any more paper?'

Hamley took it hard. 'I mean, you know the one I'm talking about, don't you? You have seen her, haven't you?'

'I'm married.'

'I promised her.'

'I can't come out tonight.'

'I've got the entire personnel desk hot for you. They're drooling into their soups.'

'Have a good time.'

'Not even a spritzer?'

'Goodnight.'

It tuned out there was more on his mind than a works outing. He had something to tell me. I stuck to my guns. In the end he had to take a lunch hour – something he never usually did. 'Let's go for a walk,' he said. Intrigued, I agreed.

In all the time it took us to walk to the Star Ferry Terminal, I don't think we exchanged more than a dozen words. Hamley had something on his mind. The further we walked, the heavier that something seemed, so that by the time we boarded the *Shining Stars* his dismal, crushed body language suggested a different personality altogether from the ebullient, sensual ogre I had known. For the first time, I was struck by the weakness of his chin.

He bought me a first-class ticket for the crossing of the harbour. I was surprised. Nobody ever rides upstairs but tourists – it takes you five times as long to leave the boat. A striped awning shaded the port-side of the double-prowed ferry. Hamley swung the reversible seat-backs to face front and beckoned me to sit beside him. A gaggle of Filipina housemaids on a day-trip came and sat in front of us, drowning out, for the *gweilos* and Japanese businessmen and Australian tourists gathered at the rail, anything we might say.

Hamley seemed pleased with the arrangement.

The crossing only took ten minutes so he made his pitch brief. 'I want to show you something,' he said. He plunged his hand into his trouser pocket, rummaged about there, double-took, rummaged some more, half-rose in his seat and plunged his fingers further in – like a best man who's forgotten the ring. At last he found it, whatever it was, and handed it over. It was a metal disc, like a large watch battery. There was a serial number stamped on the edge, half a dozen kanji, and a name: Nabeshima.

'Thanks,' I said, stupidly enough.

'It's a tracker,' he said.

'Uh-huh.'

'You know what a tracker is?'

'Uh, no.'

'Then don't pretend that you do.' He snatched the thing off me. 'God, that's irritating.'

'I'm sorry,' I said.

'It's a tracker. People use it to track people. You know: a tag.'

I looked at the thing in his hand. I looked at him.

He said, 'I found it down the back seat of my car when I was creaming the leather last Sunday.'

'Oh,' I said. I hunted furiously for something intelligent to say. 'I guess you don't know whose it is, then.' Brilliant, I thought, even before I quit speaking. Jim Rockford lives.

'Yes,' Hamley said, 'yes I do.'

I waited. I didn't trust myself to speak.

'You can buy any number of shoddy toys like this in Golden Arcade. Some of them not so shoddy. But not this sort.'

'No?'

'No.' He weighed it in his hand. His fingers closed over it. They tightened. I thought for a moment he was going to throw it overboard. Instead, he tucked it carefully back inside his trouser pocket. He folded his arms over his chest. He looked out over the water. 'It's police issue,' he said.

That afternoon I found White in his office and pinned him there a while.

He wasn't giving anything away. 'Do we have to do this in the office?'

'No,' I said. 'If you'd rather we can both go talk this through in front of the Weird Sisters.'

'I'd rather talk about this outside.'

'I bet you would.'

I wanted to know why I'd been left out of the loop. 'You should have told me you'd put him under radio surveillance. All the while you've been playing *Popular Mechanics* I've been out there with my arse hanging out.'

'Oh come on, Adam, it's a lovely day, why don't we—?'

'You told me to keep an eye on him. What's he going to think now? I don't give a shit about what you think you're on to, but if you lose me my job—'

White compromised. He hung his suit jacket over the glass panel in the door, turned on his desk fan and sat down beside it. He spoke so softly I had to lean into the breeze to hear him. It made my eyes go funny.

'It isn't us,' he said.

'But—'

'It isn't ICAC. We haven't bugged him.'

'Hamley said the tracker was police issue.'

'Did he show it to you?'

'Yes.'

'What did it look like?'

'It had the word Nabeshima on the side.'

White bit his lip.

'Well?'

'Nabeshima are our exclusive suppliers. ICAC, the Serious Crime Group, all the other spooks get their hardware from Nabeshima, via the Royal Hong Kong Police.'

'You know a lot about it.'

White grunted. 'I get their salesman drunk every quarter. Filthy job but somebody has to do it.'

'So who – who, if not us, is investigating Frank?'

White shrugged. 'If it was the regular RHKP we'd already have been told about it. One of Frank's colleagues in the Serious Crime Group, maybe? Only I don't think the SCG have the brief to conduct internal investigations. If it's not ICAC, there aren't many higher levels could order such an aggressive investigation.'

'The CIA?' I sneered. MI5, maybe? UNCLE?'

He turned off the fan. *The Spies Like Us* routine had gone sour in his mouth.

'Well?'

'Well ...' White grinned. Pure *Schadenfreude* – no humour there at all. 'I'm fucked if I know.'

'Justin's gone backwards,' Eva cried.

Justin's tiny, temporary gains, his flashes, his brief moments of connection that were all I won for all my reading, all my money – they brought him little enough gain, and Eva no comfort.

She wanted to mourn him, but I wouldn't let her. I kept wiring him up to the lightning conductor. I kept him jerking. I wouldn't let hope die. 'I talked to Dr Yildiz on Monday,' I said. I'd been doing my homework for this. 'There's an anti-convulsant called ethosuximide.'

She looked at me like I was mad.

'It's been linked to language gain. Very modest. Nothing like the DMG. But maybe a combination of that and DMG—'

'Can you hear yourself?'

'For God's sake,' I said, 'DMG's just a bloody food supplement. What harm can it do?'

Eva rubbed her face. 'How long are we going to go on like this?'

'On like what?' I had to engage her. I had to keep her enthused. Somehow.

'Justin's – it's like he's bleeding to death and we're just slapping on Band-Aids!'

'That's not fair. DMG got him talking—'

'Adam.' Her anger startled me. 'It's over.'

'It wears off, I know,' I replied, limply enough.

If I could have kept Eva in the life she was used to, things might have been easier for us. But specialist day-care and private consultants and even the workaday costs of research were pushing me so far into the red, I could barely afford to run my car, let alone my wife.

It wasn't that Eva was shallow. Material comforts weren't some kind of fetish with her. She just needed some stability in her life, some sense that we weren't spilling ourselves down the plughole of hopelessness and debt.

I hid my bank statements. Eva spent my cheques the way she had spent her mother's – on Justin.

I spent more time at home, poring over the screen in the living room. Eva, the cyberwidow, stroked Justin's forehead while he slept.

I knew she was lonely. I knew I wasn't much company for her. But I couldn't see that I had much choice. Every day I scoured the papers, looking for a loan, a deal, a way to keep our sinking ship afloat. But that, obviously, could never be a lasting solution. What I really needed was an answer, a miracle. A treatment. A cure.

That's what I was holding out for.

A cure.

The way I figured it, it was the only thing could save us.

And then, against all reason and all expectation, I found one.

'I cannot do this any more.'

She shouted it so loud, the party at the next table turned round.

'Oh Jesus Christ.' Eva hid her face behind her glass.

'So you raised your voice,' I said, 'so what?'

'For God's sake Adam, not here, please.'

I'd meant it all to be a lovely surprise: a terrace table at the Bela Vista in Macau, to celebrate our anniversary. But then, for the first and probably last time in the hotel's history, they called to confirm the reservation, and blew the surprise. Then our baby-sitter failed to show, and we had to call in the maid.

'You're right,' I said, calming her as best I could. 'Drugs and diet aren't the answer, no-one ever said they were. But Ivar Lovaas's study claims his method's *cured* some kids—'

We were under a lot of strain at the time. The Lovaas method is very time- and effort-intensive and parental involvement is vital. It's a behavioural programme, very intensive, forty hours a week minimum, at home and in special classes.

Lilly the maid was Lovaas-trained herself, as we had been, and had children of her own enough to populate a whole New Town, but something in Eva – some ingrained class-anxiety – wouldn't let her rest this evening. She fretted for her son, nursed by a mere amah …

'Adam, Justin – he's beginning to frighten me. Is that dreadful?'

'No,' I soothed. 'You're just reading into him what isn't there. You know' The cataplana arrived just then, the spices so heady, I lost the thread of what I was saying.

'Adam?'

'What were we talking about?' The things I said to comfort her were by now worn so smooth, I kept losing my grip on them.

Eva said, 'Yesterday, for example. I hurt myself. I cut myself. I was getting lunch. The way he looked at me—'

'But we *know* all this,' I interrupted, losing my patience. 'We've already lived through this. We know he doesn't understand other people's feelings. You're telling me nothing about Justin that we haven't already come to terms with.'

Eva smiled a little smile, and pretended not to mind my butting in. 'Maybe mother can help me,' she said. Her eyes glistened in the candlelight. The breeze blowing down Rua Comendador caught her hair. She was so beautiful tonight, the undisputed star of the terrace of the Hotel Bela Vista. The waiters were taking turns to serve us, just to get a look at her face. 'I know how you feel, darling, but she's so good with him—'

'No.'

'Adam—'

'Will she do the Lovaas training? Will she stick with it?'

Eva tossed her fork into her cataplana and pushed it aside. In the candlelight, the skin around her eyes looked more bruised than ever, and her lips looked bitten to a dreadful, swollen softness.

'I'm sorry,' I said.

'You want everything your own way,' she said.

'I just hate seeing you bullied.'

'Me in the house wiping food off the walls. You in the library pretending you're Nick Nolte.'

The last happy surprise I had sprung on Eva had been two tickets to see *Lorenzo's Oil*. Nolte and Susan Sarandon play parents reading up on a cure for their dying son: not, on mature reflection, a happy choice for us.

'I know I'm fucking up—'

'Don't *do* that!' Eva snapped. 'Don't back away like that. Every time I try to tell you something real, you bland me out.'

'I don't.'

'You do.'

I needed something to calm me down. To soothe me. I drank off the glass of white port I had misguidedly ordered seconds before my fish arrived. The ice had melted: I downed it in one. Alcohol, that famous marital aid.

'I can't cope with Justin in the house any more. I spoke to mother. She's prepared to pay for him to go to the Higashi school.'

Higashi's 'Daily Life Therapy'. Another very highly regarded behavioural programme, only this one is residential. And exclusive.

'*Tokyo?*'

'Adam—'

'I won't let that bitch steal my son from me.'

My time was now evenly spent smoking Silk Cut in the SCG lounge and getting vertigo in the ICAC car park. I was still reporting to the Weird Sisters about Hamley, and now Hamley, made paranoid by the tracker he had found in his car, had me reporting to him about the Weird Sisters. When Hamley found out I was working on Top Luck he must have seen the writing on the wall because he immediately began his own investigation into the company. This quickly spiralled into a major – if intractably complicated – money laundering case. Hamley had me working on it on the days I was in the SCG building. Meanwhile Daniel White had me working on it when I was at ICAC. Which meant that while I was reporting on Top Luck to White I was also reporting dizzyingly similar information to Hamley.

If I was actually getting anything out of this arrangement, it might have been almost bearable. But there were no bonuses to be had with a secondment like mine, and every month saw me eating further and further into what few savings I had put by, simply to meet the household expenses.

I was earning well, but the salary transfers barely touched my account before they were gone. Everything I earned was going on Justin.

It was the only way I could keep him.

*

In the end, Eva's mother won. Her hatchet job on her daughter was total. The Lovaas regime we were running at home broke down in a welter of tears and recrimination. My wife was wrecked, and Justin was suffering.

Eva needed time to put herself back together. A respite from Justin, she said, needlessly ashamed; and her mother repeated her offer to sweep our son off to Daily Life Therapy in Tokyo. But that, I knew, would only be the beginning, as piece by piece she reclaimed and reconsumed her daughter.

The only way I could think of to fend her off was if we sent Justin to Tokyo and I paid for the therapy myself.

So that's what we did. I'd been sitting up long into the small hours many nights now, poring over the laptop, juggling figures, trying to make things balance. It was all so hopeless, once I phoned Dad, to ask whether maybe he could remortgage his house if I paid the instalments. It turned out he had already remortgaged years before, without telling me, to pay for mum's respite care. He said he had savings. 'What do you need?' he said.

'Christ, Dad.'

'Come on. It's okay.' He knew I'd married money, but he didn't say anything. It was all I could do not to burst into tears. I said something dumb and put down the phone.

We didn't entertain any more. We couldn't afford to. It became embarrassing, not inviting people back, so Eva spent most of her time indoors.

It got so that an unannounced visit by Daniel White was a major break in routine. Eva went into overdrive. 'Another drink?' she called, hovering at the kitchen door. Her face was drawn and weary. Justin was home after his first term at Higashi, and the flight had left him nervous and irritable. But despite her weariness Eva kept on determinedly fussing around us like the perfect hostess.

'Well, I'm fine,' White told her. 'In fact it's such a nice day, shall we all take a walk?'

It was obvious White wanted to speak to me alone – appearances aside he was hardly a friend of the family, so why else would he turn up like this unannounced on a Sunday afternoon? But he extended the invitation to Eva, guessing rightly that she would have to stay in and look after Justin.

I despised him, suddenly and fiercely, for his hypocrisy. Americans are at their very worst when they think they're being tactful.

I walked him down Lugard Road. I liked White, translation problems apart, but he had begun to represent for me a nemesis I knew would come very soon, if I wasn't bloody careful.

'He's a beautiful little boy.'

'Hmm?'

'Justin.'

'Yes,' I said. 'He's autistic,' I said.

'Yeah, I know.' Absently, White broke a sprig of jasmine off a tree hanging over the path. There was a gap in the foliage here, and we stood for a moment looking down on Hong Kong. 'They have amazing faces, don't they?'

'You know about that?'

'My sister lives in a sheltered house in Delray Beach. Every once in a while Dad has to go rescue her. Fort Myers; once she made it as far as Orlando. She has an obsession with bus travel. Muriel. She's very bright.' He put his hands in his pockets and started walking again along the bridle track. 'Small world, huh?'

A party of Australian joggers tramped past us.

White was going back to the States for a week to see his father safely out of hospital.

'What happened?'

'Golfing accident.'

146

'He get hit by a ball?'

'No, an alligator bit his hand off.'

'I was—'

'Really. Bit his forefinger clean off and severed a tendon in his thumb. They sneak into the water features at night.'

'Jesus.'

'One hell of a handicap.' He turned his troubled blue eyes on me. 'I'll be away, these next six days.'

'Well,' I said, 'if there's anything—'

'Whoever's tracking Hamley, they did more than bug his car.'

I didn't need this. My life was complicated enough. 'Haven't you found out who it is yet?'

'There's a listening device in his office phone.'

I felt myself colour up. Whenever Hamley was out of the office I'd go in there and use that very phone. It was the only way, in an office as crowded as ours, that I could plead with my bank manager in private. (I'd given up my mobile. I couldn't afford the bill.)

'In his desk. In his washroom ...'

'I can't be doing with this, Dan. I work for him. He employs me. I can't hear this.'

'They're all police issue so it's a piece of piss for us to listen in on them.'

'Really.'

'Trouble is, now Hamley's on his guard, it's only a matter of time before he has his office swept.'

'Not my problem.'

'And when he finds them, he'll blame ICAC. We're the only spooks are entitled to plant equipment on him.'

'Not my problem.'

'Whoever works for ICAC and has access to his office—' White shrugged. 'Obviously, until we know who's actually bugging him, suspicion's going to have to fall somewhere.'

I couldn't believe what I was hearing. 'You're *framing* me?

'Don't be dumb. I'm just telling you how things are going to look.'

'But you've go to do something.'

He shrugged. 'What can I do? I'm off to see my dad.'

We walked on a little way. 'If you want to cover your back,' he said, 'you'll have to do it yourself.'

I laughed. I couldn't help it.

'They're only bloody microphones. They're in his office. We can tell you what they look like, where to find them. Please, Adam.'

'I don't believe I'm hearing this.'

'What's so difficult?'

'You want me to save ICAC embarrassment? Daniel, I *work* for Frank Hamley. I'm not going to put my job on the line like that.'

Your job's already on the line. If he finds them, he's going to suspect you, isn't he?'

'Hang on a minute,' I said, using anger to conceal my confusion. 'Every month since I got here the Weird Sisters have been pumping me for everything I know about Hamley. Now they have a bug in Hamley's office and they want me to pull it *out*?'

'Tomorrow,' he said. 'Without fail. Adam, this is serious. We can't nail Hamley with an unauthorised listening device—'

'You're nowhere near to nailing Hamley for anything Daniel and you never have been.'

'Oh yes?'

'It's all office-politics bullshit and you know it.'

'Really.'

'What if I get caught?' I said. 'I'm sorry, Daniel. I can't get involved with things like this.'

He let me alone until my anger dissipated. Then he started

in again: a different tack, this time. 'All your victories are on paper, right?'

'I suppose so,' I replied, sulkily. Let him insult my manhood, I thought. I'm British. I don't need manhood.

'Well,' White sighed, 'I guess that's where your strengths are.' His discoloured eyes had a saurian quality: he knew it and used it. 'I mean it. Frank Hamley's very impressed with your paperchasing, Adam.'

'Oh?'

'According to the last tape we lifted from that bug in your office.'

'You listened in on it?'

White shrugged. 'No crime in just listening, Adam. Yes I heard him. Hamley, I mean. Talking to Top Luck's MD Jimmy Yau.'

'He called—'

'He was in kind of a state. I've got the tape. Do you want to hear it?'

I don't know how I responded. White saw he was getting through. 'He warned Mr Yau about you,' he said. 'He said you were a very good paperchaser.'

'So?'

'He said you're close to breaking Top Luck's operation. He said you would have to be dealt with.'

'Dan—'

'We can't always be holding your hand, Adam,' he said. 'You're going to have to learn to look out for yourself.'

The next day, I arrived at the office an hour earlier than usual. I was the first one in.

Hamley's inner sanctum was locked. I went and borrowed the key off the cleaner, said I had some papers in there I needed. The cleaner waited for me by the door. I told him I'd bring him his keys. He told me he was leaving now, and was happy to wait. I gave him some money and told him to buy me a coffee, and something for himself. He treated me to a nasty smile and sloped off.

I looked at my watch. I had forty-five minutes.

Hamley's phone was the old-fashioned kind where the mouthpiece simply unscrews from the handset. It was stuck.

I tapped it against the edge of the desk.

It wouldn't come free. I hit it again, hard.

'Oh. Adam.' Lucy Wah, the receptionist, bit the tip of her thumb and leaned against the door jamb. 'It's you.'

'Yes.'

'You're in early.'

'Yes.'

'Do you want a coffee or anything?'

'Sorry, Lucy, I've got to make this call.'

''Hm.' She went back to her desk. Now I needed to make a call so the light would light up on her switchboard. I dialled home, got the answerphone, and let it run. I pulled my shirt-tail out and used it to get a grip on the mouthpiece.

There was a knock at the door.

'Your coffee.'

He didn't offer me any change. I didn't ask for it. 'Go away,' I said, when he lingered. 'You're not supposed to be in here.'

'I want to leave. I'm late.'

'Here. Take the keys.'

Hamley would just have to think the cleaners had forgotten to lock the door behind them. I looked at my watch.

Thirty-five minutes.

I reached forward to close the door. Lucy was watching me from her desk by the lifts. We were the only ones there still. How well could she hear from there? Could she tell I wasn't talking down the phone? I smiled at her, got nothing back, closed the door.

150

The handset came undone.

I tipped the microphone out so it dangled from its wires and looked inside.

There was nothing there.

The door swung open. 'Morning, Adam.'

Hamley put his briefcase on the desk, took the phone out of my hand, screwed the mouthpiece cover back on, and dropped it into its cradle. He sat down and put his feet on the desk. 'Lost something?'

I don't remember what I said.

'It's all right, Adam,' he sighed. 'I guessed it was you.'

19

In all the time I knew him, Jimmy Yau never went nowhere for nobody. They always came to him.

Jimmy's home was a hillside retreat near Wong Nai Chung Gap, overlooking the Tai Tam Reservoir. The exclusive, tourist-crammed beaches around Shek O were just a few minutes' drive away, but up here, the worst intrusion he'd ever suffer would come from the expats who regularly hiked over these hills back to Happy Valley. After lunch near the office I took the Eastern Island Corridor along the coast, and even though I dawdled, savouring the elevated view of high-rise beach apartments, aflame with early summer light, I reached Shau Kei Wan by two-thirty. Today was the Tam Kung temple's festival day and the streets were full of fish; wire head-dresses, costumes of card and crepe – it took me for ever to get through it all, and then I missed the turn for the reservoir.

It was just as I dropped the car into a mean-tempered first that I saw his turning. There was no sign, but then, there were no other houses. I could just see its grey tile roof, over the trees that lined the fence. They had been planted here in defiance of the landscape, lush and unlikely as the dressings of a film set.

There was an intercom beside the heavy, brutal gate. I got out and used it and something clanged. I pushed experimentally at the drab-painted bars. The gates rolled back on tracks mulched over with dead gingko leaves.

The foliage went on and on, rhododendrons and wax trees and jasmine, wild indigo: the garden seemed arranged to take all the light from the earth. The drive made its final turn.

The house was intimidating. Three storeys. A cupola above the front door. Deco mouldings round each window. A portico with pillars. It might once, but for its location, have been an ambassador's residence.

The most I'd expected of Jimmy was a minimalist apartment in Good Profit Towers. Indeed, before I saw his address, I assumed he'd conform to the usual pattern of his kind – holed up in a single, subdivided room within spitting distance of a *dai pai dong*, surrounded by boxes of kiddie-porn videos and counterfeit Dunhill lighters.

Wrong.

The door was opened by an old man wearing an apron over a cheap but well-cut suit. He smelled of beeswax. His lined, defeated face belied his strength; there was something hard and thick about the set of his shoulders. I followed him through a vestibule tiled with pink marble. I imagined him of a morning, wading treacle-ishly through his Tai Chi moves, splitting logs with his bare hands for firewood. Anyway, he couldn't have got those muscles from just rubbing down the Chippendale.

Garden urns converted to uplighters lit the neutrally-painted hall. Campaign-style curtains busied-up the narrow windows. It was a strange, chintzed-up house; like a society woman who can't follow the new make-up. More likely,

Jimmy Yau's wife had come late to the Condé Nast look, and this was her attempt to fit in.

Either the front of the house was a period fake, or the back of the house had been outraged, because the room the old servant finally led me to had a wall all of glass. Outside, a teenage girl in a black strappy swimming costume was turning laps in a kidney-shaped pool. The old man shuffled out without a word.

The room was more what I had expected, but perhaps only because it revealed so little. Low-voltage track lighting hung from taut steel wires anchored lengthways across the room. The desk at the far end wanted to be a Kubrick monolith when it grew up. A notebook computer sat ostentatiously askew on its black granite surface. Behind it, the floor-to-ceiling limed ash shelves were empty.

I went to the window. The glass was tinted, lending a greenish cast to the girl's skin as she lifted herself from the pool. Water ran off her back and her legs. She was very thin, very young. Her hips were beginning to fill. She got to her feet, water puddling the pink tiles. She crossed her arms, reaching for her shoulder straps, and pulled them down. She bent, pulling the costume away. She was evenly tanned. As she stepped out of the suit she hooked it with a toe and kicked it expertly onto the table beside her sun lounger. Water Catherine-wheeled from the damp lycra. She settled on the lounger, facing the window. Her shallow breasts hardly bobbed as she moved, they were so taut. She couldn't be more than sixteen.

She was facing the window now; I turned away.

Jimmy Yau stood in the doorway.

He was wearing chinos; his white shirt was untucked. Jesus sandals bound his powerful, hairy feet. He was eating pears out of a paper bag.

I swallowed, smiled, watched as he walked slowly across the room and around behind his desk. He pulled out his chair. He sat down. 'Adam.' It was his favourite weapon – the pause. 'You got a new job, I hear.'

Before my walk with Daniel White, I would have been impressed. 'News travels fast,' I said. Now, thanks to White, I knew just how fast it travelled.

'You're making quite an impression, for a newcomer.'

'Old job. New title.'

'Up to you.' He took the last pear, bit the stalk off and spat it back into the bag

I said, 'You know I know about Top Luck.'

He looked at me, and looked, and looked. 'Are you a cinephile, Adam?'

'What?'

He leant back in his chair. 'An enthusiast of the cinema. A movie fan. Do you follow our films?'

'Frank Hamley,' I said.

Jimmy Yau blinked.

'Sack him,' I said.

Jimmy Yau's laughter was mischievous and childish. It sent a shiver down my back. 'Adam,' he chided me, 'you're supposed to be his friend.'

'If it wasn't for Hamley, ICAC would be dangling you by your ankles over Garden Road by now. Trouble is, ICAC know it. Frank's no use to you, any more. He's a liability. Get rid of him.'

He studied me, probably wondering which of my limbs to tear off first. 'And if I don't?' he said at last, very measured, very calm. I was impressed.

'How long do you think it will be before I crack your operation?'

'Operation?'

'I work for ICAC now. I know you're layering funds through Top Luck. I know how.'

'Get to the point, please.'

'*Only* I know how.' I let it sink in a second.

'Go on.'

I said, 'You need a player in ICAC. Someone who can cover your back.'

He smiled. 'No I don't,' he said.

'Buy me,' I said. 'I've better things to spend your money on than whores.'

Jimmy Yau bit through the core of his pear, pushed both halves into his mouth and swallowed them down.

'I'm broke, Jimmy.'

Jimmy pulled out a handkerchief and wiped his hands. He screwed the empty bag into a tight ball.

I explained about Justin. 'I can't meet the school fees,' I said. They were setting me back seventy thousand pounds a year.

From a desk drawer he pulled out a mobile phone, thumbed it on, and spoke Cantonese. Seconds later the long, defeated face that had greeted me on my arrival reappeared at the open door. He was still wearing his apron.

'Take some fruit for Eva,' said Jimmy Yau. 'It's ripe.'

I must have looked a picture.

He threw me the balled-up bag. 'Willy, take him through the garden. Send her in while you're about it.'

Willy glanced at the girl by the pool, and back to Jimmy, without turning his head. A well-trained retriever.

'Jimmy, I—'

'Okay?'

There was nothing more to say. There never had been. I wondered, with a sick feeling in the pit of my stomach, whether he'd heard a single word I'd said.

I stood up. I even managed to muster up a little dignity. 'You have my number, Jimmy,' I said.

'Oh yes.' His teeth were long and grey as old bones. 'Take some fruit before you go.'

Jimmy Yau's soldier slid open the glass door. I followed him through onto the patio surrounding the pool. The girl was still naked, stretched out on her sun-lounger. Her breasts were small and round and unfinished. The hair between her legs was sparse: she had already begun shaving it into shape.

Willy barked something in Cantonese. The girl blinked at him and stretched and smiled, but his eyes were already off her. He picked a narrow dirt path between jasmine trees and beckoned me to follow.

This wasn't the way to my car. This wasn't the way to anywhere. Willy saw my hesitation and sighed. 'Sir, you wanted some fruit?'

The girl brushed my back as she eased between me and the edge of the pool.

'Yeah,' I said. 'Whatever.' I watched her go: her towel was slung low round her back, showing off her powerful shoulders. Jimmy was waiting for her at the open door.

'Jimmy likes them young,' I said, following Willy in between the trees.

'She's his daughter.'

'Oh.'

The orchard was laid out in neat, well-maintained rows. Roses bordered the plot. The air was so thick and scented here, it was like wafting a sweet jar under your nose.

'His youngest,' said Willy. 'Her brothers are stunt fighters. Karate, all that. For Top Luck films. Here.' He picked a pear for me.

'I'm sorry,' I said, taking it. 'I didn't mean any offence.'

The fruit was soft and rotten. A wasp crawled out of it

onto my hand. I cried out and dropped the pear. It landed on Willy's shoe and burst over the polished leather. Willy looked at his shoe, looked back up at me, and tried to smile. The lines on his face were so melancholy and deep, a Pierrot could not have looked more pitiable. 'You don't have to apologise,' he said. He flicked his fist into my gut.

I fell. Ash clogged my nostrils.

Willy trod on my head. My face sank easily into the forked earth. He twisted his foot over my ear, tearing it. I couldn't breath, it felt like my lungs were ironed flat.

'Message from Mr Yau.' He lifted his foot, and stamped. Blood filled the deafened cavity.

He got off me.

'Are you listening?' He kicked me again and again until I lay face up. The sky was full of insects. Little black insects, swooping and flocking between the scented, heavily laden branches.

Willy leant over me, blocking out the sky. There were insects all over his face. They were crawling out of his nose, out of his eyes; they poured out of his mouth as he opened it to speak. 'Next time you come, bring your swimming costume.' He flicked his fist into my face. My septum cracked. I gagged on blood. 'You must come round for lunch.' He turned me over so I could spit it out. 'Let me know if there's anything you can't eat,' he said. He took hold of my hair and forced my mouth into the dirt, held me there until I choked, let go and stood up again.

I sat up, spitting dirt and blood out of my mouth.

'Take your jacket off,' he said.

I blinked at him through swollen eyes.

'Dirt washes out. Blood doesn't. Take it off.'

I took it off.

'Your trousers.'

'Fuck off,' I said.

He kicked me hard in the balls. I turned over and retched and fumbled my belt free.

'Come on, Mr Wyatt.'

I unzipped my flies. He pulled my trousers down.

'Please,' I said. Not for the last time.

From his apron pocket he drew a little black box. Wires tipped with needles dangled from one end. 'Mr Yau says welcome on board.'

20

Not long afterwards, Daniel White invited Eva and I to Shek O for a day by the sea. It was a brilliantly sunny day – the ideal setting for White to show off his new girlfriend.

'*Bumpy?*'

'Her parents nicknamed her that when she was little.'

It hardly fitted her. Slim, blonde, with a honeyish, Melbourne-level tan. She was playing at the edge of the waves, showing herself off. White grinned at life in general and with a satisfied sigh lay back on his towel. I went on looking, until Eva elbowed me gently and made a face: mock-disapproval, collapsing at once into a smile. I poked my tongue out at her carefully and winked with my good eye.

It was good of White to suggest this, and Bumpy was handling the way I looked really well. It took the edge off things for me, and I was grateful. 'Where did you meet her?'

'Remember that prick Pollard?'

'Yes?'

'The consultancy his firm promised they'd bring in to revamp their due diligence?'

'Uh-huh.'

'Meet the consultant.'

'She's a bit good-looking for a job like that, isn't she?'

'Men,' Eva pronounced. 'Adam, come here.' She dabbed carefully at my face with fingers slimy with sunblock.

'Ugh.'

'Hold still, child.'

'You know, Adam?' said White. 'I think this is it.'

'What?'

'You know. *It.*'

'Have you told her?'

'God, no. Spoil the game?'

'Told me what?' asked Bumpy, hunkering down into the sand beside us. She crawled across the towel to lie beside him and water ran off her hair onto his chest. He shivered and wiped the drops away; sand sprang from his chest hair.

Eva pulled her sun dress off and headed for the sea. We slept in the sun until she got back. She was starving. 'Anyone fancy an ice cream?' Bumpy went with her to help her carry.

'Any news about who did it?' White asked, when they were out of earshot.

I shook my head. 'The car turned up.'

'Yes?'

'Burnt out in a gully north of Sheung Shui.'

'Christ, that's on the border.'

'The police say they probably used it for a drug run.'

'Even so'

'I should have let them take it, Dan, that's all it comes to. Who cares about a bloody car?'

White searched for the right words and came up blank. 'Fuck,' he said.

'Not for another week, the doctor says.'

'Christ'

'Are you kidding? It's great. I thought I was going to lose my ball.'

'How's your stomach?'

'Fine.' Since my visit to Jimmy Yau, I kept getting these

159

paralysing stomach pains. The doctors couldn't find anything. I told them about the pains, about how it felt like I
was being torn apart inside.

They asked me what time of day I had them – mornings,
evenings, after exercise, after food? – and I told them the
pains seemed to be triggered to tension.

When I said that they lost interest – maybe they figured
I was being hysterical – and told me the pains would abate
in time.

They were still with me. They were like nothing I'd ever
felt before: like little creatures aliens – swimming about in
my guts, tugging on my intestines like so many bell-ropes.
Nudging my chest wall. Nudging each other. Laughing.

I didn't complain. I hid the pain as much as possible. I
didn't want people making a fuss. As it was, I was finding it
hard to pass all this off as a street incident. Lying to Eva was
hardest of all.

'There we are. Adam?'

I turned stiffly and took the cone from Eva's outstretched
hand. Melted ice cream had dribbled across her hand and
her wrist and I bent to lick her clean.

'Behave.' She pushed me playfully away. Only her eyes
betrayed how much my bruised body disturbed her.

It was so hot, we had to eat quickly. The cold hit my
stomach. I gasped as little hands snatched and tore at my
insides.

'Adam?'

'Nothing,' I replied, with a rigid smile. I glanced at my
watch – a nasty cheap plastic number I was affecting.

('Even my bloody watch,' I wailed, when she caught up
with me in A&E.

'Oh, Adam.'

'You'd think bastards like that would know the difference
between a real Rolex and a fake, wouldn't you?')

160

'Adam?' She could see I was still in pain.

'I want to phone the school,' I said, pretending I'd mis-understood. 'Let them know Lilly's coming to pick Justin up today.' I got to my feet, dizzily. My bad ear throbbed and popped. It was blocked with wax mixed with dried blood, but the ear-drum was still working, and the doctors didn't want to mess about with it more than they had to.

'I can—' Eva began.

'Let me,' I insisted.

'She's a broker,' I told Jimmy. 'Strictly small-time.'

'So why's he seeing so much of her?'

'I think he likes her.'

'You buy that?'

I thought about it. 'Yes,' I said, 'I really do.'

'Go on.'

I read off what I had been able to piece together of White's movements the past few days.

'Very good.'

'Okay then, Mr Yau.'

'Call me Jimmy.'

'Okay then, Jimmy.'

'Is everything all right at work, now?'

'Sure,' I said. 'Thanks.'

'What about Frank?'

'We kissed and made up.'

'Has he been looking after you?'

My grip on the phone grew slippy.

'He tells me you visited North Street together.'

I changed hands.

'Adam?'

I cleared my throat. 'He showed me the sights.'

'That's good,' said Jimmy. 'You need a little relaxation,

Adam. The pressures you're under. You have to remember to look after yourself.'

'Yes, Jimmy.'

'Did you go in?'

My mouth tasted foul, suddenly.

'Adam?'

'Yes. Yes, we went in.'

'What did you think?'

My skin prickled. 'I'm not really – it's not really my style.'

I hated his laughter most of all. 'Did Hamley introduce you to Lisa?'

'I don't want this kind of thing, Jimmy.'

'I hope she took care of you.'

'I don't need it.'

'I hope she didn't disappoint you.'

'She didn't – I didn't ...'

'Aren't you curious?'

'Please—'

'Don't you want to know what it's for?'

'I know what a brothel is, Jimmy.'

'Oh come on Adam,' Jimmy laughed. 'You know it's more than that.'

There was a pause.

He said, 'Why don't you mention it to Mr White?'

I leaned my forehead against the kiosk window. The glass was hot: it branded me. I pulled away. 'Jimmy.'

'Adam.'

'I'm not a pimp, Jimmy.'

But the line had already gone dead.

21

Three weeks later I returned to work. White and I ate lunch together every day now, at a superior *dai pai dong* near the

Star Ferry terminal. Sometimes Bumpy would be there, sometimes not. When we were alone, White would insist on talking through Top Luck, hoping against hope that we'd still be able to piece together a workable case.

'I can't believe the trail's gone cold,' White fretted, and his eyes didn't leave mine for a second. He knew. He wasn't stupid. 'Oh, I meant to tell you.'

'Yes?'

White fought back a mouthful of don don sesame noodles and wiped his lips with a paper serviette. 'That Pollard kid? The one who blew the whistle on this, first of all?'

'Sure.'

'He got knifed up last night in Tsim Sha Tsui.'

I drank off the rest of my beer. The little creatures inside me rattled my ribcage, screaming for a shot of the hard stuff. The doctors had given me some prescription painkillers which didn't do anything but make me muzzy-headed. The only thing the aliens really responded to – the only thing that would shut them up – was the rum Frank Hamley had bought me, the day he introduced me to North Street.

'Then this morning two men walked into intensive care and finished him off.'

I waited. I knew what he wanted to say. About where I had been; about what had been done.

He kept quiet: he knew he didn't have to say it.

I said, 'Why didn't you tell me in the office?'

'I don't know,' White sighed. 'Since you got beaten up like that – I guess I'm just feeling cautious.'

'It's a dangerous world,' I agreed.

'I wish I hadn't been away.'

'There's nothing you could have done.'

'No?' He scooped up another fistula of gummy noodles, examined them, and with a sigh let them fall back into his bowl. 'What happens in North Street?'

It was one o'clock, the busiest time here: a party of students asked if they could share our table. I shifted along the bench to make room for them.

'Are you all right, Adam? You're looking pretty grey.'

'I'm fine.' I leant against the table edge to stop my chest thrumming so hard. *North Street*. Jimmy drew everyone there eventually. It was his poisoned chalice. 'Do you fancy another beer?'

White shook his head. His eyes never left me. His face was drawn into lines of compassion.

I said nothing.

He said, 'Maybe I should visit it.'

'Maybe you should,' I said, and prayed for him. I picked up the can again and found myself drinking air.

'Nice watch.'

I looked at it. 'Well' I said.

'Golden Arcade's best?' He grinned.

Real Rolexes are very heavy. It tugged at my wrist.

The listening devices Hamley had found in his office made Jimmy Yau nervous. Jimmy had me borrow the necessary kit from work and clean his cars, his offices, his sons' dressing rooms, his house, his garden. The poolside.

The orchard.

After a week I handed Jimmy a padded envelope stuffed with dinky silver police-issue hardware. The following week, I handed him another.

He didn't know whether to believe me or not. 'I'm thinking maybe you just raided the shelves at work,' he said.

'It's not like stationery, Jimmy. You can't just go in and pilfer it.'

Willy hit me a few more times but my story didn't change so he went and made us all some jasmine tea instead.

Jimmy remained sceptical. I could see why. Neither

Hamley nor I could tell him who had ordered the surveillance. Besides which, the Top Luck offices – surely the obvious target in any investigation of Jimmy's operations – came up clean every time we swept them.

'You're sure?' he asked me again, the following week.

'I'm in there every week, one way or another,' I said. 'Giving your accountants a bad time. Of course I'm sure.'

Willy came in and played with me a while, but only as a kind of practice.

Work for Jimmy Yau was full of little perks and incentives. North Street most of all. 'I want to pay,' I kept insisting, once my visits there had become regular. But the girls were adamant.

'You don't have to pay.'

'But I *want* to, Lisa.'

'We can't do that, Mr Wyatt,' she explained. 'We've been told not to.' When she frowned, her painted eyebrows made a fierce hieroglyphic above her heavily kohled eyes.

Outside, hidden behind muslin drapes, the cranes of Kennedy Town swung back and forth. Their chains rattled and their gears whined: strange sounds, immediate and scary, in my newly unblocked ear.

She was hard to resist: she had even remembered to wear dark, bruised-looking lipstick – the sort Eva wore when we met.

'What if we called it a tip?' I said, though I knew it was hopeless. It didn't take much psychological understanding to figure out what was going on here. Jimmy was drawing me in. Willy was the stick. This place was the carrot.

Lisa folded her left arm across her small, squarish breasts, her hand resting above her right nipple. She considered the idea, sucking absently on a carefully manicured finger. 'Uh-huh,' she smiled. She glanced to see how hard I was.

165

'Lisa, I know what you're trying to do'

She sat on the edge of the bed. 'What do you reckon?'

'Lisa'

'Smooth, huh?' She parted her legs, and lifted her bum a little. Her calves trembled, as she teetered on her shoes. The opening of her sex was very small.

'Yes,' I said, but made no move to join her.

She pouted at me, reached over to the bedside table, and pulled a needle from its case. 'Well?' she said.

I shrugged and made for the door.

'Hey, Adam.'

'What?'

'Watch.' She pulled her left nipple taut and screwed the needle into it.

She smiled.

'If you want,' she said, clipping the wire.

It was about four when I left. The cloth factors who occupied the ground floor took no notice of me. They were too well trained.

I pushed through the plastic ribbon curtain. A thin, toxic haze had drifted South from the mainland to filter the sun.

I reached into my pocket for the car key, and my fingers closed around a crumpled heap of dollar bills. My tip to Lisa. She'd palmed it back on me somehow. I stuffed the bills back in my pocket, shucked off the jacket and threw it onto the passenger seat.

Though I arrived early, Zoe was already waiting for me outside the school gates. All blazer and sensible skirt, she was unrecognisable as the lolita I had watched lolling about by Jimmy's poolside. She leaned in through the open window. 'Willy sick?'

'He's still down with the flu.'

She opened the rear door and threw in her satchel, then came round and climbed in the passenger side.

'Just chuck the jacket in the back.'

She picked it up and the wad of dollars fell out into her lap. She laughed, and counted them. 'You been at the races?'

'I don't bet.'

'You steal it?'

'Don't be silly.'

There must have been some problem in the Cross Harbour Tunnel because the traffic started to lock almost as soon as we fed onto the Corridor. The haze had thickened, filtering all the goodness out of the light. Where Lisa had slid her needles – where before it had felt like bolts of pure light had burnished my insides and set my tendons humming – now rods of lead and mercury leaked poison through my veins.

'What do you do for *Ah-Bah*?'

'Nothing much.'

'Are you in film?'

It dawned on me then that I was. 'Yes,' I said. 'Sort of. I keep Top Luck's visiting executives entertained.'

'You take them round the sets?'

'No. They have studio people to do that.'

'Where do you take them?'

'Oh, you know.' It was very hot in the cabin, even with the windows open. We weren't going fast enough to make any breeze. I loosened my tie. 'Restaurants and that.'

'Do you get them girls?'

'Zoe!'

'Do you?'

'Sometimes.'

She looked out the window. There was nothing to see. There was fog over the harbour. 'You should send me,' she said. 'Give me my big break.'

'They'd eat you alive,' I said and, quickly changing the

167

subject: 'What do you want to be, anyway?'

'Oh, I don't know.' She yawned.

The traffic picked up. We passed the turn-off for the tunnel and the road got clear enough for me to speed a little.

'Do you ever use girls my age?'

'No.'

'I bet you do.'

'No,' I said, 'I don't. Jesus.'

'Sorry.'

'Look it's just corporate entertainment, okay? It's just helping out your dad a few hours a week. I work for ICAC, for Christ's sake.'

'Okay, okay.' She folded her arms, and quickly unfolded them again. 'Christ, it's hot today.'

We drove through Shau Kei Wan and took the turning up towards the reservoir.

She kept tugging her skirt down to keep her thighs, sheened with perspiration in the intense humidity of a Hong Kong summer, from scratching against the upholstery.

'What are you looking at?' she said.

'Nothing,' I said.

'Yeah, right.'

I fixed my eyes on the road. My mind raced. There was a hot feeling in my throat.

'Look, Zoe,' I said, 'I'm really sorry if I—'

'If you want to look at me like that,' she said, 'you'd better stop the car.'

I tried to be casual. I laughed.

'I mean it.'

I looked at her.

She took off her tie.

'Stop the car,' she said.

I kept my foot on the gas. I kept my eyes on the road.

'I don't bite,' she said. 'Stop the car.'

168

3

LONDON

AUTUMN, 1998

22

'And you haven't *any* idea what it's for?' Loh's steel-rimmed glasses flashed in the sunlight streaming through the glass roof of his office.

'Can you tell me how your TV works?' I said.

'I'm not being asked to patent my TV.'

It was a fair point. I had turned up at his office – the tarnished husband of his wife's not-very-close friend – with an anachronistic lump of bakelite wrapped in a Sainsbury's carrier bag; now I was trying to convince him that it could be patented – promoted, even. That this shoddy box was the clockwork radio and bag-less vacuum cleaner of the alternative health market.

So, to convince him, I wired up his hand and handed him the carrier to crumple between supersensitive fingers.

'I really can't feel anything,' he complained.

'You must.'

He sucked his teeth. 'It tingles a bit.'

'I guess the battery's wearing down.' I was a bit drunk. Approaching Loh had always been a long shot, and when the time came I'd needed Dutch courage even to get through the door. I wasn't being very convincing.

When Loh had first greeted me, he was in a high humour. He'd finally won that minidisc case; a high-risk gamble not to accept Nabeshima's out-of-court offer had paid off, and with the money he'd earned he had secured a mortgage on a former antique bookstore off Bishopsgate. It was badly lit, and dust lay thick on empty shelves. Maybe the forty watt light bulbs in every anglepoise lamp had been chosen to preserve the book bindings, or maybe the previous owners just enjoyed being depressed. Now that Loh had moved in, electricians were installing strip-lighting in the offices on the other side of the high, wall-length bookcase that divided the office in two, right up to the ceiling. Twice they had dropped a tube and it imploded in a cacophony of splintering glass.

Loh's side of the office, meanwhile, had a glass roof so filthy, the little light that bled through was as dark and felty as pigeons' wings. Each time a tube shattered Loh and I winced and cowered, thinking the roof was crashing in.

Loh plucked the alligator clips off his hand. His fingers were thick and callused: he and his wife spent three evenings a week hanging off Bendcrete flakes in a climbing gym in the East End. Maybe his skin was too tough for the machine's signals to penetrate.

Maybe I should have brought a spare battery.

A couple of accounts girls entered the office. They were carrying those little brown paper carriers Italian delis give you so your Diet Coke falls out the bottom. Loh stuffed his hands in his pockets as they went by. He didn't want to be seen playing with toys during office hours.

'You know,' he said, carefully, not wanting to give offence, 'developing a patent isn't usually such a hands-on business. We deal with blueprints here. The closest we get to handling the material is talking on the phone to the engineers who mocked up the prototypes. Even then, most of the products we handle are software ...'

He was letting me down gently.

Well,' I said, 'as I told you, I'm really here just for advice.'

That was true enough. I'd given Zoe the impression I knew something about product development. I'd audited enough R&D companies in my KPMG years, after all. But all that was years ago, and in Brazil, for heaven's sake – half a world away. I was all at sea.

We sat there in silence a while, Loh and I, not knowing what to say to each other. Zhenshu's brown box sat between us on Loh's beaten-up oak desk, small and frayed an unprepossessing: a very unlikely grail.

Zhenshu's invention – was that why Zoe had turned up to meet me that day in Wye? Had she known all along that there, in the loft of Zhenshu's beautiful but derelict house, was the solution she craved? The lever she needed to prise herself free of her troubled family?

A business of my own – her ticket to Hong Kong?

The idea to base a business round Zhenshu's invention, such as it was, was mine. 'We could market it,' I said. I figured, if Cognitional could sell 'remyelinisation' pills to autistics and plastic bubble-suits to neurotic office workers stricken with sick-building syndrome, if shops in Bristol could sell crystals for healing and palmists in King's Cross could advertise in the back of *Vogue*, why shouldn't Zhenshu's invention have its day in the sun? At least it worked – in its own strange fashion.

Yes, the idea was mine – but just how hard an idea was it to have, given the way that day had gone? I'd merely stated the obvious, and Zoe – she had been if anything too surprised, too slow on the uptake. I couldn't help thinking, in the back of my mind, that she had known all along what I'd say.

'Look …' Now I was saying it again, for Loh's benefit, and a bit desperately. 'Look, my client and I have only just come across this prototype. As far as we can discover, it's the only one of its kind. There is nothing else like it on the market. Given its age, it must be relatively uncomplicated. Which means, I suppose, it's cheap to produce. If we can only find out what it's for – I really think we have something special here,' I concluded, feebly enough.

'If there was any paperwork at all—'

'Oh, there's paperwork,' I butted in. 'Too much bloody paperwork. And none of it in sequence. We don't know what relates to what.'

Loh prodded the device. He was getting exasperated.

I said, 'If we knew what this machine was for we wouldn't be approaching you so soon, and in such an unprepared state.'

Loh's look only darkened. I wished I hadn't drunk so much.

If our wives hadn't been old Hong Kong cronies I'd never even have made it as far as Loh's secretary. (She was off in some back room now, making what I hoped was something approaching coffee.) Loh had no reason to take me seriously – the last he had seen of me I was pottering around Eva's dinner party pouring everybody too much wine and taking a lifetime's disappointments out on a limp-wristed antiques dealer.

But Loh was polite. Hugely polite – luckily for me. He was so busy worrying about my feelings, it didn't seem to occur to him that he could just show me the door.

'Well,' I said, figuring attack was the best form of

defence, 'how do you suggest we go about developing fresh paperwork for this device? There must be a way.'

Loh shook his head, like a garage mechanic, or a plumber. 'Reverse-engineering is expensive.'

'Loh,' I said, taking my cheque book out my suit pocket, 'this thing was put together in the Fifties. How complicated can it be?'

He followed my chequebook with his head like a snake follows a charmer's stick. 'Now this does mean I'll need the device,' he said.

'Can you say for how long?'

Loh shook his head. 'How can I? First I need to contact some consultancies, see if we can put together a suitable team for us.'

'Can't we just loan it to some hard-up university physics department?'

Loh's spectacles flashed. 'Sure, if you want a six-month wait and have the specs smeared across the internet.'

I smiled. 'You wouldn't be trying to cost me money, would you?'

Something of his old, wry humour returned. 'Trust me,' he said, and his spectacles flashed. 'I'm a lawyer.'

When I showed Zhenshu's box to Eva, I remembered to put in a fresh battery.

'Ugh!'

'What's the matter?'

'My fingers feel sticky.' She wiggled about uncomfortably, and her chair scraped against the kitchen tiles.

She was feeling the sweat and soap in her skin – or maybe even the gluey ecosystem of fungus and bacteria that skin contains, no matter how much you wash.

'Rub your fingers together.'

'Oh – *God!*' She jerked compulsively, tearing off the wires.

The box bounced and I had to grab it to stop it falling off the table.

'Eva?'

'I got a shock.'

Not from the device – it was her own static. I'd got the box turned too high.

'I'm sorry, love. Here.' Reluctantly, she let me wire her up again. I looked around for something to give her. Something she could feel in all its magical richness. Something that would show her how extraordinary the world was, when you perceived it through Zhenshu's wires.

The trouble was, now we were back from our annual weekend break (Florence: the Palazzo Pitti for her; Montepulciano for him), Eva had entered tidy-up mode once more, launching herself into it the way a drunk launches into the bottle after a weekend on the wagon. Everything was put away. There was nothing around for her to feel: not a plate, not a spoon, not a loaf of bread, not even a tea-towel.

'Adam?'

There was a bowl of fruit on top of the fridge. 'Hang on a second.'

I carried it over. I picked out a pear. I turned the dial to three, waited till she had stopped wriggling and grimacing, and then I laid the pear in her hand. She bit her bottom lip. She went white. She turned her hand over and the pear fell onto the table, rolled off, and connected wetly with the floor. 'Oh, *Christ!*'

'What is it?'

She tore off the wires and rubbed her hands together, ridding them of disgusting sensations. 'What on earth is that thing?

'It's a kind of sensory amplifier,' I said. Well, it sounded good to me.

'It felt like my whole hand was caving in.'

I didn't understand.

'The pear – it was so heavy. Oh, the bloody pear …'

She lifted her chair back and started scrabbling about under the table.

'Eva, if you could just leave that—'

'Oh no.'

'What?'

'I've scratched the tiles.'

She looked up, her eyes ablaze with accusation. 'Look what you made me do!'

She wasn't against the device in principle. She thought it was a good move, my software company acquiring this extraordinary new output device.

'But what is it *for*?' she kept asking.

I hazed and hazed.

'A kind of what?'

'An amplifier of nervous response. It's a spin-off of some new medical kit they're developing for use with spinal injuries patients.' I made a mental note to suggest that to Zoe. Physiotherapy – it was as good an application for the box as any other, though nothing on Zhenshu's CV suggested he'd thought in those terms.

'Who's they?' Eva asked me finally, as I drove us in to work.

'It's just a kitchen-table outfit,' I said. 'They don't have much clue. I think they must have got me out of the Yellow Pages.'

'How does it work?'

'They've cooked up some really neat feedback algorithms,' I said, blinding her with cod science.

'But the box, it looks really old.'

'It's the casing off an old radio,' I said. 'They thought it looked cool. They're only postgrads.'

'Where are they studying?'

Well, it went on and on like this.

23

Incredibly, life got a little bit simpler. The following day the *South China Morning Post* carried a short article announcing the close of the judicial enquiry into the Top Luck affair. Of course the report has still to be prepared, but I could take comfort in the fact that I hadn't, after all, been required to give evidence. I should have been relieved; as it was, I felt onscurely disappointed.

The enquiry had at least been a tangible threat. Whenever Hamley or Boots came to mind, I could pin what had happened on the effects of the enquiry. But it had never developed into the showdown we'd all feared and expected.

Money's protection of me, the none-too-veiled threat that was Boots' death, Hamley's 'accident' – now the enquiry was over, none of this made much sense.

I felt the way you do when music is switched off half-way through a track. It left an ache behind.

Or like a Catherine wheel when the touch-paper gutters out prematurely: approach it, it might go off in your face.

Eva was glad of any extra help I could offer her at the café. For my part, while Loh was arranging to have Zhenshu's box investigated, there was little I could do except wait. As long as I kept up the pretence of having a job to go to now and again, Eva was more than happy to have me around, while she planned the café's redecoration.

The press's off-and-on relationship with the South Bank was on an upturn in '98. On the back of every whinge about Mandelson's Dome, there'd be some tyro columnist singing the praises of this restaurant or that warehouse conversion. The Tate's Bankside was nearly finished. At lunchtime you couldn't move in the Oxo Tower at for all the superannuated Voguettes, recharging their batteries after Anish Kapoor at the Hayward.

Libby Brooks, the *Guardian* journo, interviewed Eva and other businesswomen in the area for the women's page. There were documentaries. *Time Out* started scouting for writers to produce a guide to South London. Things were happening, and as always Eva, with her appetite for things, was poised to make the best of them. A restaurant. A guest house. Her ideas made sense. We had the money. We had the credit rating. We had the location.

We spent most evenings at home, talking her ideas through. She exhausted me. I couldn't keep up. She'd be talking about poaching some bright young chef from Andrew Edmunds, or ringing *The World of Interiors* for the name of someone to design an indoor market in a disused garage on Stoney Street; meanwhile I'd be worrying about all the little things. The decor, the furniture, the shape of the lighting.

'So draw it for me,' she said. 'So pick a colour.' 'So find out the cost.'

She had the walls of the café painted white, and the woodwork a deep greenhouse green. I stencilled the floorboards myself, a repeating rose pattern, the red a subtle translucence over the darkly stained boards, so that you had to catch it in certain lights to really be sure it was there.

'It's terrific.'

'Too subtle?'

'I don't think so.'

'Too camp?'

'We're near the National Theatre. Who cares?'

It was a good time.

*

'Adam?'

'Hello?'

'It's Loh Han-Wah.'

'Hi.'

'I just wanted to touch base with you about the box, about the technical work we need to do to prepare the patent.'

'Sure.'

'There's a team at Nabeshima were working on that mini-disc format I took to court this spring—'

'Your client sued them.'

'Sued Nabeshima. Yes.'

'And won.'

'Yes.' There was a pause. Loh chuckled. 'Adam, it was a civil suit over a technicality, not some great moral crusade. We can still do business with them.'

But that wasn't what was worrying me. 'They're a potential buyer, Han-Wah.'

'I don't think so, Adam, to be realistic—'

'The inventor's flat is full of correspondence with Nabeshima. He used to work for them. They were interested in him.'

'I know all this, Adam, you've already told me. But it was over forty years ago ...'

'I don't want Nabeshima to handle the device until we have a water-tight patent. And then I want you to try and sell it to them.'

Loh sighed. 'Adam, I really think a smaller company, maybe a Scottish Power subsidiary or someone we find through Investors In Industry, is much more likely to—'

'Han-Wah. We are going to sell this thing. To a major.'

'You'll find—'

'Han-Wah. I know you think I'm deluded, but this isn't your problem. Just concentrate on the patent.'

'That's what I'm trying to do.'

'Please. Find someone else to study it. Go to a university. Please.' I put the phone down to find Eva watching me. She was just out of the bath. She smelled of sweets.

'Sorry,' I said. 'Was I loud?'

'You were fine,' she said. 'You sounded like – you sounded fine.'

Like I used to sound. It was sweet of her to think it, sweeter of her not to say it.

'Let's go to bed,' I said.

'Get off!'

'Just playing.'

'Daft sod.'

I swung the tap on full. Water ricocheted off the tiny new enamel sink in the Ladies and sprayed us from head to foot.

Hannah twisted out of the café's new bathroom, squealing. It was Sunday. The heavy work was done and she and the other waitresses had agreed to come in on double time to help unpack the new crockery, the hand towels and the trendy marbled soap.

Hannah's mother breezed by us like a cold north wind, bearing bowls of pot-pourri. 'All right there, Mr Wyatt?' she scowled at me, disapproving as a chaperone. I tried to behave myself.

'Adam,' Hannah called from the bar, 'is Eva coming in again?'

'Not this morning.'

'A man rang for her.'

'Take a message?'

She handed me a Post-it note. I glanced at it. I didn't think anything of it at first. I looked at it again. Something at the back of my head started to itch. A nagging, paranoid itch. 'Give me the phone,' I said. Eva had the car today, so ...

'Is everything all right?'

'The phone, Hannah, please. It's right behind you.' I snatched it off her. 'Thank you.'

Behind me, Hannah's mother sucked her teeth.

My head began to pound. I punched in the number of a local cab company.

I found Eva waiting in the foyer of an hotel in Sloane Street. She was wearing a business suit from Sogo; she must have gone home to change. She didn't see me straight off; she was reading a magazine. I got close enough to smell the Iron Buddha tea. It must have been a good article. *Company* – hardly her usual style. There was a sofa free opposite her, on the other side of the glass coffee table. She glanced up, smiling.

Her face fell.

'He's not coming,' I said, dropping into the upholstery. It wasn't nearly as soft as I thought it was going to be; it practically bounced me onto the table.

'Who—?'

'Loh phoned the café.'

She tried to explain. I really wasn't in the mood. A waiter passed and I ordered two doubles.

'Adam.' She leaned towards me, trying to draw me in. 'He thinks it could really help!'

It was so like me speaking, I almost smiled. I had spent years hunting up treatments for Justin. Losing us money. Hunting for more. Wading deeper and deeper into Jimmy Yau's filth. So I suppose I had this coming. In fact, as poetic payback went, this was positively mild.

My drinks came. I used them.

'Loh's engineers think the device sets up sympathetic frequencies in the nervous fibres ...'

I wondered if she could hear what she was saying. Had I, ever?

'It focuses his attention. I spoke to Francis. He even volunteered in class today!'

I said, 'I'm not interested in how the device works. I'm not interested in how it's supposed to help Justin. I want to know why I'm only hearing this now.'

She swallowed. 'I meant to tell you.'

'Of course you did.' She hated my sarcasm. I did, too: it wounded her too deeply. Maybe it reminded her of her mother or something. But I couldn't stop myself. 'I go see him Thursdays. Tomorrow I'd have found it clipped to him.'

'I had to know it worked.'

Heads turned. Eva coloured up. I murmured sorry. The waiter was giving us the basilisk eye so I picked up the second double and toasted him with it. He thought about coming over, looked into my eyes, and changed his mind.

'I just couldn't find the right moment ...'

Our marriage had foundered because I was constantly putting Justin through one treatment or another, whether we could afford it or not, whether it helped him or not. Now it was her turn to be tempted by an exciting long-shot. How could she have told me about it, without hopelessly undercutting herself? Face was everything with her.

It was Loh I was worried about. His secrecy I didn't understand. Why had he approached Eva first? Why had he left me out of the loop?

Eva experimented with a laugh. 'You've been here before,' she said. 'Haven't you?'

Her honesty was disarming.

'How does it feel?' I asked her.

She studied her hands. 'Horrible,' she said. 'Dirty.' She looked up at me. 'It's exciting, isn't it? I didn't expect that. Thrilling, like betting on horses. Only it's not horses, is it? It's not a horse that'll win or lose.'

'Don't beat yourself up,' I said, losing the last of my anger. 'You're entitled to hope. Tell me what Loh said.'

Eventually Loh and I had agreed the box should be taken apart and examined at Southampton University, where Kevin Leicester's team were blue-skying everything, from herding behaviours to the digitisation of facial expressions.

Now Eva seemed to know better than I did what they'd found out.

Autism is a pervasive disorder. There are as many explanations for its symptoms as there are specialisms interested in them. Everyone from optometrists to acupuncturists to neurobiologists has an explanation for the condition, and the devilish thing is they're all (partly) right. Where you start to tackle the condition is almost arbitrary: every treatment regime feeds into the next. And, because autism is a spectrum of widely varying conditions, no child with autism reacts the same way to any one regime.

Eva had been fed one explanation. It had to do with myelin.

Myelin is a coating covering nerve fibres. It's like the plastic sheath around an electrical wire. It keeps signals running down the nerve, the way plastic keeps electric current running down a wire.

If a live wire isn't sheathed in plastic, the electricity it carries is free to short out on any nearby conductor. Imagine the sparks if a load of live electrical wires, all bunched together, lost their plastic coating.

Nerves come bunched together. All the nerves in the body eventually bunch together in the brain. Imagine the sparks that would fly if that lot were improperly insulated.

The worse the insulation, the more trouble you're in. Many autistic children have problems with epilepsy. And even if it's not severe enough to cause epilepsy, every little discharge, every little stray spark, is a piece of nervous information lost forever. A tiny epileptic fit, wiping out a signal here, a signal there.

We rely on those signals. Those signals are our only connection with the world, and with our bodies.

An autistic life is a life drowned in static, a life spent struggling to tune into a distant radio station. You're straining the whole time. Your nerves are on edge.

Then, without warning, a signal comes in. Not a clear signal – never a clear signal – just another burst of particularly heavy static. There's meaning in it somewhere, but the first thing you're aware of is the signal strength. Unfamiliar noises deafen you. New smells assault you. Bright lights blind you. Rough objects sting your hands.

As partial explanations go, it's a good one. It explains why it's so hard to get through to an autistic person. It explains why they shy away so much from the world. Why they're so slow on the uptake. Why it takes so long to get their attention. Why they can only concentrate on one thing at once, or one part of one thing.

When Eva started explaining it all, my heart was in my mouth. Surely Zhenshu's box was the worse thing for Justin: a sensory amplifier for a child who couldn't handle normal input, never mind a turbocharged version.

But that wasn't how Zhenshu's amplifier worked. It didn't amplify the signal at all. It clarified it.

'It generates solitons in the nerve fibres – stable waves that don't decay, no matter how far they travel.'

For the first time in his life, Justin was getting a clear signal.

Eva said, 'I've never been so certain in my life that this is the right thing to do.

'Yes,' I said, 'that's how it starts.'

'Adam—'

'I'm sorry.' I should have said more. A lot more. About using untested kit on our baby. About putting so much trust in Loh, who wasn't even an engineer, let alone a doctor. About leaving the device with Justin, where any curious nurse or teacher might play with it and wonder what it might be for, or even what it was worth.

But something in her look stopped me. A naïveté I recognised as mine, long ago, when I too believed that there might be a cure. A magic bullet. A grail.

'Just see him,' she said. 'Just see what you think.'

24

Justin hadn't taken to the PlayStation, but he enjoyed the kaleidoscope. Broken or not, it had pride of place on top of his new chest of drawers. He liked looking through the eyepiece, at a world blurred and bloated through the magnifying lens. It was the seed he had needed: the core of his new obsession. He opened the drawers one at a time to show me his collection. They were stowed away in shoe-boxes: spectacles, binoculars, cheap magnifying glasses, some not so cheap, even a school microscope.

'Such a lot. Where did you get them?'

He slid the last drawer shut, ignoring me, and picked up the kaleidoscope. He crossed to the bed and settled it on his lap. He turned the tube uselessly with wired fingers. I sat beside him and watched. I thought he might want a hug, but he didn't. Every once in a while an alligator clip slipped from his skin; Justin paused, pinched it to the back of his hand again, and went on with his game.

'It's very nice,' I said.

'Present,' he said.

It was a day of small miracles.

I hadn't had to ask him to show me his collection. He

had showed me himself. All on his own, he had done that. He had wanted to share – or maybe not that, but he had known, somehow, it was what he should do. Other people had begun to exist for him. We were breaking through.

'Yes,' I said. 'Present.' I pointed to the chest of drawers Francis had brought in to house his collection. 'Justin?'

He glanced at me, ignored my outstretched finger, and turned back to his kaleidoscope.

'Are they presents?'

'No.'

Francis had got them for him. He scoured boot sales. What made the kaleidoscope a present, and not Francis's gifts? Was it shape? Colour? Size? Could it be – miracle of miracles – something to do with the way the kaleidoscope had been wrapped, and presented to him on a special day? Had he remembered that? Was he able now to understand its significance?

I got off the bed and crossed the room for my bag. 'Justin?'

'Tiny.'

'Yes, Justin.'

His eye, absurdly magnified, blinked at me. He lowered the spectacles from his eye and picked up another pair.

'Tiny.'

'Yes, Justin.'

Another.

Another.

'Do you like the photographs, Justin?'

'Tiny.'

'Yes, yes.'

He started arranging spectacles and loose lenses in long meticulous rows along his bedspread.

I unfastened my bag. Justin glanced up. I pulled out a wallet of photographs – holiday snaps from our Florence weekend that I'd just had developed. 'See photographs?'

Nonchalantly, Justin performed another miracle: he put down the kaleidoscope and crossed the room to see what I had brought him. I handed him the packet. He sniffed it. He licked it.

'Oh Justin ...'

He opened it. Carefully, he withdrew the photographs. He went back to the bed and sat down. He was surrounded by old spectacles. I began to wonder, guiltily, how much Francis was spending at those boot sales he went to, picking up all this garbage for his charges. Justin started to leaf through the photographs. I came and sat beside him again.

Manipulating the photographs meant the crocodile clips kept slipping off his hands. It was painful, watching him put down the photographs, clip on the wire, pick up the photographs, turn one over, drop the clip, put down the photographs again.

Justin picked up a photograph. I looked with him. It was of Eva, the day we visited the Uffizi. She was sitting on a low grey stone wall, studying the Ponte Vecchio. Behind her, beyond the town, the hillsides, some wooded, some terraced, were sheathed in mist. There was something lush and primeval about them: a landscape from a dinosaur movie.

'Mum's sad.'

I didn't say anything. I didn't breath.

He put down the photograph and picked up another.

'No, Justin—'

He flapped my hand away like it was a dead branch. The hat-stand that responded to the sound 'Dad', always getting in the way.

'No, Justin. Look.'

He snatched the photograph off me and looked at it again.

'Mum,' he said.

I reached round behind him, picked a magnifying glass

188

from the orderly row he had made, and held it in front of the photo. 'Look. There.'

Justin flapped his hands. I had raised my voice. I was overloading him.

I took a deep breath. I calmed down. I sat very still, and I waited.

He looked at the photograph.

Eva's eyes were slitted against the sun, which had just then broken through the noon haze.

He saw the magnifying glass in my hand. He plucked it out of my hand, the way you'd snatch a pen from a pot. He held it over the photograph.

'Sad, Justin?' It shouldn't have been in his vocabulary. How can a hat-stand be sad? How can anything, in a world full of static and inanimate terror, be sad?

Justin laid the photograph in his lap and studied it through the glass. He pulled the lens back from the photo, magnifying the image. Eva's head swelled and broke up into blurred, pigmented surfaces. He frowned.

He looked at me.

He pointed.

He looked back at me to see if I was looking.

'Sadder,' he said.

25

I met Eva that evening in the Ravi Shankar on Drummond Street. I remembered the name from my student days but I hadn't been back since. We sat by the window, looking out. It wasn't what I remembered.

J. Vine the butcher's was closed down now, and its red and white striped awning was grey with dirt. Soon enough it would be another restaurant – a Diwana, or even a Spice Café. The road was lined with expensive cars: a Mercedes

E220, a BMW 925i. It was getting more like Chinatown by the day here – a Chinatown for the Indian middle-classes, as first-generation graft – a lifetime's late opening at the Viniron Europ Spice Market and the Ambala Sweet Centre – blossomed into second- and third-generation conspicuous consumption. There were all here tonight, the sons and daughters of the first, dour, diligent shopkeepers, eating paper-thin dosas and small steel dishes of bhel poori smothered in cold tamarind gravy.

'I think it's a wedding,' said Eva, as the taxis rolled up one by one, disgorging them all. Some of them were Italian. 'Do you think it's a wedding?' Table after table was added to the growing line. Eva horrified a waiter by offering to move upstairs. He spent the rest of the evening trying to make us feel comfortable, asking us if everything was all right

Above the Islamic Book Centre a white girl in a grey silk suit was leaning out of an upper-storey window, a mobile phone pressed to her ear. The upper floors of the terrace were all flats, and the windows of most were freshly polished, bright with orange and lemon-yellow shards of late sunlight. The window frames on many were painted in period black paint, even the ones above Vines.

'An Indian Summer on Drummond Street': the hacks sniffing round Southwark could certainly make something of that.

The party was laid-back, funny, bizarre. The young men all wore gold earrings and heavy watches, but they still favoured the white collar-less dress shirts they would wear to work tomorrow, waiting tables in their own restaurants. The girls were more radical. Some wore their long hair permed. One had an Indian silver choker round her neck, and her translucent embroidered blouse was pure Bollywood sauce.

The Italians didn't know what had hit them.

'Please, Adam.'

'I'm sorry,' I smiled. 'Window-shopping again.'

'Pig.' She laughed.

'What's wrong?' I said.

Her smile came apart.

'Darling?'

'I—' She looked away, and her eyes were wet and full of lemon light.

I took her hand. 'Eva,' I said.

'I should have told you about the box.'

'You were going to tell me.'

'I should have. I'm sorry.' The wave gathered itself up inside her.

'Eva—'

'The things Loh told me. Do you really think …?'

I held her hand, tight, held her together, as the wave broke her to pieces.

'Do you really think—'

'Yes,' I said.

'I'm sorry, Adam.'

I leaned forward across the table, and kissed her hand. 'I love you,' I said. 'I love you.'

The wave retired. She smiled. Someone on the big table cracked a joke and the laughter distracted her; she blinked away tears and glanced at the wedding party and I had never seen her so happy. She let go my hand and grabbed my lapel and pulled me forward across the table. She kissed me. Her mouth was full of garlic and coconut relish and salty lassi, and I stuck my tongue in her mouth to taste it all.

'Hey,' she said, fingering my lapel. She laughed and wiped her eyes. 'Nice jacket.'

I sat down, out of her reach. I looked round for the waiter. I ordered another beer.

'Is it new?'

*

Zoe and I had been shopping. While Loh was wheeling and dealing (and sneaking around behind my back – I still hadn't confronted him about that) we had little else we could do.

She was worse than Eva. 'All your trousers sit too high round your middle,' she'd decided.

'They do?'

'Come on.'

Ted Baker's were hopeless – they make clothes for stick people. Zoe bought a World Cup exploitation T-shirt so small you'd think only a child could get into it.

Paul Smith had a pair of jeans as blue as an Yves Klein dream and as soft as fur. Anyway, that's what the assistant said.

'Go try them on,' Zoe insisted.

I wore them out of the shop and steered us towards Covent Garden. Only she dragged me into Blakes and we spent the next hour trying on leather jackets.

'Try the trousers too.'

'No.'

'Go on, try them.'

'I am forty-two years old.'

'Go on.'

I had inherited my father's genes: I was immune to middle-age spread. I never exercised much any more but decorating the café had shed what little flab the pub had put on. They were tight on the leg – not too tight. I squatted obscenely; and the calf-skin gave in the all the right places. I pulled back the curtain.

Zoe wrinkled her nose.

'What?'

'Looks like your arse is in front,' she said.

Zoe had a long talk with her mother and they agreed that she could have Zhenshu's old house. Her mother found her a chi-chi decorating firm in Tenterden. They knocked the Spanish hacienda-style arches from the corners of every knocked-through wall, rewired from top to bottom, and laid a new damp-course. Under the unpleasant beige fitted carpets, the original floorboards were good enough to stand sanding and varnishing.

Zhenshu's house was well-aired by the time I visited, and the smell of paint, which normally tore out the back of my throat, was a distant tang. The rooms upstairs were still wet with varnish. Her bedroom – the first room she'd finished – was full of unopened boxes from Heals and Habitat.

'Help me unwrap,' she said.

The crockery was deep red, the glaze as rich and translucent as toffee round an apple. Neotu rugs, a terracotta tea-set, a stone door-stop from Habitat ...

'What the hell is this?' I said, swinging it from the chunky steel eye screwed into its top.

'A door-stop. It's hand-carved in India.'

'Christ.'

'Help me put this stuff away,' she said. She led me into the kitchen.

A bleached pine table from Viaduct. A daybed from SCP. 'Where do you think this should go?' she asked me, holding up sixty quid's-worth of Nick Munro pepper mill.

'How would I know?

'Oh, come on, Adam.'

I didn't want to play house with Zoe. But her smiles were infectious. 'I bought some bed linen,' she said. We fought the duvet into its striped cover. 'Well?' she said.

'It clashes with the lampshade.'

'No it doesn't.'

She threw a couple of acid green scatter cushions against the headboard. 'There!'

*

Zoe didn't invite me to stay, and if she had I don't think I'd have accepted. I think we both understood what was going on; and each of us, for our own reasons, felt the need to limit the damage it would do.

The Xedos was uncomfortable, but Zoe's MX5 was plain impossible, so we used the Xedos. What Eva made of the greasy stain on the passenger-seat is anyone's guess.

'Turn the light on.'

I reached up, balancing awkwardly, crushing Zoe's arm, fiddling with the switch, slipping out of her ...

'Oh come back,' she laughed, reaching up for me.

I couldn't think for the life of me what she saw, looking at me that way. Surely not a lover.

She didn't take her eyes off me once. Grey hungry eyes flashed gold in the cabin light. Sometimes they seemed to be smiling. Not often. She never closed them. They burned me. When I reached my climax I kissed her hard on the mouth so I wouldn't have to look at them.

'Can we turn the light off, now?'

'I want to look at you,' she said.

'Zoe ...'

She stroked my chest. 'Your hair's growing grey here.'

'Like my heart.'

She laughed. She had blind grey eyes. Cocaine eyes.

26

While electricians installed strip-lighting in his side of the building, Loh conducted as much of his business as he could from a table in the window of a café-bar off Farringdon Road. It called itself a bistro, the way most places do around the Barbican, though I never saw anyone eating anything fancier than a baguette. The interior made the usual cursory continental gestures: Toulouse-Lautrec posters on the walls;

'Hommes' and 'Dames' stencilled on the lavatory doors; sugar crystals for your coffee.

He ordered a bottle of wine.

'If I'd known you and Eva weren't talking,' said Loh, genuinely wounded, 'I wouldn't have said anything to her.'

'Eva and I *are* talking.'

'So why didn't you know about Justin? Why are you laying into me just because Eva didn't tell you? Why are you saying I went behind your back just because I talked to your wife? Be reasonable, Adam, she's a friend. She's how we know each other in the first place.'

Loh wasn't giving an inch. It was my fault I knew nothing about Justin using Zhenshu's box. It was me who was overreacting. He made a good case. I was just about to write the whole thing off to paranoia when he dropped another bombshell.

'Nabeshima!'

'It was you who recommended them.'

'I know, but—'

'To be honest I didn't think they'd give me the time of day,' he chuckled. 'Shows how much I know.'

It turned out Nabeshima had become interested in the treatment of spinal injuries. 'A couple of years ago, a medical archivist came across Zhenshu's research papers and something clicked. They've been trying for over eighteen months to recreate Zhenshu's device. And you know what?' He recharged my glass and topped up his own. I noticed he wasn't keeping up. But I hardly expected him to – if nothing else, he lacked my years of dedicated practice. 'They haven't been able to do it.' He raised his glass to me. I picked up mine and drank, draining the glass, while Loh said, by way of a toast, 'A clever little bastard, your Zhenshu.'

It was good news, but I was still in a bad temper. 'It's too early for this,' I protested.

'The patent application's gone in. You have a working prototype. How is it too early to meet a major?'

'Loh, for the last time, we either talk strategy through together or—'

'Did you read that prospectus I sent you?'

I studied his face for clues. Nothing.

'What?'

'Did you read Nabeshima's prospectus? I posted it to your office.'

I had not. I hadn't been in the office for over a week.

Loh smiled a wry smile. 'Or did you not find the time?' he said, not unkindly, and his spectacles flashed.

I rubbed my face. Little alien hands nudge-nudged my diaphragm, making sure I got the joke. 'I've been busy,' I said.

I was busy now. A delegation from Nabeshima's medical arm was visiting for a Wellcome-sponsored IT conference, and Loh had arranged for me to give them a demonstration of Zhenshu's amplifier. At first I thought he meant I should show them Justin, but even Loh, in his enthusiasm, wasn't suggesting that. The idea was I let Nabeshima's suits play with Zhenshu's box for a few minutes, get them good and curious, good and flummoxed, then left-hook them with an idiot's guide to autism and the improvements to Justin's condition.

'It's the best we can do without formal data.' Now I was in the café kitchen, mobile pressed to my ear, explaining this strategy to Zoe.

'I thought they made CD players.'

'They do.'

Beyond the glass door, as though to prove my point, Hannah turned up the Keith Jarrett mid-whine.

'Will you come?' I said. I wanted her with me at the

meeting. I was very nervous. I wanted someone other than Loh by my side – someone I could trust.

'What about your wife?'

'What about her?'

'I thought you said she and Loh were friends.'

'So?'

The door opened and Eva leaned into the kitchen, her face red and damp from a morning spent leaning over the steam spigot. 'Are you going to be long?' she said, not seeing the phone pressed to my ear.

I waved her away.

Hurry up! she mouthed.

'So if I turn up at the meeting,' said Zoe, 'it'll get back to her. Won't it?'

For the would-be Jeffrey Archers gazing over the Thames from newly finished apartments in Manhattan Lofts – an expensive, modern complex barely two streets away – we were proving something of a godsend. Where do you get a quick working lunch in Southwark Market? Gabriel's Wharf was too gimcrack for them; the Oxo Tower too aspirational. More and more of them were chilling out with us: city boys and girls drowning stress-days and sickies with macchiato and ristretto from Eva's new steam-engine size espresso machine.

'Grind some beans,' she said.

'Grind dem beans. Tote dat danish.' I only wanted to be funny but Eva was well strung-out.

'For fuck's sake, Adam,' she said.

Zoe wasn't my mistress. She was more like a car accident. You see this tree-branch fallen into the middle of the road and you know you should avoid it, you know you can avoid it, if only you'll look where you want to go. Only you keep staring at the branch, unconsciously tilting the wheel to follow your eyes, until it's too late, and the collision when it comes is almost a relief.

'Come with me to the meeting.'

'Your wife will find out.'

'Why should she?'

'She might.'

'Please, Zoe. Be with me.'

That's what it was like for me. For Zoe, God knows. Her hunger was cryptic. Her brothers carried their scars on their arms, as wounds from martial-arts practice and knife-fights in Tsim Sha Tsui. Zoe carried her scars all on the inside, behind the pin-pricks of her fur-grey eyes.

'Is this a salad?'

'Table four, Adam, quickly, we lost their order once as it is.'

'This isn't a salad, it's a garnish.'

'Adam, please.'

Nabeshima. Everything from hospital intranets to animation hardware for Pixar and Dreamworks. Global. Exciting. The sort of company whose MD is made to look like a rock star on the cover of *Wired*.

'No, Adam, *four* capps, *one* espresso.'

I wanted Eva with me at the meeting, instead of Zoe. I wanted someone I could trust. But taking Eva along wasn't a realistic option, and besides, Zoe had finally agreed to go along with me. Instead, I told Eva what I could about this important business meeting I was having. I figured that if she knew, she could at least be with me in spirit.

But I only made things worse. 'That's wonderful,' she kept saying. 'How much will they want to know?' she asked me.

'Will they want to make an outright purchase?' she asked, 'or do they want to invest?'

A little more of that and the aliens started playing cat's-cradle with my innards.

'Are you all right, love?'

'I have to go to the bathroom.'

'Darling?'

'I'm fine.'

I went into the kitchen and shut the door. I propped a chair against the handle. I crossed to the sink and I bent down and I reached into the hole at the back of the unit.

It was empty.

Eva was a worrier – her ambition was like a nervous disease, it kept her fidgeting, scratching at old sores.

'Are you sure of your legal position in all this?'

I took the chocolate shaker out of her hand. 'Cinnamon,' I said. 'She asked for cinnamon.' Or was it nutmeg?

'Are you sure the inventors worked on their own? Are you sure they didn't sell any rights?'

'They don't need milk, it's lemon tea.'

'Adam?'

'It's fine,' I said. 'Everything's fine.'

'Adam?' she said.

'Oh for fuck's sake, what now?'

She wiped foam off the steam spigot with a wet rag. 'If you take the device to show them—'

'Yes? What?'

She laid a hand on my arm. 'What about Justin?' she said.

27

Guy Criville, Knox Lodge's headmaster, was a pale man with a face so uniformly cylindrical – lips and nose sewn on, an afterthought – it might as well have been an extension of his neck. He was older than me and his lack of adult experience showed in the weakness of his jaw and the slackness of his tie. I'd learned to respect his understanding of autism but I had yet to get any impression of him as a man. He cleared his throat. His secretary smoked and clearly it bothered him. 'It's not tested?' he said. Through the closed door came the unmistakable bonfire stench of Gauloises.

I shook my head. 'It's new,' I said.

I was taking the device away again, for the meeting with Nabeshima. I hadn't been looking forward to today. I'd expected Justin to fight me, to be upset, even angry. But he had hardly blinked when I explained what I wanted it for. And when I told him he'd have it back within a few days, he'd merely shrugged. 'Okay,' he said. I couldn't help but wonder whether this wasn't another little miracle: that his time sense had improved to the point that the idea of a few days' wait was comprehensible at last – even bearable.

No, the real struggle of the day turned out to be Criville.

He sighed, and sank his generous arse into the edge of his desk. He started to fold his arms then thought better of it. Body language 101 – avoid barrier gestures. 'We thought it was a toy,' he said.

'So did I,' I said, affecting a casual air.

'Did you try using it yourself?'

I thought about my hand, swelling like some Dali neurosis to fill the attic air. Then the other times. The girls. Willy Lam, Jimmy – I only just stopped myself in time. The machine – because of the signals it sent, or because of some deeper, more sinister magic Loh's pet engineers had yet to uncover – spoke to the lizard-brain; memories of it were hard to control.

'Because I did,' he said, and his few words were pregnant with meaning. But he couldn't hold my blank stare for long. He looked away. 'I ... did.'

'I don't blame you,' I said. Brazening this one out wasn't going to be easy. 'Did you enjoy it?'

'I don't feel easy with this,' he said, not rising to the obvious bait. Whatever experiences he had had with the device, they had spoken deeply to him. He was so reluctant to meet my eyes, he practically offered me his profile.

I wondered: had he interpreted his experiences sexually? After all – uneasily, it occurred to me – I had. Maybe the sex response was the only possible response to sensations so strong and so pure.

'We know how it works,' I said. 'My company. We received a report from Reading yesterday.' I told him what Eva had told me about the signals Zhenshu's machine sent up the nerves. Pure, undegradable messages. Snatches of lucid, liberating sensuality ...

'I can't have you conducting trials here,' Criville said. Unease, shame and hunger fought for control of his face like the beginnings of an emotional outburst. But he held it in. He even managed to look at me. 'We haven't got the facilities.'

'I'm not conducting a trial,' I said. 'Eva brought it for Justin to play with. We considered it a toy.'

'If it hasn't been tested then I'd have thought—'

'We didn't know it would have the effect it had,' I said, too loudly.

'I understand your enthusiasm,' he said.

I knew then that I'd have to withdraw Justin from the school. The device was too effective. It was generating too much curiosity. A stronger man than Criville would have muscled in on the research weeks ago.

I made some placatory noises: things had moved faster than I could ever have hoped, and Criville wasn't the only one who was scared by it all. I left him with the impression I wasn't bringing Zhenshu's toy back this time. The least that would give me was a couple of days' thinking space. I wondered if Eva would agree to us bringing Justin home for a while.

And I wondered, uncomfortably, whether I really wanted that right now.

When I arrived at Zoe's house she was out. I let myself in with the key she had hidden under a flowerpot and went into the kitchen.

There had been more deliveries. Glassware, this time: on the kitchen table, wine bulbs as big as my head rang against each other as I walked over to the kettle. A loose floorboard already: so much for rural workmanship.

They stood next to a pile of torn tissue. Zoe was so like a kid at Christmas, no patience at all. She had to play with her toys straight away, never mind the mess.

While the kettle boiled I went through to the bathroom and rifled the cabinet, looking for things to help me freshen up. The meeting with Nabeshima was still a couple of days away but already the tension was beginning to show.

I dashed water in my face and hair and shaved with a disposable Bic. I looked round for a towel to dry myself off. There wasn't one. I used a dry flannel. I looked in the mirror: my face was pale and dry and overstretched, and there was a line of stubble like a streak of dirt down the corner of my mouth where I'd missed it with the razor. The skin under my chin was sagging more than usual, and when I swallowed, my Adam's apple bobbed about painfully in my throat, a knot of gristle I couldn't swallow down. God knows what kind of impression I'd make when I finally made it to Nabeshima's offices.

I found a jar of vitamin B12 and took half a dozen with water from the tap. I went back into the kitchen and finished the coffee and burned my tongue so badly I couldn't even taste the bitterness.

It was strange, wandering through Zhenshu's house now, with its Designers Guild wallpaper and Neotu rugs and Zoe's clothes discarded in odd corners of almost every room. I hadn't had a drink all day and the coffee wasn't doing me any good at all, it was making me shake, and my head was throbbing like a ripe egg. I looked out the living room window, like that would make Zoe less late, then headed back to the bathroom for a shower.

I sat under the flow for a long while, as the downpour numbed my face and forehead, until I started to get the shivers. It would have been so easy to go fix myself a drink, there was so little else to do, and I had to keep going over and over in my mind what it would be like, sharing the first with Zoe, drinking with Zoe, being with Zoe, touching her, tasting the rum on her mouth – all to stop myself heading for that cabinet in – truly, my mistress had the low-down on me – the bedroom. The hot water was almost gone and my teeth started chattering before I got up the energy to soap myself up and wash. Then I stepped out and of course there wasn't a towel. Cursing and dripping, I traipsed upstairs to the bedroom.

There were no towels.

The room next door was going to be Zoe's dressing room but there'd been another delivery and the room was full of boxes. I padded downstairs. Zhenshu's old bedroom was next to the bathroom. I went in.

It was still as it had been: a wheatmeal carpet, white woodwork, plastic coving round the walls. I opened his wardrobe but it was bare, of course. The bed was stripped so that was out. There were drawers built into the base, though, and when I pulled the drawers open I found a stack of bath-sheets and some jumpers wrapped up in dry-cleaning bags. I pulled the drawer wider and pulled out a towel. It was wrapped round something because it was heavier than it should have been. As I pulled it out it unwrapped and a package slipped out and nearly struck my foot.

I picked it up.

The wrapping was oil paper, tied round with twine. I sniffed the towel and it stank of creosote. I threw it on the bed – I was practically dry by this time anyway. I sat on the bed, picked up the package and worried the knot free. Beneath the oil paper there was a cardboard box. I pulled the lid open.

The handgun appeared to be unused, but what would I know?

The bluing was unworn, the mechanism slick with oil. Gingerly, I turned the gun over in my hands. There were Japanese characters stamped into a lozenge riveted into the rosewood butt.

The front door opened.

I dropped the gun back in its box, shoved the oil paper over it and closed the lid.

'Adam?'

I dropped the box into the drawer, grabbed the towel and wrapped it round myself. 'In here.'

She stepped into the room, saw me there half-naked, and stared.

'I was freshening up.'

'Yes.'

'I couldn't find a towel.'

'Try the airing cupboard?'

She didn't believe me. She had her own theory.

She pulled her dress over her head.

'You're bloody keen,' she said, and kicked off her shoes.

28

She wanted to use Zhenshu's box.

'No.'

'Oh come *on*.'

'No,' I said.

'It's great!'

I knew how great it was.

Did she know that I knew?

Paranoia ruined any chance I might have had of losing myself in her. I couldn't get Zhenshu's gun out of my mind; there it was, sitting in its shoe box under the bed where Zoe was trying, without much success, to arouse me. Did it work? Probably – it had been well cared for; it probably hadn't been out of its oiled wrapper since the end of the war. A nasty sort of memento but there were still enough of them around, I guessed ...

I wondered if it had ever seen action. I wondered why Zhenshu had felt the need of it. Wasn't he the Kempeitei's darling? Wasn't he their spy?

Not if the story he's told Zoe was true. How five teenage Kempeitei, drunk on blood and boredom, had frogmarched him and Eva's father out to Sidney Beach. How with sticks and rifle-butts they forced them to their knees, facing each other, in the surf. How they made Zhenshu watch. '*He never betrayed Eva's dad,*' she told me once. '*It was just a sick joke. A sick practical joke. You must have heard what they were like.*'

'Yes.'

'What?'

Zoes's panted question, her red face, her thin, starved arms, fingers clawing at my chest like a cat's claws, brought me back to the present. 'Nothing,' I said. 'Nothing.'

'It would give you an erection.'

'I don't want to use the box, for God's sake, Justin uses it.'

It hadn't occurred to her, that I might feel awkward about it; the excuse seemed to satisfy her.

It was a clumsy, gimcrack sort of lovemaking, but out of it came something graceful and sad and a little decadent: a lot of wine, a lot of stroking, a lot of staring. I did most of the staring.

'Jesus Christ you're beautiful.'

'I know.'

'What do you see in me?'

She pressed her fingers to my lips. 'Don't dare,' she whispered. 'Don't bloody dare,' and she kissed me deep and then, too late to matter, I felt myself engorge.

Afterwards, crazy and drunk, I fed her wine from my mouth and poured the dregs inside her body straight from the bottle and I knelt and drank her down until she bucked and came. I let her rub herself against my thigh and she left a friction burn there I would have to hide from my wife. We fell asleep tangled up in each other in a position that started as 69 and twisted itself as we dozed into some bizarre, magical number that gave me a crick in my neck that lasted a week.

About four in the afternoon I woke with the entire back half of my head on fire.

'Huh,' said Zoe, struggling to vocalise through the fug of her hangover. At some point that afternoon she had decided to match me glass for glass. It had seemed like a good idea at the time.

'What, my love?' In the late afternoon light: her skin had the fullness and bloom of a ripe peach

'Huh,' she said again; or it may have been 'Help'.

'You want a glass of water, baby?'

'Huh.'

I groped my way out of bed, my mind and spirit freed

from Zhenshu and his toys, his unquiet spirit laid to rest by sex and the taste of Zoe's mouth. I padded to the door. It was open, held there by that toe-crackingly brutal Indian stone doorstop which I had learned, through bitter experience, to avoid. I stepped out onto the landing and I heard glasses tinking.

Those new wine glasses – the ones Zoe had left un-wrapped on the kitchen table – were zinging against each other again. I must tell her about that floorboard, I thought.

They zinged again; now I got the message.

The gun was worse than useless. There wasn't any ammunition anyhow. Whoever looked after it that well wouldn't have left any in the chamber.

I leaned back into the room. Zoe was dozing, none the wiser. It was safer to leave her that way. I squatted down and picked the Habitat doorstop up by its heavy steel hook. I eased towards the top of the stairs, weighing the cylindrical slug of stone in my hand. None of your child-friendly rounded corners from these Indian stonecutters,

I eased my weight onto the first step. Below me, through the banisters, shadows moved against the wall.

Behind me the bedroom door, unstopped, swung shut. It squealed. It slammed.

Below me, a glass shattered.

I ran down the stairs, swung on the banister, and sling-shotted into the kitchen.

It was empty.

The floorboard gave a little under my foot. On the deal table, another glass travelled, and toppled, and fell.

I dropped to my knees. It hit the floor. I caught it as it bounced. It trembled in my hands like a living thing. It didn't break.

'Are you all right?'

'Christ,' I shouted. I stood, swinging the doorstop

blindly. It was so heavy it didn't get higher than my waist. Zoe stepped smartly out of its way.

My heart hammered in my throat. 'For God's sake,' I said, 'I nearly brained you.'

'The door slammed. It woke me up.' She blinked dozily, taking in what I had in my hands. A wine glass, the stone doorstop ... She looked at me. 'What?' she said.

The windows were shut. So was the door. I tried it. 'It's unlocked.'

'I know.'

'You left it unlocked?'

'Adam. Look out there.'

The last leaves burned like fire in the late afternoon light. Low mist eddied round the trees.

'I've never seen it so beautiful.'

'Someone was here,' I said. I went out the back door. Autumn was taking hold today – the air smelled of wet and spores and earth. The tarmac was cold on my bare feet.

'Adam?'

'Go inside. Lock the door.'

Undergrowth rustled to the left and behind me. I turned in time to see a stag, fully antlered, disappearing into a stand of fern.

Then, beyond the avenue, out on the public road, a car engine turned and coughed.

'Adam?'

I ran down the drive.

'Adam!'

Out on the road, the engine coughed again. It was cold. It didn't want to start. The engine turned again and caught. There was still time. The air burned my lungs.

But the wind that night had tossed the chestnut trees, and it only needed one, sickeningly deep lancing pain before I realised my mistake.

When Zoe found me, I was still hopping about the drive in no particular direction, inventing vocabulary. She laughed. The image stuck with her. She was always reminding me about it afterwards, joshing me.

How she'd caught me that day, singing and dancing barefoot among the conkers, with their pale green barbs.

29

Around the middle of November, Money and her sons Brian and Eddie got ready to move back to Hong Kong.

The police had already questioned Eddie about his sports gear importing business. And at first I thought Money had seen the writing on the wall; that she was getting the boys out of the country before their fast friends in Hoxton landed them in even deeper trouble. But the reality – as Zoe broke it to me, the night of their leaving party – was far stranger.

'*Producers?*'

'Adam, be nice.' Zoe chided me, between dabs at her freshly lipsticked mouth.

'What the hell do they know—'

'Adam?'

'Okay,' I said. I leant back and watched Shaftesbury Avenue slide by the cab windows. 'Okay, I'll be nice.' Patrick Marber's *Closer* was still running. Lonely old men were shambling through bargain book stores. The queue for cigarettes stretched out of the old 7-Eleven onto the pavement.

'Here. Here we are.'

The cab let us out just before the Circus. We crossed to the north side of the road and weaved our way through the last, laggard flock of Japanese tourists, sitting and shivering while street artists caricatured them in charcoal.

'Is it far?'

'I can't believe you've never been to the Atlantic.'

209

Getting past the door wasn't so bad, but the bouncers inside were beyond parody. 'I know it's in a room here somewhere,' Zoe fretted, crossing and recrossing the plush lobby like a cougar in a baiting pit, but the apes at the entrances of the private rooms let it be known in their own language that we weren't welcome. They had things in their ears that looked like cybernetic enhancements and they probably needed them.

'Maybe we're eating,' I said, 'isn't that a restaurant through there?'

The public bar was an old wartime dance hall, or maybe a cinema: sprung floor, high ceiling, a lot of gilt, a lot of uplighting. The walls were aubergine. There were some dining tables, hiding behind all these gelatinous brewery executives and their metallic seventeen-year-old girlfriends. But no-one we knew was eating there.

'Adam. Zoe.' Eddie was sweating so hard it looked like he'd taken a shower. 'Come on through, come on through.'

He led us out of the main bar, across the lobby, and ushered us into a private room. The doorman butted in. Eddie grabbed him by his ponytail and said something I didn't catch. The doorman blanched and stepped away. 'He must have a death-wish,' I murmered to Zoe.

'Are you kidding?' Eddie clapped me round the shoulders, taking my remark as meant for him. 'Money arrived about 8 p.m. to set things up here, would you believe she had to show them her credit card to get in?'

I took in the room. De Palma wouldn't have dressed it any more outrageously; the sofas were pure Vegas and the flunkies with their dainty brooms and nifty long-handled dustpans might have constituted some sort of East European mime ensemble, there were so many of them; but at least you could breathe in here, and there was a vibe to the place – the way people knotted and mingled and waved to each other – that suggested the conversation might extend beyond skiing accidents.

'Who comes here, anyway?'

'Footballers, soap stars, assorted fuckwits. Buy into it. We did. It's fun.'

Eddie certainly wasn't coming across as someone running from a peddling charge. He didn't dress that way, either.

'Nice suit.'

'Gordon Happ. Dublin.' He snapped his lapel between his fingers and winked at his sister. 'Hello, beautiful.'

The change in him seemed to surprise Zoe as much as me.

He led us over to the bar and ordered us a bottle of champagne. Brian was there, sitting next to a white girl in a dress made of strips of brown velvet so narrow she had to keep nudging her tits back into place. He glanced at us and nodded, and said something lugubrious to the girl and she made a sound like a laugh. There was powder on her fingernails when she picked up her glass. All in all, it was a far cry from Hannah and the café.

'Come say hello to Mum,' said Eddie, and led me to the back of the room.

She was sitting in state, the way Jimmy used to. I didn't recognise any of the faces adoring her, but I recognised the type. They were new to their role and it took a little while for Money to dismiss them, but they got the message eventually.

'Come sit down here.'

The contrast between her immaculate blue and silver cheongsam and her lined and sunken face should have been terrible; it wasn't. The Chinese have a way of carrying age – Chinese women in particular. Next to them old British women look like stricken children: unfinished and immature.

211

'The inquiry's over.'

I looked down at my glass and it was empty. I wished Eddie had brought the bottle over.

'You can go get yourself another drink in a minute.'

'I heard,' I said. 'I mean, I read about it in the *Post*.'

Money sniffed. 'I take it you want to know what really happened?'

For all her build-up, though, Money's story wasn't much different from the one I had read. The inquiry into the police handling of Top Luck and the money laundering operation had reached its bureaucratically constipated climax. Top Luck's lawyers had thrown one or two of Jimmy's more dispensable colleagues in the police community to the legal lions and criminal charges were expected. No further action was contemplated.

Incredibly, Top Luck was to be allowed to continue to trade.

'Is that who they were?'

'Who?'

'The fan club.' I pointed over my shoulder at the men who'd been sitting with her.

Money smiled. 'Actually they're from the British Film Institute. What was the British Film Institute. Now it's combining with British Screen and God knows what else and I really can't see what Top Luck can do for them.'

They were, she said, schmoozing up sponsorship to save a masters course they'd been running. I looked around and saw that Eddie had gathered them up. They smiled and nodded and laughed: he was charming them. The scene was so civilised, so ordinary in a strange, Soho-ish way, I wondered dizzily if I hadn't stumbled into some bizarre alternate reality.

Had Money really achieved her dream? Were her interests legitimate at last?

As if to assure me that some things never change, Brian got up from the bar and pulled his shirt off, showing off his scars to the girl in the strappy brown velvet.

A murmur went round the room.

Knives and whips and the odd cigarette end had left an indelible impression on Brian's back. They were the badges he carried of his struggle: his life-long labour to become as tough as his dad.

Money sucked her teeth.

The girl in the brown dress hid her face behind her glass.

Eddie went to the rescue.

'What's the film about?' I said.

'*Kowloon Takedown*,' said Money. 'About the developing friendship between a Triad boss and a detective.'

'It sounds exciting,' I said.

'You know they're starring?'

'I heard.'

Zoe had gone for a beer with her brothers a while back, when they first read the script. Zoe told me they liked it; that they saw themselves in the characters. They spent the whole evening swapping one-liners from the script. But how could we have guessed it would inspire such a change in them? Such dedication?

'Top Luck's first feature of the new millennium. Its first since the Handover.'

'You must be very proud,' I said.

It was a *Heat* rip-off. Brian wanted the De Niro role; Eddie, Al Pacino. During a bank raid, the maverick new recruit of a Triad gang led by Brian cuts out the tongues of three witnesses during a meticulously planned bank raid. Eddie's wife, a bank teller, is one of his victims, and Eddie, the detective, swears revenge. Michael Mann meets the Yau brothers: it didn't bear thinking about.

Money was looking at me levelly: maybe she thought I

was soft-soaping her. Eventually, though, she relented. 'It's good that they have a professional career,' she agreed.

Eddie had managed to get Brian to put his shirt back on. Then, to show Brian wasn't the only freak in the room, he rolled up his shirt sleeves so the punters could see his own scars. Money drew in a hissing breath, but I thought it was clever of him. There he was, smiling, chatting, normalising everything. I could imagine what he was saying. Martial arts are our business! Oh, we've earned a few scratches in our time!

'This is the last month I'll be paying you, Adam.'

I watched her.

'Of course, I expect you to take an appropriate cut of the proceeds Zoe makes from Zhenshu's little toy.'

'All right,' I said.

Money laughed. 'Don't look so shocked, Adam. You did a good job. And as you can see' – she looked around the room – 'you did it admirably. You helped us reinvent ourselves, Adam. Thank you.'

I thought about it. The truth was, I was afraid to let go. 'The inquiry—'

'Adam, if you needed protecting, I would protect you. But it's over now. And you don't need me any more.'

I let it sink in, because I knew it made sense, but it took a long time. 'You know,' I said, 'I wish we'd found out who it was you were protecting me from.'

But Money, ever the practical one, had no time for my philosophising. 'Don't look a gift horse in the mouth, Adam.'

'Will I see you again before you leave?'

Money smiled and shook her head. 'Shooting begins next week,' she said.

The girl in the brown velvet had disappeared. Eddie had his arm around Brian's shoulder. Brian was trying to smile.

'Look after them.' I said.

Paranoid or not, I couldn't shake the creeping feeling that slowly, subtly, things were slipping out of control. The next two days, I couldn't have made myself more unbearable if I'd practised.

'What do you mean, you don't know whose car it is? It's been sitting out there every day for a week.' I was back at the café, back being the good husband. Well, a husband.

Hannah retreated behind the counter. She only wanted a bit of pin money working in a nice coffee house and suddenly she'd found herself slap bang in the final reel of *The Shining*.

'Wha's-a-matter?' I said, trying to placate her with a ghastly smile. What did she think I was going to do? Batter her to death with a ham and cheese croissant? 'Give me a coffee,' I said. I slumped down at a small table by the window, watching for the owner of the Saab to return. A Saab. Why a bloody Saab? Like God was suddenly handling product placement for all the really bad moments of my life. Seeing my glowering face through the window, no wonder nobody came in that afternoon.

'Cappuccino?' Hannah's hands were shaking. Froth dribbled down the side of the cup.

'Coffee. Black coffee, damn it, you know how I take it by now.'

'I was trying to be nice.'

'Don't,' I said.

Eva came in around four. She asked me where Hannah was and I told her she'd walked out. But Eva had already had it up to here with my foul mood and she guessed straight away what had happened.

'I'll make it up to her.'

'Too fucking right.'

215

Two tourists, lingering by the door, blanched and walked on.

That night, Eva tried again and again to break through. But I was closed to her, and far, far away.

'Please Adam—'

'Sorry, love.'

'Not that.' She kissed my unresponsive sex. 'You know I don't mean that.'

'I know.' I tried to pleasure her, but there was no fooling her: she knew I was only trying to avoid her eyes.

'Come up here. Look at me.'

I looked.

She took a deep breath. 'Tell me,' she said.

I made the usual excuses. Worries at work. The meeting with Nabeshima.

She said, 'I know that's not the truth.'

She said, 'I know what it is.'

'What is it, then?'

She shook her head. She wanted me to tell her.

'It's nothing.' I kissed her on the eyelids, the way I used to. 'It's nothing. It's too much booze again. It's nothing.'

I woke up in the middle of the night and found her watching me. She smiled the saddest smile. She stroked my hair.

'Go back to sleep,' she said.

'Nothing,' I said.

'I know.'

30

The next day, around eleven in the morning, the Saab appeared opposite the café. I was busy in the kitchen; I didn't see it arrive.

'Adam, will you give me a hand?'

I slouched away from the window.

'What is it out there?'

'Nothing.'

'You're giving people the creeps. Here, take these.' She pushed two manchego ploughmans across the glass counter and I carried them to the table in the back.

I didn't recognise the two suits lunching here today, but they seemed to know me.

'Thanks, Adam.' said one.

'Ta,' said the other.

'Oh I think this salt's run out,' said the first. He handed me the cellar. I took it without looking at it. He looked up at me. He tried a smile. It didn't work. 'What?' he said.

I smiled.

'What?'

I handed them a full cellar from the neighbouring table and went back in the kitchen. My hands were shaking so much I spilled salt all over the floor.

There was a letter waiting for me when I got home.

It said, 'I'm sorry you didn't make it to Hong Kong.'

It was from Daniel White.

'You would have been much safer here in my spare room.'

He was trying to not be angry with me. He was trying to not feel betrayed. He changed the subject. His father had died: a coronary on the links. 'They've still got an alligator problem, which I find oddly comforting. Muriel insisted on riding in the back of the hearse.'

He had just arranged for his sister to come live with him in Hong Kong. There were good schools and day-care centres; she was settling in as well as could be expected. 'I hope to God it takes her a while to discover the tram system. I can hardly make it out myself.'

Between the lines you could feel this new responsibility weighing him down: no more late nights and easy dates for him now – not with an autistic teenage girl sharing the apartment.

There was no mention of Bumpy.

Right at the end, just as he was getting to the hugs and the kisses and the please-write-soons, he lost it.

'Most people who need money for their kids – and I KNOW that's why you did it – remortgage their house. Not you. Oh no. Nothing so obvious from my oblique limey chum.'

I threw the letter away, tore the stamp off the envelope and fed it carefully down the kitchen plughole, tore the envelope into little pieces and threw old coffee grounds over it all.

It was strange, how much I missed him.

The next day, the day of my meeting with Nabeshima, I looked out of the window and there were three Saabs parked outside the café.

'Christ, Adam, what's the matter? You look as though you've seen a ghost.'

We were miles away from the Millennium site at Greenwich, but the lunch-time talk this week was full of the Dome and the laser show and God knows what else. I wondered what had brought them here – all these little Mandelsons in their expensive cars.

'If you can't be civil, stay in the kitchen.' Eva hissed. She was furious.

'For God's sake, Eva, I was only making a little light conversation.'

'Those two have had lunch here every day for a week – we'll never see them again the way you're carrying on.'

'I only asked them what they did.'

Hannah came in from the kitchen and hesitated at the door.

'What is it, Hannah?'

'It's my break, Mrs Wyatt.'

'Of course. Sorry, love. Adam?'

'I'm on it.' As I walked past Hannah the air chilled perceptibly. I was trying to be nice, but she was only back and working here because Eva bribed her with a raise.

When I got to the counter and looked out the window, all three Saabs were gone.

'Dan here.'

'It's Adam.'

'Adam? Adam. Christ.'

'I need you to tell me something.'

'Goddamnit, how are you?'

'Dan, I haven't got time.'

'What's up, pal?'

'Did you ever find out who conducted surveillance on Frank?'

'Oh, Adam, relax, it's all water under the bridge now.'

'Dan, tell me. It's important.'

The line was so clear, it was like I could hear him thinking. 'What's the matter?' he said.

'Did you find out or not?'

'No. What's this about?'

'Did you ever stock-take the RHKP stores? Did you ever cross-check the consignments?'

'Of course we did.'

'And?'

'And nothing. Nothing was missing. Christ, Adam, don't tell me you—'

My hands were shaking so much, I could barely hang up the phone.

So. About a year too late, I had my answer. I knew, now, who had been spying on Hamley and Jimmy Yau, and I had a fairly good idea why.

And it hadn't got anything to do with Top Luck.

The day dragged by. My mind wasn't on my work. Loh had arranged for Zoe and I to meet the Nabeshima people at his office. It would take me maybe an hour to walk there, past Blackfriars and St Paul's, and since the sky was clear and I needed the time to wind down, that's what I decided to do.

'Good luck,' said Eva, and kissed me, and looked proud.

It was a clear night, and cold, and because I'd driven over to the café with Eva that morning I hadn't got a coat. I turned up the collar of my suit jacket and began marching to warm myself up. The box, jammed not altogether safely into my wallet pocket, dragged at the thin fabric so that my collar chafed the back of my neck

Southwark's reinvention – the new office buildings east of the South Bank, Hay's Trocadero, the Clink, the Globe – there was something brash, facile, and Eighties about it all, and profoundly unconvincing. But around Southwark Market, the streets still held the authentic tang of what had been here once. The tops of the old warehouses still sported lifting gear, and behind thick walls of old, pollution-softened brick, through barred and dust-bleared windows, set too high to see through properly, lay disused garages and storerooms, market halls and dead wholesalers' offices. The railway arches leading east to London Bridge station were most of them adapted into wine bars now, and architects' offices; but the upper parts, well above the identikit plate-glass fronts, and out of reach of the streetlamps, were nailed over with panels of garishly painted clapboard. Into these, badly measured windows had been sawn, and grilles of chicken-wire nailed over them. I studied them as I walked.

I looked at all the old and broken places and I smiled.

I knew I was being sentimental. I knew it was wrong, to prefer dead places to living ones. I knew, too, that it was just my sort of shallow, fag-end Romanticism that had brought planners and developers – and café owners – here in the first place. That and the low property prices.

I knew I was part of the very process I was despising; the trend that would, one day in the not too distant future, obliterate the old entirely, and make of this another Islington, Portobello, Clapham, Hammersmith. Another strangely inauthentic middle-class preserve. It occurred to me, as I walked, that I was thinking like a café proprietor.

It was strange, to catch myself doing that. But why not? The café was the one solid thing in my life. That, and Eva, and the endless, generous second-chances she kept giving me.

Right then, as I passed beside Southwark Cathedral, and climbed the stone steps that led up to London Bridge, if someone had asked me what I was doing, what my errand was, why I was doing it – I could not have answered them.

My suit was a summer suit, and the wind was blowing downriver. I put my hands in my jacket pockets and tried to wrap the fabric tighter around myself, but the wind ignored it, and blew straight through. So I glanced back along the bridge thinking there might be a cab I could hail.

There was a lull right then – one of those strange London lulls that, for a few eerie seconds, might almost persuade you that you are alone. There was only one car on my side of the bridge, and it had pulled up against the kerb, and a man with a ponytail was climbing out of the car. They had pulled up between streetlights, but in the maladjusted headlamps of a Transit van heading south, I saw that the car was a Saab.

I kept walking.

From Monument to Moorgate is one stop on the City branch of the Northern line. The city's lull broke and the escalators into the bowels of the station were clogged with office-workers. I wanted to walk down but it was so crowded we all just had to stand there two abreast and wait for the mechanism to deliver us like so much airline baggage to the lower floor. I looked back, up the escalator, and hunted among the blank, incurious stares for the pony-tail. I didn't see him. I was nearly at the bottom now. I put my hand in my jacket and tried ramming the box deeper into my pocket. It wouldn't go.

They have a whole new set of tunnels connecting Monument to Bank via the DLR; but the Northern Line, whatever the signs say, lies somewhere else, at the ends of old passages, clad here and there in shiny enamelled panels, but carrying about it still the smell of dry plaster and old billboard glue. According to the illuminated board suspended over the platform, the train was only a minute away. We must have waited ten. The platform was crowded by the time the train arrived, but I muscled my way to the front. The carriages weren't so busy – there was even a free seat – only the pony-tail got there before me.

He wore a Gap fleece, the collar turned up round his chin. His shoes were expensive and formal and looked silly against his blue-jeans. He was thin, in an unhealthy, coked-up way, and in the dead, grey-yellow light of the carriage his eyes glistened schizophrenically.

I stayed on at Moorgate, and so did he. I stayed on at Old Street. He crossed his legs, and he tugged his jeans leg up an inch to protect the crease. At Angel, just as the doors were closing, I leapt up and got off the train. I bent to tie my shoe-lace and he walked right by me. His arse was so narrow his jeans hung in two ugly, shapeless folds below his belt.

I didn't see him in the corridors and when I got on the

main escalator he was trotting up the steps far above me; he was nearly at the top. I was surprised at his energy. When I got to the ticket hall I found it lined with lost-looking twenty-somethings waiting for their dates – but no pony-tail.

He knew I had sussed him.

I crossed to the entrance barriers and fed my ticket in and went back down into the tube system. I glanced behind me on the escalator but I didn't see him. I walked onto the Southbound platform. There was a five-minute wait for the train to carry me back to Moorgate. This time it was punctual. The doors opened. There were plenty of seats this time. I sat down.

He was sitting at the other end of the carriage, on the same side I was, and I could see him reflected in the glass of the door.

I looked at my watch. I was thirty minutes late for Loh's meeting. I felt nothing.

I thought about the suits from Nabeshima, tapping their Mont Blanc pens impatiently against their even, white teeth, and I still felt nothing.

I thought about Zoe, sitting there as the minutes ticked by. Fielding them. Fielding Loh. Waiting for me.

I had had enough.

I rode back to London Bridge.

He was right behind me as I exited onto Tooley Street. He stood beside me as I waited to cross the road, and as I descended the stone steps into the precincts of Southwark Cathedral I could hear his shoes tap-tapping behind mine.

There's a dead space at ground level beneath the huge iron pillars supporting the Charing Cross line. There's a sign calling it a car park, and a gate across the entrance that always seems to be locked. I waited for him there, and when he walked past me I ran out and grabbed his head and drove it into the side window of a nearby BMW 5 series.

The car's alarm was so loud I could barely hear him cry. The window was crazed but not broken and I took a minute to mash his scalp against the shards still sticking to the laminate. He broke free of me and ran but the blood must have got in his eyes because he hurtled straight into a pillar.

I picked him up and helped him down Winchester Walk, towards the café. He was heavier than I expected and I had to support him by holding onto the belt of his jeans. I asked him who he was but he was sobbing so hard he couldn't speak. So I sat him down on the kerb, among the broken vegetable boxes and Styrofoam fruit trays, and kicked him all over until he recovered.

He fumbled in the pocket of his fleece and pulled out his wallet. He drew out a card and handed it to me. There was a smear of blood over the name; I wiped it away.

His name was Tommy Parker and he worked for Fred's Bureau of Investigation. The company initials were outsize embossed blue type, making a familiar acronym.

'Cute,' I said.

He made to get up, but I dissuaded him.

'You owe me a dog,' I said. 'Cunt.'

'Dog?'

'Cunt.'

'Wha'?'

I swung a fist low and he fell back on the pavement.

'Nabeshima so fucking paranoid they have to hire wankers like you now?'

'Who—'

'Don't they tell you anything, you little shit? I'm *bringing* it! I've got a *meeting*! You can all stop following me you little shit, I'm *selling* it, you understand?'

'I don't – Ow.'

'Stop wasting my time.'

'Oh Jesus Christ I think you've broken it.'

I let him get up. I didn't want him choking.

He gobbed up a mouthful of blood and spat it into the gutter. He was hugging his stomach. I hadn't touched his stomach.

'What's the matter?'

'I think I'm going to throw up.'

I let him throw up. I stood well out of the way.

He touched his nose and winced. 'Can I go now?'

'Who hired you?'

'Mrs Wyatt.'

I just stood there.

He looked at me. 'What?'

I thought about it. 'Zoe's house—'

'Yeah, yeah, yeah.' He was bored. I was boring him.

'Eva—'

'She knew you were fucking around.'

I swallowed.

'So can I go now?'

'When?' I said. 'When did she hire you?'

'A couple of months ago.' He licked around his mouth. 'I think I'm going to be sick again.'

'Why'd she hire you?'

'She found a petrol receipt from Wye in your pocket.'

I thought about Eva. I thought about what she'd said and the way she'd said it. She had known all the time. She even told me that she knew. How could I have been so stupid?

I said, 'Come with me to the café. I'll get you cleaned up.'

'Fuck you.'

'Come on.'

'Fuck you.'

'Please. I thought you were someone else.'

'I don't want to have to sit through some shitty little marital scene.'

'She'll have gone home by now,' I said. 'Come on. I'll make you a coffee.'

We walked together down the road into Stoney Street. The lights were off in the café.'

'You see?' I said.

'Okay,' he said, 'okay,' and he pulled away from me and stepped off the kerb, right into the path of Eva's car.

31

Eva had only just pulled away from the kerb so even the ambulance men had a hard time believing Tommy Parker's injuries were all down to the accident. But a policeman noticed that though the Xedos's engine was running the headlamps were off, and that distracted them all awhile.

The ambulance left and we followed in the car. Parker was already in theatre by the time we arrived. We waited in the lobby of the A&E. The coffee machine was broken.

She said, 'I know who it is.'

'The little prick came right inside the house,' I said. 'He came snooping through the kitchen. He's lucky I didn't kill him then.'

She said, 'I saw what you did to him.'

'You didn't even have your headlights on,' I said. 'You saw fuck.'

'I know who it is,' she said.

'So you know.'

'So do you want me to spell it out?'

'Why bother?' I said. I spotted another drinks machine. 'Do you want a Coke?'

'No thanks,' she said.

I bought myself a diet Lucozade Sport and I spent the rest of our little chat hiccoughing and burping.

'Christ,' she said.

'It's not my fault.'

'You disgust me.'

'Oh, tough.'

I could have tried to explain, I suppose. But if I started, I wouldn't be able to stop. I would have to tell her everything. About Zhenshu's box, and Jimmy, and what had really happened to me in Hong Kong. Any justification I made would only be a window on another set of lies. So I sat there and let her have her say.

'It's Jimmy's daughter, isn't it?'

'It's Zoe, yes.'

'Did you bed her in Hong Kong?'

'She was a teenager.'

'Did you bed her?'

'No.'

'Did you want to bed her?'

'Yes.'

'I am just trying to understand.'

'I've wanted to fuck her through the floor for years, okay?'

Well, there wasn't much to say after that.

She knew about my software business. She knew I was doing some kind of deal with Zoe and the family. 'You can't do anything straight, can you?' she said. 'Frank told me that once. At our wedding. He warned me you were a buccaneer.'

Frank Hamley. Now there was a blast from the past. I thought about telling her what had happened to his head. But I just couldn't see what good it would do.

'All this time,' she cried. She was beginning to enjoy herself. 'All this time you've been experimenting on Justin.'

'*What?*'

'Just so Money gets a good deal from Nabeshima.' She was still obsessing over that bloody kaleidoscope.

'Honey,' I said, 'it was you who gave Justin the box. Remember?'

'And now you're trying to take him away from me.'

'Who? Justin?' I drained the can and gulped air. 'Come again?'

'I swear if you pass wind again I am going to vomit.'

'The only one who ever cut you out of caring for Justin was your bloody mum,' I said. I crushed the empty can in my fists. 'It's no good being angry at Money just because she reminds you of how crap your mother was.'

She looked at me oddly and no wonder, I was talking complete rubbish, I was just opening my mouth and letting the words tumble out; anything, to avoid what I knew was coming.

She stood up. I got up after her. But her eyes could always stop me. Even now, they stopped me.

'I know what you're doing,' I said. 'I know why you hired that prick.'

'Then get ready,' she said.

'If you want we should part then we'll part,' I promised her. 'I won't contest it.'

Her eyes gave nothing back. It wasn't that she was withholding anything. There was just nothing left for her to give.

The moment had come. There was nothing left for me to do now but face it. 'But that's not all of it,' I said. 'Is it?'

'He's not your son,' she said. 'He's your hobby.'

'That's enough,' I said.

'Like your dad and his bloody medals and stamps. You're all the same, the three of you. What do they call it?'

'Shut up now.'

'Asperger's. That's it. Nerd's disease.'

'Please don't take him,' I said.

'You've hurt him enough.'

'Please.'

'You expose him to things. To bad people. He needs protecting.'

'He's getting better!'

We were only going to get louder, so maybe it was as well the police came over when they did. There were two of them, both young, both absurdly handsome, the sort who get shot in ITV drama serials. 'We'd like a word, Mr Wyatt,' they said.

'Adam?' said Eva.

I ignored her. 'Sure,' I said.

'Adam, what did you do to him?'

They took me to an unoccupied dressing room and drew the curtains and took down my full name and my date of birth. 'I'm afraid I didn't see very much,' I said.

'What was your argument about?' said the first one: his blond hair was out of a bottle, no question.

'We weren't arguing.'

They might have learned their silences from Jimmy Yau.

'I was the one called the ambulance,' I shouted. 'Well, ask him.'

Outside, in the corridor, a baby began crying.

'My wife ran him over.'

As it turned out they were just having a bit of fun. Parker wasn't dead. He wasn't even unconscious. Only the doctors didn't want him questioned while they were drilling a hole through his skull.

'They're putting a drain in,' the second policeman told me. He was blond too, but of a more realistic kind. He was excited. 'They do that these days. When they think there might be bleeding. You know. To avoid brain damage.' He wasn't being nasty. He was just enthusiastic.

'We were just talking,' I said.

'Take off your shoe,' the first policeman said.

'What?'

'Your left shoe. Take it off.'

Why?'

He sighed. 'Because some silly bastard left their footprint on his neck.'

4

LONDON
WINTER, 1998-1999

32

The night I was arrested they gave me one phone call, so I'd phoned Zoe. Zhenshu's box had fallen out of my pocket, of course. Zoe found it at five-thirty the next morning. One of the stallholders in Southwark Market had found it and was holding it to his ear, turning the little dial back and forth, trying to tune in Capital.

I wasn't much use to Zoe after that. Somehow I lost interest. Besides, Eva was piling it on. I did try to contest the divorce at first, but it was a non-starter. In the end it was all I could do to get decent access to Justin.

Zoe, meanwhile – well, Zoe had a business to run. I think her brothers' success in the film industry had made her antsy. She had things to prove, and fast. She rang Loh, got on a proper business footing with him, went with him to Southampton and met the engineering crew – generally played the young go-getting businesswoman.

I tried to tell her.

'You're not still dealing with Nabeshima?' I said.

'What do you care?'

'They were the ones planted listening devices on your dad and Frank Hamley. In Hong Kong. It was Nabeshima. They've been spying on your family for God knows how long.'

Zoe was sceptical. 'Well how the fuck do you work that one out?' she said.

'They were licensed suppliers to the Royal Hong Kong Police. Of course when we stumbled across the bugs we all thought they were part of some secret police op. But it wasn't. It was Nabeshima.'

'Why?'

'I don't know.'

'How do you know it was Nabeshima?'

'Well, if it wasn't the police, who else could it be?'

'Christ, Adam.'

'What?'

'Do you know how paranoid this is?'

'I'm serious.'

'I know you're serious. Tommy Parker knows you're serious. You had him down as from Nabeshima and all.'

'Oh, fuck him.'

'I wish you could hear yourself,' she said.

'Oh well,' I said, 'fuck you too if you don't want to listen.'

'Adam?'

'Fuck you.'

Eva lent me the Xedos so I could ferry my things over to my new flat. She even packed them for me. I didn't crash, so when I drew up outside the house in Shaftesbury Road I made sure I scraped the passenger door against a lamp-post.

I'd found the place through an ad in a newsagent's window. The owner, a Cypriot with David Essex hair and a growth on his lower lip, ran a dry-cleaning shop on Stroud Green Road. He wanted me to pay him in cash every Saturday morning and he wanted four hundred pounds' deposit. A sign on the wall behind the counter explained that refusal often offends, so I paid him.

Archway wasn't nearly far enough away. It didn't take me more than an hour to dump my boxes in the first-floor room and find that the door lock didn't work, before I was back again, handing Eva her car keys.

'Where's your set?' she said.

'I want to phone for a minicab,' I said.

'I want the keys to my car. I want the keys to my house.'

'I threw them away,' I lied.

She came out with the phone and made me stand out on the stoop while I dialled the cab company. I handed it back to her and she slammed the door in my face.

I punched it till the skin over my knuckles was broken and then I started kicking it. The cabbie pulled up, saw what I was doing, and drove off again at high speed. So I walked: past Pentonville Prison and over the rail lines heading east through Finsbury, and up along the Holloway Road.

The flat wasn't a flat at all, but the first floor of a terraced house in Shaftesbury Road. It looked pleasant enough from the outside. Even before I got to the front door I could smell curry, which I figured for a promising sign. But by the time I'd negotiated the sacks of sand and old motorcycle parts and sofa cushions the neighbours had thrown over the fence, the smell had turned rank and sooty. I opened the door and the thin smoke that greeted me stank of cumin.

The house was supposedly three flats but they weren't subdivided in any way; at the end of the hall by the stairs, smoke dribbled from under an old panelled door. Carefully, I swung it open.

The kitchen was a lean-to, tacked onto the back of the

235

house. There were windows on all three sides. Two gave onto an overgrown back garden, the one on the right to a narrow alley where nothing grew in the shadow cast by a weathered fence. A neglected rose-bush had clawed its way up to the left-hand window and tap-tapped against the bird-messed glass. There were brown marks and peeled paper near the back door where the rainwater came in, and the lintel was rotted through. I turned off the gas under a pan of blackened onions.

I hammered on the living room door. It swung in.

The room's woodchip paper was painted magnolia, to which cigarette smoke had added a shiny, tea-coloured patina. The furniture was mismatched, picked up at one of those junk shops that advertise house-clearing and always have a cardboard box by the door full of Hammond Innes and one George Best annual.

Three plastic trolls, two with pink hair, one with green, stood on the mantelpiece, under a fly-spotted oval mirror. A 1997 Diana memorial wall-calendar hung to one side of the chimney breast. Six white chrysanthemums had rotted to a pale brown in a jam-jar full of pond-green water on the shelf beneath.

The chef was asleep in his shirt and underpants in front of *Ski Sunday*, a bottle of synthetic wine clamped between his thighs. Every once in a while David Vine got excited and a Euro '96 commemorative mug, perched on top of the set, buzzed in sympathy.

I walked into the room, watching him. His white stubble had got almost to goatee length. Once, he must have been handsome. The hairs round his mouth were stained purple. I kicked his bare foot, gently. It was so grubby and thin, I was afraid it might come off. He began to snore.

*

Up in my room, I began to unpack, only I realised I had nowhere to put anything.

There was one hanger in the chipboard closet which, apart from the bed, was the only article of furniture. I hung my jacket up and swung the door shut and the whole closet tipped back and banged against the wall. A few seconds later the chef knocked a broom handle against the ceiling.

I leant out into the hall. 'Hallo?'

It was as silent as the grave.

My living room – you could tell it was the living room because there were old sofa cushions propped up along the bed to make it look like a sofa – had a chest of drawers, three of which opened. It was light enough I could carry it through single-handed into the hall. But it wouldn't turn the corner into the bedroom, so I had to carry it back. There was some more knocking.

Singh grew friendly enough after I took his broom away from him. Life following sarcasm the way it sometimes does, he turned out really to have been a chef. He used to work in a curry house off Brick Lane, only it changed its image, painted its shutters lime green, renamed itself 'The Spice Mill' and started calling its curries 'Bangladeshi cuisine', so he left.

This, apparently, was a high moral stand he had taken – so high, it was a wonder his family bothered to make the climb. But every week or so they'd come round: his father, an aunt; a boy so young they could only be bringing him along to give him a dreadful object lesson on the evils of drink or careers in catering; and a woman who said she was his sister once when I met her on the stairs. But when I mentioned her to Singh it sent him off on an enormous silent binge so I figured she was probably his wife. They'd come round and scream at him for a couple of hours and go away again. I don't think they actually enjoyed giving him such a hard time. It had just become a habit with them; a habit with him, too, perhaps, to wind them up the way he did. I felt sorry for them. They looked so gentle, getting in and out of their Volvo, the old man so solicitous, opening the door for the women, the little boy so well turned-out. When it was dry he used to go play in the garden at the back of the house.

I'd go up to the kitchen and watch him through the window as he beat the long grass disconsolately with a stick. I don't think he saw me.

33

Most days I stayed in. If it was fine I sometimes walked along the old rail-bed that runs along the back of Hornsey Lane. Once I went as far as Highgate Wood, but I started enjoying myself so I came home again.

Singh had videos. One was little more than an old man in a foreman's beige coat, beating a girl's buttocks with a length of garden hose. It was called *Are You Being Served*? I let Singh come up and watch once but he started playing with himself so I threw him out. He came back upstairs with an apple corer and when he found I'd mended the lock on my door he stabbed the wood. The blade snapped and went straight through his hand.

Singh had it in his head that Shazia was going to be there waiting for him by the rubber doors of the A&E, waiting there with needle and thread ready to stitch him up.

'She doesn't work here. She works with the elderly.'

'I'm elderly! I'm *fucking* elderly.'

'Sit down and shut up.'

The triage nurse came over.

When we got back from the A&E, Singh's phone was ringing. The telephone was supposed to be for both of us and stood out in the hall on a battered console, onto which someone had scratched the words 'Thatcher Fuck'. But Singh had craftily fed the wire under the hall carpet and through a nick in the bottom of the living room door. The phone only reached a foot or two beyond the door, and Singh knocked it over every time he entered the room.

Singh fumbled around on the floor for the receiver. Old habit got the better of him and he dropped it straight back in its cradle. Then he picked it up again and raised it to his ear. 'Uh,' he said.

He was suspicious, full of hows and whos. His gas had only been reconnected that week and the electricity was on a key meter, so how he kept a phone in working order was anyone's guess. Maybe his family paid for it.

He turned to me. I thought he was going to tell me to go away. Instead he said, 'It's for you.'

I thought about who it might be. I took the receiver off him and rammed it into the cradle.

I went into his kitchen and unscrewed a bottle of wine. I didn't stop drinking until it was empty.

I woke the following afternoon and all the doorbells were ringing, one after the other: Singh's, mine, and the one for the empty rooms on the top floor. I sat up in bed. The TV was still on, and the video: the screen was blue-screen blue.

'The screen,' I said aloud, 'is blue-screen blue,' but it didn't make me feel any more real.

The bells kept on ringing. What was Singh's family doing here on a weekday? Then I remembered the phone call. The penny dropped, taking my stomach with it.

They went away eventually – whoever it was. I prised my fingers free of the duvet and got out of bed. Singh was curled up like a cat by the door and hardly stirred when I stepped over him. I knelt at the top of the stairs and studied the front door. Nothing moved against the frosted glass. I went into the bathroom and locked the door. I ran the taps and caught sight of myself in the bathroom mirror. I shambled towards it, poking and prodding my face. It was still there. Ears, nose, lips, all there.

Next door, in the bedroom, I heard the TV go on.

I flexed my hand, feeling the stiffened tissue in my palm where, almost a year ago now, Money had stitched my cut. It felt the way it had felt that night, but without the hurt: a perfect hemisphere, nicked in one corner. As though a sharpened coin, minted in the shape of the moon that night, had sliced my palm.

She had used no anaesthetic, I remembered. Surgical stitches and swabs, but nothing to take away the pain. I thought of Brian and Eddie, and their scarred arms. They had no use for painkillers. They had no fear of pain. Pain was their friend, their ally. Pain made them what they were – just like their father.

I opened the cabinet and took out a bottle of *eau dentifrice*. I plucked the toothbrush mug from its ring on the wall and tipped the brushes out into the sink. I rinsed the mug out with tap water, poured myself three fingers of medicinal alcohol and topped it up with tap water. I downed it in one.

My stomach fluttered. I crouched there, not understanding what it meant. A loud dry fluttering filled my ears, like a flock of startled pigeons. The aliens had grown wings. Big leathery wings beat against my ribcage. I gagged. They were trying to escape. I clutched my stomach to keep them in and I pressed my forehead on the cold rim of the toilet bowl. I didn't throw up. A minute or two later they quieted down. One still pecked in a desultory way at my sternum, but I managed to ignore it; I got in the bath.

The doorbell went a second time. I jumped so far, half the water slopped over the side. Back in my bedroom, Singh scrambled heavily to his feet. I wrapped my arms around my shins and pressed my face into my knees. He thundered out of the bedroom. I wanted to stop him but I couldn't think how. If he told me to fuck off one more time I knew I would break down and cry.

His bare feet slap-slapped on the hall linoleum. He fell down the stairs without a cry and when he landed it sounded like a library stack toppling over.

The ringing stopped. I listened for some sound of motion, but heard nothing. I concentrated harder, thinking I might hear the sound of a car pulling away, but all I heard was a bike accelerating past the house towards Crouch Hill. I stayed there, hugging my shins. There was still no noise downstairs. I imagined Singh, his body snapped and broken, crawling slowly and spastically towards the phone – the phone he couldn't reach because he kept it in his bedroom and now he couldn't reach the door handle.

The thought revived me. I grinned and washed my hair.

About thirty minutes later I wrapped the towel around myself and stepped into the hall.

Singh was lying at the bottom of the stairs, crumpled in a meaningless heap like a bundle of laundry.

I went back in the bedroom and locked the door.

At about eight that evening I heard Singh stumbling around downstairs. I turned off the video and wrapped my arms around my shins and listened closely. The shuffling sounds stopped, and soon I could smell the familiar smell of burnt spice. I was just feeling around for my clothes in the dark when the doorbells rang again. I put my hands over my ears. When they had stopped I edged towards the window.

A silver MX5 was parked in front of the house. As I watched, Zoe stepped out from under the porch and negotiated the path back to her car. She got in.

I waited for her to drive away before I put on the light.

34

The hapless Mr Parker did not take things lying down. Not only did he press charges, he sued me in a civil court for loss of earnings.

That and the otherwise trivial cost of the flat in Archway had me going cap in hand to Loh's new office looking for a job. Any job.

'Zoe and I have made quite a bit of progress recently,' Loh told me.

'That's good.'

'We got talking the evening you missed the meeting.'

'I don't doubt it.'

'It's just difficult to see where you'd fit in now.'

'I'm just looking for a job. I'm not interested in the box any more.'

Loh had chosen to meet me in the foyer, which I took to be a bad sign. But as luck would have it his receptionist had just quit. 'She seemed a bit upset that she nearly burned to death,' he commented, glumly. His old offices had recently been gutted by fire.

'I wouldn't mind that,' I said. 'Really. It would be a kindness.'

'Have you spoken to Eva?'

'What do you mean?'

He meant he didn't want to play piggy-in-the-middle with us again – or with me and Zoe, for that matter – but before he could say any of this his mobile peeped at him. He reached into the handkerchief pocket of his suit and pulled out a silver phone so small it looked more like a lighter.

The call was something about an appointment, I didn't bother to listen.

'Is that one of the new Nokias?'

He pulled it out of his pocket again to show me. It was new, he couldn't resist showing it off. It wasn't a Nokia; it was a Nabeshima.

'I didn't know they made one this flash,' I said.

'Home market only.'

'How much?'

'I don't know. It was a present.'

I thought about it. 'They sending you freebies, now?'

Loh shrugged.

'Please, Han-Wah. I need the money. Let me help you out. Just for a few months while you get yourself sorted.'

'I don't—'

'Please. I don't know anyone else to call.'

The lighting contractors blamed old wiring for the fire which had forced Loh's move. 'They told me it needed replacing,' he said. 'I thought they were trying to pull a fast one.'

'What did the insurance people say?'

'Well, they paid out.' He gestured at the new furniture in its bubble-wrap, stacked up by the lifts.

He said, 'You don't want to be a receptionist.'

'I do. I do.'

'I don't know.'

'Come on Han-Wah, for Christ's sakes.'

Incredibly, he gave me the job.

I went to the pub to celebrate and Zoe was waiting for me.

She'd had her hair cut boy-short – in a short grey velvet skirt and a black shirt open at the neck, it was a provocative combination; a little girl, dressing as a woman.

'Hello,' I said.

'I called for you last week,' she said.

'I saw the car,' I said.

'I phoned you,' she said, trying to provoke me, but I wasn't going to be drawn.

She tried harder. 'The night you missed the meeting—'

'Look at that prick,' I said. A man with a grey, smoke-cured face and a Moody Blues haircut was rigging a couple of microphones inside the sound-box of the piano.

'Adam?'

'He's got the loudest instrument in the combo and he has to tannoy it all the way to bloody Plaistow.'

'Don't you want to know how I found you?'

'Tell me if you have to,' I said. 'What are you drinking, anyway?'

'I didn't come here to drink.'

'Please yourself.' I ordered a rum.

'I rang your wife,' she said.

I hid my face behind my glass.

'I needed to talk to her about the amplifier, about what we're going to do with it.'

'"We"?'

'Me and Loh.'

'Oh.'

She said, 'I don't know why you got so worked up about Nabeshima.'

I said nothing.

She said, 'They're letting Justin use the box, still. They've been very good about it.'

'I've noticed that,' I said. 'When I've visited.'

'It's nice of them, isn't it?'

'Oh, yes,' I said.

She tried a different tack. 'Eva told me where you were living.'

I put my glass on the bar.

'How long did she know about us?'

I began to tell her about Justin, about her getting custody, but I managed to bite the words off. 'The bass player's really good,' I said. 'But thanks to that prick you can never bloody hear him.'

'Wyatt.'

Singh was waving at me from the opposite side of the horseshoe bar. I raised my glass to him.

'She told me where you were living. Who was it answered the phone?'

I nodded at Singh.

'Is he your landlord?'

'Apparently.'

'Adam, what did I do wrong?'

'Shall we go over and say hello?'

'Why won't you look at me?'

Singh pointed at the door through to the saloon. I gave him a thumbs-up.

'If you want me to go,' she said, 'I'll go.'

'Go,' I said. I looked at her. It wasn't easy. 'Go.'

She stared at the beer rings on the bar, thinking about it. 'Fuck you, Adam,' she said. 'Fuck you.' She wasn't going anywhere, so I put my arm around her shoulders. She stiffened under me.

'Come on then, now you're here.'

'I don't like this place.'

'I do.'

She let out a ragged sigh and let me lead her into the saloon bar.

It was the usual crowd: Singh, Tony, Steve, Winston. Steve was well into one of his monologues – a bizarre loser variant on the 'I was a driver for the Krays' number, according to which he'd installed a sun-roof in a Jag belonging to Reggie and Ronnie's gormless older brother Charlie. As though making the lie boring made it more believable. In a corner by the door to the gents, Nicki was thumping the cigarette

245

machine slowly, over and over, like she'd forgotten how to work it.

I sat down between Singh and Tony. Zoe looked round dully for a stool and pulled one up next to Winston. I performed introductions. 'Zoe's a student,' I said.

'Oh. Yeah?' said Winston, staring frankly at her crotch. Zoe crossed her legs.

Nicki came over. 'That's my seat,' she said.

'So?' I said.

She came over and settled herself slowly into my lap. 'Enough?'

'Mercy.'

She got up and I hunted out another stool for myself. As I pulled it over to the table Zoe brushed past me.

'Bye, then,' I said.

I made an effort to be early on my first day at work.

'Good God, Adam,' Loh said, when he rolled up, shortly after ten. He thrust his hands deeper into his expensive lamb's wool overcoat. 'You must be taking a pill or something.'

'Hurry up, get the keys for God's sake,' I muttered, shivering. The portico gave no protection against the wind when it came from the east, and I'd been cowering here under the stained concrete awning for the best part of an hour. All his other employees were on paid leave until the following Thursday.

'How long have you been here?'

'Since nine-thirty.'

'Jesus Christ. Here,' he said, handing me his keys. 'Go across the road and cut yourself a set.'

The wind was blowing forbidding black clouds over the street, and while I was waiting for my keys, a gust of hail made the whole store-front tremble.

I ran back to the office and got soaked, but at least there was a cappuccino waiting for me. Loh said, 'I won't be in the office Monday next.'

'You want me in anyway?'

'Wouldn't mind. You can tackle the filing.' He had had hard copies made of all his documents and they needed putting away. He went into his office.

Wednesday was my usual day to see Justin. I sipped the chocolate skein off the foam in my cup. If I took Monday off instead I could be around to help Loh the day before his staff arrived. 'Where are you going?' I asked him.

'Southampton,' he called back.

Where Zhenshu's box had been examined. That threw me. 'Kevin Leicester?'

He didn't reply. I turned. He was leaning against the door frame. He was looking at me carefully, without his spectacles: they were in his hand.

'It's okay,' I said.

'I wish you and Eva were talking.'

'We'll get round to it,' I told him. 'It's okay.'

He nodded, but he wasn't satisfied. He went back inside his office but he left the door open. 'Southampton want to renegotiate their fee,' he said.

'How's it going?' I asked him.

'Okay,' he said.

Loh must have been over-insured, because the carpet in his new foyer was so thick you could lose pens in it, the windows were tinted and the instruction manual for the switchboard had the weight and clarity of a PhD thesis.

It seemed the box was Loh's main business now. That and other bits and pieces of Nabeshima business. Most of the recent correspondence I was filing was back and forth between Loh and the medical arm of the company. Most afternoons there'd be a meeting in Loh's office, and when I brought in the coffee and biscuits the Nabeshima executives sitting there would give me these odd looks – appraising, humorous looks, the kind that made me wonder if Loh had told them who I was. Yes, that's the man who stood us up, that autumn night. That's the one. The one who couldn't hack it, let it go, withdrew, retired. Fucked up.

Loh's spectacles flashed. 'I didn't say anything to them!'

'I'm not stupid.'

'Believe it or not we had more important things to talk about.'

'You laugh at me again you'll be laughing on the other side of your face.'

'If you're not happy here then you know where to go.'

The rest of the week I rolled up each morning only just before eleven, but Loh didn't mind. I was on an hourly rate but he never deducted the hour. We even went together to a bar after work once. I tried to apologise but he wasn't interested.

'They're going to buy it, you know.'

'Nabeshima?'

'They want Kevin Leicester, too. They've offered him his own lab.'

'Is he going?'

'He can't decide.'

I nodded. 'One hell of a wrench, I suppose.'

'What?'

'Tokyo.'

'Tokyo?'

'Well where else is this new lab of his?'

'A greenfield site outside Coventry.'

'Oh.' I thought about it. 'Is Justin going to have to go to Coventry, then?'

'Relax. We haven't even begun to discuss that side of things.'

'Because I think I have some say here.'

'Adam—'

'What?'

'Have you spoken to Eva?'

I hid behind my glass.

Loh wrung his hands. 'This is all so unnecessary.'

I put it down empty. 'Do me a favour,' I said. 'Just shut up about my personal life.'

So, after a couple of beers, he went home to Angelica and I rode the tube up to Archway and changed my clothes and went to meet Singh in the King's Arms for some rather more serious drinking.

35

On Monday I set off to see Justin.

I was fucked if I was going to spend the day in the office on my own filing Loh's bloody papers. And since Loh was only paying me for the hours I actually worked, I figured I'd pull a fast one, see Justin today on the sly and get paid for my trouble.

I was still pretty hung over from the weekend, and the bar prices on the train were so high I had to wait until Staplehurst before getting myself some hair of the dog.

The sun was behind the main building as I floated up the drive to Knox Lodge. The flower-beds by the road were leaf-strewn and bare, the house dark and impermanent-looking.

I felt ropy. I'd woken up late and hadn't had time to bath. I leaned against the school entrance trying to rethread my tie and finally I tore it off and shoved it in my pocket. I shot my cuffs and rubbed the points of my shoes against my trouser legs and figured it would have to do.

But they still didn't let me see him.

They sat me in the secretary's office and opened the windows and someone brought me a coffee; they left the door open and I heard someone say my wife's name. I played stupid and when they were gone I walked back out into the corridor and wandered around a while, trying to get my bearings.

I only had a couple of minutes at the most before they realised I was loose. But if I could only find Justin's room, they'd hardly drag me out with him looking on.

But when I got there, everything had changed. The pictures were gone from the walls. The chest of drawers, the desk, the TV and his PlayStation had all been removed. The bed had been replaced by an outsize cot. Plasticated curtains hung over the windows.

'Mr Wyatt?'

I turned. It was Francis. 'What have you done with him?'

Francis laughed, but so weakly he can't have convinced even himself.

My hands were shaking. I didn't want him to see so I reached back and took hold of the bars of the cot. There was a roughness under my fingers.

'Mr Wyatt?'

I ran my fingers over the marks. I turned and studied them.

'Adam, can we do this somewhere else?'

I went to the curtains and studied the chewed half-moons there.

'Adam—'

'He's nearly eight years old.'

'He's not here.'

'He's better than this. He doesn't do things like this any more.'

A hand squeezed my shoulder. I turned. Francis was all blurry – I couldn't read his face. 'Adam, what's going on?'

'I came—'

'You must know. You can't not know. He's not here. You know he's not here.'

I blinked.

Criville was hovering nervously at the threshold. In as much as his muppet face could express anything, it expressed trouble. 'Mr Wyatt—'

'What—'

'Mr Wyatt, he's not here.'

I blinked at him.

'Did you not know?'

'What do you mean, he's not here?'

Criville swallowed.

'For God's sake,' I said.

Criville walked me to the lobby. 'Mrs Wyatt called for Justin this morning,' he said. Francis walked with us. He was watching me carefully. 'She told me you knew,' Criville said.

'No,' I said, as evenly as I could manage. 'No, she hasn't called me. We're living apart now. When are they coming back?'

'Mr Wyatt?'

'When's she bringing him back?'

'Mr Wyatt – ' Criville rubbed his hands together. Washing them. 'Justin's not well.'

I imagined him, chewing the bars of his cot. 'Francis?'

Francis just looked at me.

'He doesn't do that. He's not a baby. He doesn't do that any more. Where are his pictures?'

Criville said, 'We don't know when he's coming back.'

'He ate them,' Francis said.

My palms were wet.

'Since he hurt himself – Mr Wyatt, how could you not know about this?'

'*Hurt himself?*'

Criville just stood there. He wasn't saying anything.

I wanted him to tell me what had happened, but when I opened my mouth to speak, the words came out all wrong. 'It wasn't the box,' I said.

'Mr Wyatt—'

'It wasn't the box. I know what you're thinking. It wasn't even my idea. It was Eva's idea.'

Francis tried to touch me and I brushed him off. 'Fuck you, Francis.'

'Mr Wyatt I think we should talk in my office—'

'Fuck you.'

'Adam,' said Francis, 'please—'

'Let go of me.'

Francis let go of my shoulder.

'Mr Wyatt.'

'You're lying. Both of you. You just want it for yourself. You're trying to steal it.'

Criville was standing in front of the main door now. I made for him. He stepped smartly out of the way. I threw open the door and found myself outside. It was sleeting again. Infuriated, I turned, but Criville was in front of the door again.

'Give it back to my son.' I screamed. 'Give it back to him now.'

'Mr Wyatt,' Criville was appalled. He was outraged. 'Have you been *drinking*?'

There was a pay-phone in the railway station and I had a handful of change left from the pub so I called Zoe.

'I rang you,' she said. 'I waited for you—'

'It isn't about that.'

'What happened, Adam? Where did you go? Why, damn it?'

The sleet had turned to rain and the air was so cold my hand was numbing solid round the phone. 'Justin.'

'What do you mean, "Justin"?'

'Justin. Where is he?'

'Are you all right?'

'I'm freezing my balls off. I'm fine.'

'Adam, you're crying.'

'Whose idea was it to take Justin away?'

'Away where? Adam, are you drunk?'

I was nearly out of change. 'Justin's hurt himself. Done something.'

'What?'

'Eva's taken him out of school.'

There was a pause.

'Give me your number,' she said.

She phoned Southampton for me. Loh wasn't there. Kevin Leicester wasn't even there. His entire team was off in Glasgow for a robotics conference.

She phoned Hemingford Road for me. There was no reply.

'Where's the box?' she said.

'I don't know. With Justin.'

'Jesus Christ.'

'I don't know what to do.'

'Give me Loh's office number.'

'Nobody's there. Nobody's due in until Thursday. They're all on leave while we set up the office.'

'Can you get in?'

'What do you mean?'

'There may be something there to say where Loh's gone.'

'You should know, you've been working with him.'

'Negotiations collapsed weeks ago.'

'Why?'

'I don't know. I'll meet you there,' she said. 'What's the address?'

I got to the office around 5 p.m. I was still there before Zoe. I rapped on the door but the security man wasn't about so I unlocked it myself and slipped inside.

There was enough light from the landing to see my way to Loh's office door, and luckily for me he wasn't in the habit of locking it. Some while later my fingers connected with the light switch.

Loh had so much space in his office he didn't seem to know what to do with it. His desk was crammed up against the window. A couple of easy chairs sat regimentally straight against the opposite wall. It looked like a film set: an unimaginative corporate interior out of one of Brian and Eddie's kung-fu films.

There was a cocktail cabinet by his desk, for corporate entertaining. I had no idea any more where the steady point was – that ever-shrinking period of drinker's equilibrium. Maybe I had to have more. Yes, that was it. Ceremoniously, I pulled open the doors. I might have known he'd only have brandy. There were four fingers of Courvoisier left in the bottle. I uncorked it. It smelled of must and sweat and hangovers. Two fingers, I told myself, raised the bottle to my lips, and drank one.

The aliens yelped and splashed around in it. The room lurched. Everything got brighter. Every drink of the past year came and shook me by the lower intestine. My stomach yawed like a mouth. Alien talons stretched it wide and fluttered there, expectant, open mouths upturned beneath the straining sphincter. I had to close it somehow, before my heart and my brain fell through the gap, so I drank another finger, and another, and then I put the bottle back in the cabinet and flaked out on Loh's natty new chair.

Dimly, I heard the lift clank into action.

I sat up.

The lift stopped. The doors scraped open. I had one thought. Loh.

I had to hide. I had to turn off the light. I had to get to the light switch. I could barely crawl off the chair. I took hold of the edge of the desk and levered myself to my feet and I tripped over the waste-basket. It fell and rolled, shedding paper everywhere.

I froze, waiting for something to happen.

The lift doors guillotined shut once more and the lift descended.

Silence.

It was only then it occurred to me that the person in the lift might be Zoe. But it wasn't.

No sound.

The night-watchman arriving, maybe, on the first of his infrequent rounds.

I crossed to the cabinet again without major mishap. There was about a finger left. I took a couple of small swallows. I felt steadier now. I drained the bottle, screwed the cap back on and put it back in the cabinet.

I set the bin straight and threw the rubbish back in. I came across a torn scrap of envelope with a green travel-company decal in the top left corner. I recognised it. Trailfinders. One whole marriage ago, they had sold me two tickets to Florence.

I emptied the bin on the floor and started flattening out everything Loh had screwed up. I came upon a Mastercard bill with the counterfoil already torn off; a statement of bank charges from the Abbey National; the offer of a gold card from MNBA; an airline confirmation.

I turned off the lights in the office and took the stairs to the ground floor. The night-watchman was away from the desk. I heard a kettle whistling in the cubby-hole beside the lavatories.

I let myself out. It was snowing again. I didn't have very

long. I ran all the way to the Barbican tube. I slipped a couple of times and I tore my trousers. Northbound services were disrupted. I had fifteen minutes to wait for a train. There was a phone on the platform so I called Zoe's mobile. 'Don't bother with the office,' I said.

'You were supposed to call me an hour ago.'

'Don't bother with the office.'

'But I'm already there,' she said. 'I'm just looking for a place to park.'

'Forget it,' I said.

I looked at my watch. It was 6.45 p.m. We didn't have long. Loh's flight to Tokyo left Heathrow shortly before ten.

'I'll go to the airport,' she said.

'But I'm already—'

'You go see Eva, find out what's going on. I'll stop Loh.'

'I don't know where she is.'

'Home.'

'Home?'

'Hemingford Road.'

'How do you know?'

'Well, there's somebody there. I just tried there. The phone's engaged.'

'Forget driving,' I said. 'The shuttle only takes half an hour.'

'I'm not stupid,' she said.

36

I'll say this for Eva: she had the guts to open the door herself. Loh was hanging around behind her in the hall, in case there was trouble. As if.

I didn't say anything. I was too full of things to say. She should just have shut the door. It would have been easier on all of us. But she didn't.

'You've torn your trousers,' she said.

'Thanks.'

'Keep him out,' Loh said, but I was already in the hall.

We stood there for a minute, the three of us, not saying anything. Eventually I realised they were waiting for me to speak. What I said was, 'I've been to Knox Lodge.'

'You were supposed to be filing,' said Loh, which was about as stupid a thing as he'd ever said.

'I've taken him out of school,' said Eva.

'What's he done?'

'If you'd answered the bloody phone, you'd know.'

'Eva?'

'I kept calling you as soon as I heard.'

I remembered the night Zoe ambushed me in the pub. The phone, ringing and ringing, the moment I stepped through the door. The spiteful staisfaction I had felt, imagining that it was Zoe.

So.

'Tell me now,' I said.

Eva bit her lip.

'Loh?'

Loh didn't know what to do with his hands so he put them on his hips.

By now I had worked my way into the living room. I sat down.

She was already packed. Her Samsonite suitcases stood by the door.

'We're going to Tokyo,' Eva said.

Loh stared at Eva.

I stared at Loh.

Loh put his hands in his pockets.

Eva said, 'They have a programme in Tokyo. Nabeshima have a programme. They're going to help Justin.'

I said, 'He doesn't need help. He needs the device. You

stole it from him. You stole the thing that makes him better.'

'He's still got the box,' said Loh. 'He's dependent on it. That's why Eva had to take him out of school. That's why we have to get him to Tokyo. Get him some help.'

'Zoe's going to want it back,' I said.

They were only waiting for their cue. Sooner or later, something would have set them off.

Eva was appalled: 'Which is more important to you?' 'Nabeshima owns the box,' Loh insisted. 'The box or Justin?' Eva demanded. 'Zoe has no business approaching you,' Loh said. 'Zoe's not interested in you,' Eva said. 'Eva has custody of Justin,' Loh said. 'She just wants to make money,' Eva said, and Loh said, 'She can do what she likes, it won't make any difference.' Something like that. I guess you had to be there.

'I think you'd better go,' said Loh.

I stood up. He moved towards me. Eva screamed.

'*Mum?*'

Loh froze. Eva froze.

'*Mummy?*'

I ran.

There were footsteps on the stairs behind me, Loh's footsteps, but I was already on the landing. Our bedroom door was open. I stepped inside.

Justin was sitting on the bed, swinging his feet against his overstuffed *Godzilla* rucksack. His Parka lay on the bed next to him. He had on a heavy cable-knit jumper; the sleeves were so long they practically covered his hands. He had one leg crossed over the other, the leg of his brown cord trousers rolled up to his knee. He was studying his shin. The wires from Zhenshu's box were pinned to the skin with fine acupuncture needles.

When I entered he stared at me, startled, and whipped his left hand behind his back, hiding something.

Another little miracle, that he should want to keep a secret from me. Deceit is something autistic children never master – why would they? They're alone, they've no use for lies.

'Justin.'

'Dad.'

'Oh, Justin.'

Justin smiled. 'Daddy.'

I settled on the bed beside him. He tore his Parka from under me and dropped it casually over his lap, covering his leg.

'What happened? Are you hurt?'

He turned to me. He smiled.

I kissed him.

'Dad.'

'Tell me.'

'I don't hurt any more.'

'That's good.'

'They gave me pins, not clips.'

'I saw.'

'It stays on better.'

'Doesn't it prickle?'

'Oh no,' he said. Then, 'Only at first.'

It was strange, talking to him like this. We had never had a conversation before.

'What happened at Knox Lodge?

'Nothing.'

'No one took your box away?'

'Oh no.'

'Justin?'

He looked at me. He wiped my face. 'Don't cry,' he said.

He reached forward to stroke the tears from my cheek.

'Don't cry,' he said. 'I bet mum can mend your trousers.' His sleeve rode up, and his arm was a mass of deep, regular scars.

I suppose I made a lot of noise. I don't remember.

'Justin.'

Loh stood in the doorway. His shadow fell across us. 'Go see your mother,' he said.

Justin was backed into the corner of the room, white as a sheet. 'Justin?'

Obediently, Justin picked up the box and turned it off. He bent, plucked the needles from his shin, and rolled his trouser-leg down.

He tried to slip past me but I wouldn't let him. I hugged him, held to him, rocked him, willing away what I'd seen. On the bed behind him, I saw what he'd been hiding.

Another bitter little miracle, that: scissors had always terrified him before.

Justin pushed against me. I hung on to him. Gently, he pulled free.

'Go on,' Loh said. 'There's a good boy.'

Justin glanced at Loh without expression and left the room. I picked up the nail scissors and wiped the tips against my fingers. They came away red.

'Oh Jesus,' Loh sighed, but he wasn't surprised.

I found my voice. 'Justin?'

Loh came over and put his hand on my arm. His grip was surprisingly strong. 'Let him be.'

Justin didn't even look round. He took the stairs one at a time, not reluctantly, not eagerly; but steadily, his gait more natural than it had ever been before.

I recalled how Justin had beaten his head, the night of the bust-up with Eva's mother, on the leg of Eva's chair. 'Autistic children hurt themselves,' I said. 'That's all.'

'Not like this. It's too methodical. It's deliberate. It's over his arms, his legs.'

I sank onto the bed. 'It's Eva's fault,' I said.

'Let's get you a drink,' Loh said. 'You look like you could use one.'

'She's the one gave him the box.'

'Come on, Adam.' He took me by the arm and led me down the stairs. 'I told you two to talk to each other,' he said. 'What did I say to you? Jesus.'

The next thing I remember I was following Loh down to the kitchen. Someone had slapped a coat of white emulsion over the stairs. I ran my hand along the banister. All the work my father had put into smoothing the wood had been obliterated. That, and the puddle of wax he had worked into the wide bottom step.

'My dad built these stairs,' I said.

Loh seemed to know his way around. He poured me a rum.

'We never got around to waxing them.' I sat down at the kitchen table and he put the glass in front of me.

'When we came back from shopping we found him lying on the bottom step.'

'Shut up, Adam.'

'Look,' I said. I stood up and pointed to the bottom step. The puddle of waxed wood showed through the paint. 'See?'

'Sit down.'

'That's as far as he got.'

'Drink your drink.'

I drank. 'I need some Coke in this,' I choked. Loh got me some. 'She painted the stairs,' I said.

He poured a mild shot for himself and sat with me at the table. 'They look crap if you ask me,' he admitted.

'Why'd she do that?'

He poured me another. 'You can see we have to get Justin to Tokyo.' He was like a doctor, explaining a dangerous but necessary operation. 'You see what he's like.'

'It can't be the box.'

'It can be. It is. What else is it?'

'Kids are always doing stuff—'

'Two nights ago he practically circumcised himself.'

The room seemed to turn.

'It could be his tongue next. It's a compulsion. We don't even know what it is. That's why Criville phoned Eva. That's why Eva phoned you. And when she got no answer, she phoned me. We don't know how to stop him. We didn't have time to go crawling the pubs of North London for you and bring you up to speed. Not in your condition. Eva wanted to. I said no. Don't blame her. If you really need to blame someone, blame me.'

'Okay,' I said. I threw my glass at his face.

It ricocheted off his forehead, landed on the tiled floor and shattered.

Loh whipped off his glasses and rubbed his eye. 'Fuck,' he said.

'Sorry.'

'*Fuck.*' But he wasn't even scratched. When he'd finished feeling sorry for himself he adjusted his spectacles, recharged his glass, added a thin skim of Coke, and pushed it across to me. 'You need this more than I do,' he said.

I drank it and poured myself another. 'This isn't about Justin.' The aliens sat up straight inside me and got ready to listen. They didn't even snigger. Well, not much. 'This is about the box. Sooner or later you were going to steal it. That's why you gave me my pissy little job. To keep tabs on me. To keep me in the dark. That's why you stonewalled Zoe's negotiations. You had no intention of cutting her in on her granddad's invention. You never did.'

He took a deep and calming breath. 'Whatever,' he said. 'The fact is, Justin's sick. If anyone can help Justin, they can. They've spent months gathering specialists to work on this thing, damn it. Stop working yourself up into such a state, *please*, it's giving me an ulcer.'

I looked at him. The silence dragged. He looked at me. We both knew he had done it. He had confessed.

'One way or another, Nabeshima were going to take it, weren't they?'

Loh tried to sneer the moment away, but he couldn't. Eventually, he nodded. 'Yes,' he said.

'Since when were you on Nabeshima's payroll?'

'Oh don't be so overdramatic,' he laughed, or tried to. 'They hired me merely to recover a piece of their lost property.'

'What do you mean, *their* property?'

'You should have paid a bit more attention to those papers in Zhenshu's attic, Adam. If you had, you'd have discovered that Zhenshu's box belongs to Nabeshima.'

'Bullshit.'

'It's not bullshit. Zhenshu invented the Interrogator in 1944 while under a binding contract of employment with Nabeshima.'

'*Interrogator?*' I must have looked a picture.

'That's what he called it when he demonstrated the prototype.'

I thought about it. 'He wasn't—'

'He was employed by Nabeshima twice. Once in 1944. Again in 1951.'

'But he was in Hong—'

'Occupied territory, Adam. The Kempeitei? Eva's grand-dad? Sidney Beach? Remember?'

The glass rattled against my teeth. I remembered.

'I don't suppose he meant it as an instrument of torture. But that's how Zhenshu justified his work to the occupying forces back in '44. War work. Only the prototype didn't induce much more than severe itching, and anyway he couldn't explain *how* it worked. So they said he was wasting their lab-time and the only way he saved his neck was by telling tales on his friends and neighbours. You know the rest.'

I knew. It was the scene I had replayed, with horrified fascination, each time the gilt-framed photograph of Eva's grandfather caught my eye.

I lifted the glass to my lips and there was nothing in it again. The aliens in my gut yawned and lay back and stretched their mouths, ready, as ever, for more.

The front door clicked.

Loh coughed to cover the sound. He harrumphed. 'Look, Adam,' he said, and a lot more besides, all the while trying to steer me away from the kitchen window. He was too small for me. I walked through him.

The window was frosted with condensation. I wiped it aside and looked out.

It was snowing in earnest now. It was settling. Above us, at street-level, a car's headlights limned the gateposts of the drive. The front gate squealed. I turned, and rubbed the mist away, and glimpsed Eva, drawing our boy away from the house. Justin scuffed abstractedly through the snow, shapeless and absurd in his Parka. Eva was wrapped up in the fun-fur I'd bought her in Florence. A figure in a black suit climbed out of the car and held the door open for them.

Loh knew what he had to do. When I got to the door he was standing in front of it, barring the way. I felt almost sorry for him, but I didn't let him stop me.

The air was so cold it hit me like a hand. I pulled myself out of the house and tottered frantically down the path to the garage and the drive. Strands of dead buddleia wound their fingers around my face. I flung my hands out and flailed them aside. The night was so cold, it had frozen the sleet to the gravel. Above me, on the street, the car engine revved. I screamed something. I don't think there were any words in it. I drew breath to scream again, and the air scooped up a fistful of needles and shoved them down my lungs. My head spun. I spun. The aliens screamed, poisoned by all the oxygen, and the car pulled away from the kerb. Its brake-lights were red rockets in front of my eyes, and when I put my hands out to save myself, my palms slipped on the ice and my head hit the concrete.

I don't think I passed out, but there was so much oxygen in my bloodstream now, the alcohol didn't know what to do with it all. The sky was spinning both ways at once. I couldn't hear the car – I couldn't hear anything but the pulse in my temples.

I didn't have much co-ordination, but after a lot of spastic flailing about I managed to turn onto my front. I looked up: there wasn't the slightest trace of tail-light anywhere. Holding my head up like this was draining it of the little blood it had left. I felt like I was falling. I scrabbled for purchase on the concrete drive, and snow and grit forced their way under my fingernails.

Behind me, the kitchen door banged open. I turned onto my back and waited. Loh was in his shirt-sleeves now, and he had a tea towel pressed to his eye. He stood over me, panting hard. His breath, clouding in the freezing air, almost touched me.

'Han-Wah?'

'Why don't you mind your own fucking business?' He looked up at the street. 'Fuck,' he said. He'd missed his lift.

I tried to sit up.

Han-Wah pushed me back down with the toe of his shoe. 'Justin'll be fine, Adam. Put up with it.'

'Zoe—'

'They dealt with Jimmy; they can deal with Zoe.'

The words hung in the air like crystal.

'Jimmy—'

'It was too easy. They should have put him in a bloody coffin, sunk it slowly the way he sunk his girls.'

'You—'

'Oh …' He shook his hands, like he wanted to wash them. 'I don't know. What would I know?' He took the cloth away from his eye and shook it out. Ice cubes fell out of the folds. I'd split his eyebrow. It was dark already; a dirty bloodstain smeared his upper lid like eye-shadow. 'I just say what they tell me to say.'

'Tell me.'

'They've known about the box from the beginning. It was their property only Zhenshu kept it for himself. They've been trying to get it back for years. They tried to broker a deal with Jimmy—'

'So they were spying on him! In Hong Kong!'

'Were they?' Loh shrugged. 'If you say so.'

'It was them planted the devices in Hamley's office. It wasn't Hamley they were after, or Top Luck. It was Jimmy.'

Loh was disconcerted. 'Do you want to hear this story or not?'

All that shouting had made me dizzy. I lay back and listened.

'They figured if Jimmy wouldn't sell them the box then they could get one out of North Street. Jimmy made sure they couldn't.'

This time he let me sit up.

'Don't fuck with them, Adam,' he said. 'They've lost people already over this. One of the girls was theirs.'

I remembered how the sea-water poured out of the container. I remembered the girls, flopping about like fish in a bucket. 'Then?'

'I only get the rumours.'

'Tell me.'

'They knew there still had to be a box somewhere. It was just a question of forcing it into the open.' He shoved a hand in his trouser pocket and pulled out something, a scrap of tissue or something, Something black. 'Remember this?'

He dropped it into my lap.

'They gave this to me. In case you needed softening up any time. They expected me to ...' He looked away. He wouldn't meet my eye.

I studied the thing in my lap.

'They knew you'd turn up a box eventually, Adam. They just had to find some way to get you involved again.'

I recognised it.

'They had to persuade you. Get you back under Yau family's wing. I'm sorry.'

It was Boots's tongue.

37

Loh went back inside to collect his things. It was snowing in earnest now. It was collecting in the creases of my trousers. A few flakes blew in through the rent I'd made in the knee, when I was running for the tube. They melted against my bruises and trickled down the back of my calf.

Loh didn't have long if he was going to make his plane. When he came out his coat was only half on, and the wires of Zhenshu's box were spilling out the sides of his attaché case.

'Use the shuttle from Paddington,' I said. 'It only takes half an hour.'

He stared at me. 'I know that, Adam,' he said. 'Jesus.'

I waited as he climbed the steps which ran up beside the drive. I bent my head back and watched him up to street level, and then he disappeared.

I waited until I could no longer hear his footsteps. Then, I waited some more.

I picked Boots's tongue out of the snow. It was leathery and stiff. I bent it across my thumb. It split the way liquorice does. I threw it into the tangle of dead budleia.

Zoe would be waiting for them. When Eva and Justin arrived at Heathrow, Zoe would be there, alone. When Loh, and Nabeshima's muscle arrived – the men in grey suits, the escort, the muscle – Zoe would be there to stop them. I knew her. She'd be there. She'd try.

And Nabeshima? They'd brush her aside like a child – if she was lucky.

I sat up and rubbed my hands clean in the snow. My fingertips were bleeding where I'd scrabbled the drive. I sucked on them, but that only warmed them and made them more sore, so I stopped and pushed them into the snow again to numb them. I wasn't shivering, and it occurred to me that if I didn't do something fast I was going to fall asleep out here. I scooped up a good handful of snow and rubbed it into my face. That wasn't enough so I got onto my hands and knees and crawled over to the little patch of absurdly sloping lawn and squeezed a handful of snow into a popsicle. I took a bite, forcing my teeth through the gritty ice. I rubbed snow in my hair and forced it down the back of my neck. I still didn't feel awake. I thought about making a coffee, but I didn't have time.

Not if I was going to stop them.

I got to my feet and felt in my pockets for my keys and fanned them out and found the one for the garage. I swung the door up and there was the Xedos. I unlocked it and climbed in. It smelled like an office washroom; there was a scent tree dangling from the rear-view. I hate those things. I tore it off and the perfume etched my bleeding fingertips like broken glass. I opened the door and threw it out and slammed the door again. I turned the key in the ignition. It caught immediately. I turned on the headlights. Only one came on. I grinned; I could guess how Eva had smashed it. She never could handle our driveway.

I dropped the handbrake, depressed the dinky little button on the side of the stick, and pulled it into Reverse. I floored the accelerator.

The Xedos leapt like a stallion, tyres screaming, and bucked out of the garage. It hit the sloping drive so hard the whole back end jumped clear. The tyres landed, screamed like saws through the snow and hoar-frost, and rushed the car up the incline so fast I fell forward and hit my head on the steering wheel. I remembered my seat belt. I relaxed on the accelerator. The back wheels skidded. I hit the brakes. The car slid down the drive. I swung the wheel and hit the accelerator. The car lurched backwards and rammed the gatepost. I hit the brakes. The car slipped again and I wrestled the wheel around. I hit the corner of the garage and glass shattered and the other headlamp went out. I hit the accelerator again and the car swung round and reversed into the earth bank by the side of the drive. I let go the accelerator and the car slid and slammed the opposite corner of the garage. The counterweight for the garage door bounced and landed on the bonnet. The door swung down and shattered the windscreen. I hit the accelerator. The car lurched and the engine cut out and I hit my head on the steering wheel again.

So that was out.

I went back inside and climbed the stairs to the bedroom. My feet felt hot and heavy and huge so I kicked off my shoes, but I didn't have the co-ordination to undress any further. I tried unbuckling my belt and somehow I only succeeded in loosening it. After a few minutes' tossing and turning my shirt and trousers were so screwed and rucked, it felt as though I'd been bound with strips of filthy rag.

I tried lying with my head off the bed, thinking I could drain some blood back into it, but I couldn't sleep. Every time I dozed off I was woken almost immediately by the sound of rain.

38

I sat up in bed and looked around, trying to work out where the hell I was. The alarm clock on the bedside table said 2.30 a.m.

The bedroom window was dry. I slitted my eyes, because focusing was still difficult, still something I had to think about. Light from a half-moon streamed in, washing the crumpled duvet with silver.

I could still hear rain. How could it only be raining on one half of the house?

I reached out blindly and swept a glass of water off the bedside table onto the bed. Water seeped under my fingers and into the sheets.

I felt around for the glass. It had rolled away. I sat up, too fast. My brain slopped back and forth inside my skull like a sock-full of pennies. Even in the light coming through the open door, I couldn't see where it had rolled to.

Strange, I thought, that light. I remembered climbing the stairs in the dark.

The rain changed tune.

It wasn't rain.

Outside, the half-moon shone in a clear sky.

It was the shower.

I climbed off the bed. I used the door to prop me up as I went into the hall. The light was on. The bathroom door was ajar. Steam billowed and receded there like desperate hands. I swung it open.

The shower curtain was drawn back and there was water all over the floor of the bathroom. Zoe was sitting in the bath and the shower was jetting straight in her face.

She turned to me. She was bright red. Her skin was raw like someone had thrown a kettle over her.

She smiled. There were needles in her face. In her cheeks, through her lips, through an eyebrow, through an earlobe. There were wires dangling from the needles and they led back over her shoulder to a small black box, perched unsteadily on the tiled bath surround.

'Hello, Adam.'

I came into the bathroom and hunkered down beside her. Her clothes were piled in a heap by the side of the bath and I kicked them aside. Jeans and a jumper: not her style at all. She leaned towards me and water spattered off her face into my eyes, scalding me.

I moved away, and I saw that the dial on the box was turned all the way up.

With steady, delicate fingers, she pulled the needles out of her face. 'Come on in.'

I tried to shut off the water but the tap was so hot I burned my hand. She reached forward and turned it off for me.

'It's lovely,' she said. 'Come on in. Have a try.'

I backed out of the bathroom.

She found me in the kitchen. She wasn't dressed. She wasn't even dry. I was nursing the rest of the rum. Water dripped from her breasts. She smiled. She said softly, 'Any left for me?'

I looked at her. I didn't know what to say. She came towards me. Barefoot. Something snapped. I leapt up.

Zoe stopped where she was. 'Oh,' she said. She looked down. The floor was covered with broken glass. 'Oh. Bloody hell.'

She hopped back to the bottom step and sat down and crossed her left leg over her right knee, studying the bloody mess in her heal.

'Zoe! Christ ...' I looked around for something to staunch the bleeding, for a tea-towel, anything, but the towel was outside somewhere, probably under the Xedos, and there wasn't any kitchen roll.

'It's okay,' she said. She took hold of the largest shard and pulled it out. I watched her. She didn't even blink.

'Zoe?'

'Have you got a pair of tweezers?' she said. Blood dribbled from her heel. A pool of it spread across the terracotta floor tiles. A red grid fanned out along the grouting.

I lay on the bed.

'Adam?'

I put my hands over my ears.

'Adam, come down here, I'll get blood all over the stairs.'

I pushed my face into the pillow.

A while later I felt the mattress give and she climbed onto the bed with me and I felt her hands on me, tugging my shirt up, and I felt her lips on my back.

I turned over and sat up and there was blood all over the sheets. Gently, she undid my belt. She pulled down my fly. She drew off my trousers, my pants, she unbuttoned my shirt, the air had dried her, her skin was still pink, and she pressed her breast to my mouth.

There was blood everywhere. I tried not to look.

She hobbled into the bathroom and came out with the box and laid it on the bed beside me. 'There,' she said.

'There, there.' She was trying very hard but her eyes refused to smile.

'Where are they?' I said.

'Over Africa,' she said. 'I guess.'

'They made it? Justin? Eva?'

'Of course they made it.' She sat up. She tried to laugh. She rubbed her foot down my calf and the blood was hot then cold against my skin. 'Adam, what it is that you think I did?' The first needle went into my arm, the second into hers. She turned the dial and scratched a third needle down her arm so it bled. I screamed and bucked and came.

She plucked the needles out and sat up in the bed. She pushed a needle in her bleeding foot, right into the cut, another in my lip, and turned the dial.

I bit my tongue so hard blood oozed between my teeth. She touched me and I came again into her hand. 'My turn,' she said, licking her fingers clean, and pushed a needle through her sex.

It tasted like Hong Kong.

39

'Get dressed,' she said.

It was dark, still. She put on the bedside light. The clock radio said a little before 5 a.m. She stalked around the bed, all muscle, all motion. I hunched up under the duvet, watching her.

'Get dressed, come on.'

I massaged my tongue against the roof of my mouth. It was swollen and sore, and my face felt like it had been peeled off and then stuck back down again with a staple gun.

'I want to borrow a shirt,' she said.

I watched her. I should have guessed what she was like.

I could have guessed. It would have been so easy – only I hadn't wanted to. Her scars were obvious, if only I had dared to look.

She opened the wardrobe. Eva had left some old things behind and she tried on a dress. It didn't look any better on her.

'What do you think?'

'Was it Jimmy?'

'What?'

'Was it Jimmy,' I said. 'You know what I'm talking about. Was it Jimmy taught you?'

'Taught me what?'

She was as familiar with her granddad's box as she would have been with any child's toy. She had grown up with it. It had opened her up.

'Oh get up, Adam, please.'

To sensation, to pleasure.

'Adam, what's the matter?'

To pain.

Jimmy explained it to me once. 'You know,' he said, 'when I was sixteen I went to visit Daddy in Japan.' I remembered the feel of his hands. 'I met a girl there. Nice girl. A clerk in Daddy's office. We ate sushi in a café where the dishes come round on a little conveyor belt. It was expensive. These angel-fish would come by us and sometimes they were so fresh their fins would still be fluttering.'

'Get up, Adam, we haven't the time.'

Jimmy had a room to himself in the brothel in Kennedy Town. He had me visit him there. He had us all visit, at one time or another. A bed and a box with a dial and wires. That was the thing about Jimmy. He never went anywhere for anyone. Sooner or later, for fair reasons or foul, it didn't matter – you came to him.

'Anyway,' Jimmy said, settling himself against me. 'We

shared them, mouth to mouth. The angel-fish. You know, like those Disney dogs with the spaghetti.'

'Yes. Yes.'

'And I fed her a fish, pushed my tongue deep inside her mouth, like this—'

'Adam.'

'Yes, yes.'

'Like this.'

'Come on.'

I clambered from the bed.

'And you know what she did?' Jimmy said.

His breath smelled of cloves and stale brandy and cigarettes.

'She bit my tongue, Adam. She bit down on it. She thought my tongue was a bit of fish. She bit my tongue. You know what the worst part was? It was knowing, right then, right then as she did it, that I'd never be able to forget it. It was one of those things, one of those moments, that stick. My tongue wasn't even bleeding, and five minutes later I was laughing the whole thing off and eating again. But it marked me. A moment had been fixed in me. I was changed. That is what pain is, Adam. Big unforgettable experience, all in a tiny flash. Just like pleasure.'

'Is that it?'

'Just like this,' he said, and spread me.

'Yes,' I said, 'that's it.'

He entered me.

Zoe frowned. 'No jacket?'

'Downstairs,' I said, doing up a shoelace.

'Have you got any money?'

I tapped my trousers: my wallet was there. 'Not really,' I said.

'Let's get moving,' she said.

'Nothing hurts me,' he said. 'Nothing can hurt me more

than I have learned to hurt myself. You see?' He turned the dial up and stubbed a cigarette out between the needles in his arm and didn't scream.

Brian and Eddie; their scarred arms were their fortune now. They looked great on camera.

Willy Lam came in. His body was as hard and shiny as brass.

'You'll see,' said Jimmy, plucking the wires from his arm and, one by one, screwing them into me. Willy wore a crucifix. It dangled in my face. 'Welcome on board,' he said.

'Was it Willy?'

We were half way down the stairs to the living room. Zoe had Zhenshu's box in her hand, the wires wrapped casually round her wrist.

'Was it? Zoe?'

Zoe stopped suddenly and turned to me. I nearly stepped into her. 'Willy who?' she demanded.

'Willy Lam.'

'What about Willy?'

'Was it him did it?'

'Did what? Adam, can we talk about this in the car?' Zoe was getting nervous. As soon as Nabeshima found Zhenshu's box was missing, they would be back here, retracing their steps. Me, I didn't care either way, but Zoe wanted to be long gone.

'Will you remember me, Adam?'

'Yes, Jimmy.'

'Will you?'

'Yes. Yes.'

'And what will you feel when you remember me, Adam?'

'Pain.'

'What?'

'Nothing, Zoe.'

'Where are you going?'

'My jacket, I told you, it's downstairs. In the kitchen.'

'Hurry up then.' She waited for me at the head of the stairs.

The kitchen stairs were wet with blood. There were bloody footprints all over the kitchen floor.

'Kiss me, Adam.'

'Jimmy.'

'Kiss me on the lips.'

I kissed him. I pushed my tongue inside his mouth. Willy turned the dial. Gently, Jimmy bit down.

I got my jacket and climbed the stairs and followed Zoe out of the house. Her MX5 was pulled up at the kerb. It hadn't snowed any more: the canvas roof was dry. The silver body gleamed like still water in the streetlight. 'Wrap up warm,' she said. 'Don't you want anything?'

'I'm alright.'

It was the coldest night of the year: didn't the temperature affect her at all?

Of course it didn't: no more than the glass in her heel. No more than the pain that was her pleasure in bed. That was the point. She was hardy, like the rest of her family. Zhenshu's box had made them all that way.

She gathered the wires around her hand and thumbed them around each other in a loose bundle. 'There.'

I held my hand out for the box, so I could put it in the glove compartment; but she ignored me and stowed it behind her seat instead. She undid the crook-lock and shoved it in after. 'Ready?'

'Who taught you?' I said. 'Who did it to you? Brian? Eddie?'

'What about them?'

'Did they teach you?'

'Adam, you don't know anything about it.'

'What did they do?'

'Get in the car.'

I tried to read the truth from her eyes, but they were as blank and hungry as they always had been. Cat's eyes; predator's eyes.

The Yaus had used granddad's box to make them stronger, more resilient, more alive. It had only made them monstrous. They weren't brave. They weren't wise. They were numb.

That's what made Jimmy unstoppable, and his children after him. He was used to pain; he had learned to handle and even enjoy the way pain objectified the body, parting self from flesh, so that his tongue, once bitten by the girl, could never quite be his again, but only ever *almost* his; an appendage he used, and understood, and, at worst, could afford to lose.

How can you possibly stop someone like that? Pluck the leg off a spider, it still keeps walking.

'How did you get the box off Loh, anyway?'

'It doesn't matter,' she said. She started the engine. There was a hot metal smell in the cabin. 'Are you in or out?'

I shut my door and strapped myself in. I couldn't stop her, any more than I could stop Jimmy. Pluck the leg off a spider, it still keeps walking.

Why?

Because it is too stupid to care about pain.

Zoe drove as badly as she always did.

'How's your foot?' I asked her.

'What foot?' she said.

Then, 'Yes, it's fine.'

40

'Where are we going?'

'We're going to Brighton,' she said. She looked exactly the way she had, the day we went to Dover.

We got as far as the M3 and I asked her if she had any cigarettes.

'You don't smoke,' she said.

'It's that or more booze. I'm getting the shakes.'

'We'll stop at a services,' she said, but she didn't. The moon hung in front of us as we drove through Camberley, and silvered the fields around Winchester. I glanced at the fuel gauge. We only had about a quarter of a tank.

I couldn't persuade her to turn off at Winchester, or Eastleigh, and we were half way to Salisbury on the A36 when it occurred to me we were going the wrong way.

'Does it matter?' she said.

'Doesn't it?'

'Why should it?'

'Where're we going?'

'Anywhere!' Her voice was high and strident, like a gull's. 'What's the matter with you?'

I began to smell that burnt-oil odour again. I glanced at the handbrake. It didn't look as if it was engaged at all – maybe a brake disc was rubbing. 'Zoe, can you smell it again?'

'It's nothing.'

'Zoe?'

'Just forget about it.' She braked and we turned off on a road signed to Amesbury, then down a tiny lane off to the left. It was uneven, much-patched, lathered with mud from a winter's worth of tractors and farm plant. The mud had frozen solid, and the car bounced and jolted from one tread-pattern to another.

'For God's sake, Zoe, can't you slow down?'

There was definitely something wrong with the car. The smell wasn't getting any worse, but it was there, and the handling seemed sluggish, the rear end dragging dangerously around every curve.

The next turning she took was a lethal affair, right at the apex of a hairpin bend. We overshot. Zoe stomped the brake. She snapped the stick into reverse and floored the gas, slewing us back around the curve. She slipped into first and put a full lock on the wheel and still we didn't clear the verge. The left front wheel bounced sickeningly against a rock and something heavy thudded about in the boot.

'Do you know where you're going?' I said.

It took Zoe maybe twenty minutes more to admit she was lost. 'You'd better navigate,' she sighed.

I reached for the glove compartment.

'Not in there.' She reached behind her seat and pulled out a large format AA gazetteer. 'Here.'

When you opened it out it was as wide as the cabin.

'Mind your elbow.'

'I'm trying.'

'Try harder.'

Swindon. That's where we were headed now. Swindon. Seventeen industrial estates and a Little Chef. Any further and we'd be back on the M25.

'Christ.'

'What?'

'Christ,' I said, 'is this your idea of running away? Is this your idea of disappearing?'

She looked at me. Her eyes held no intelligence at all.

'I'm sorry,' I said.

'It's all right.'

'Look, Zoe, I'm sorry. Let's drive on, there's a junction up ahead.'

I got us onto the A4 towards Chippenham and this, soon enough, took us past a service station. Zoe pulled in at last.

It was cold, waiting there while Zoe filled the tank, and to make things worse she'd left her door open. I undid my safety belt and leant across to close it. Behind me, I heard her wrestling the cap back on. I clambered back in my seat and looked out the side window. She was already heading across the forecourt. I wished she'd limp, even a little bit. I unwound my window and yelled across, 'Camel Lights!' – but she didn't respond.

Though we'd stopped driving the smell, which was never more than a troubling hint, still hadn't gone away. Maybe it was something electrical.

Burned oil.

Something electrical, maybe.

Burned oil.

I knew what it was. I knew what was coming. Wrapped up so neatly there, under her bed: I knew. Leaving it there, pretending not to know, I had practically pulled the trigger myself.

I opened the glove compartment. The handgun – Zhenshu's lovingly oiled wartime souvenir – was the only thing in there.

I pondered it a while. I didn't touch it. I glanced out at the garage. There was a queue inside, waiting to be served. Zoe was at the back of it.

I shut the glove compartment.

A minute or so passed, and the queue hadn't moved.

I got the gun out of the glove compartment but I didn't know how to open the chamber. I was frightened to fiddle with it too much. I might blow my kneecap off. I put it back.

How many shots had she fired?

I thought about Eva, and her smile, and the way after a day's work at the café her hands smelled of honey.

I looked out the window. Zoe had been served. She was walking across the forecourt towards me.

I wrestled across to the driver's seat. I fumbled for the ignition. I couldn't find the key. It occurred to me maybe Zoe had needed it to open the petrol cap.

I looked out the window again. Zoe passed under the lights of the first row of petrol pumps. I could see her face. She was watching me. I think she realised. Anyway, she walked faster.

Maybe the key was in the cap, still. Maybe I had time to get to it before she got to the car. I unclipped the door and rolled out, bumping hard into the steering column, and something rattled.

I recognised the sound. It was a key. It was the key rattling. *The key was still in the ignition.* Then I remembered: Zoe, on a previous occasion, opening the petrol cap with the lever by her seat.

I glanced out the window.

Zoe was running towards the car. I hunted frantically for the key. It was further forward than I'd expected; you had to reach right around the steering wheel for it. I ground the key round and dropped the handbrake and floored the gas. I went nowhere. I was still in neutral.

She shouted my name. I heard it, over the sound of the engine's dying whine. *'Damn!'* That's what it sounded like.

I leant across the cabin and locked the passenger door. She tugged the handle. I slipped the stick into first and floored the gas pedal. Zoe still had hold of the door. The rear wheels span, fighting for traction on the oil-slick surface of the forecourt. The tyres engaged and the car bucked and slewed across the tarmac. Zoe screamed. I glanced in the rear-view but it was set for someone Zoe's height – I couldn't see a thing.

I swallowed, and I braked. I leant forward and back,

hunting for Zoe in my side-mirrors. She was sitting on the forecourt. In the fluorescent light, her face was unreadable – a white mask. Men were running out the garage towards her. I hit the accelerator, more gently this time, and I didn't even bother to look as I pulled out onto the road. Eight seconds later, rounding a shallow bend, I glanced at the controls, and watched mesmerised as the needle passed seventy.

41

I was all at sea after that. One of the sad things about drink is it makes you think you're some kind of free spirit, totally unpredictable, a romantic loner – but the truth is everything you do is mechanical and obvious and everyone else can see it coming a mile off. Every drunk in the county probably ended up on this stretch of tarmac sooner or later. If the police patrol hadn't found me, it would have been only a matter of minutes before the next loser happened by.

The trick in these circumstances is to not slow down. If you slow down they know you're shitting yourself. I got that from a Hunter Thompson book. I wasn't much more than ten over the limit and I stuck to it religiously, forcing myself not to look back more than normal. There were traffic lights up ahead, which gave me a great opportunity to demonstrate my smooth braking technique, and at the roundabout, about a quarter-mile further on, I even remembered to signal. Which is when they decided to turn their lights on.

I pulled to the kerb. It was hours since my last drink and I was still as pissed as hell. I hadn't run over any small children – leastwise none that I'd noticed – so provided I didn't try anything stupid, there was no reason they need know anything about the handgun in the glove compartment. That could wait for the men who came in the morning to tow the car away.

I engaged the hand brake, undid my safety belt and got out of the car.

The police had disappeared. Where were they hiding? I stood there a while, trying to work it out, and bright blue light flickered and faded in the foliage of distant trees.

It was after five now and I didn't know where the hell I was. Which didn't matter much because – it was time I faced it – I didn't have anywhere to go. In my current state it seemed the safest thing just to get off the road as quickly as possible and stay there till first light. I took the quietest roads I could find, expecting that I would have to kip in a farmyard or someone's driveway. But someone threw me some luck finally and after about twenty minutes I found myself in the New Forest.

There was even a camping sign at the entrance to the car park, which was gilding the lily as far as I was concerned because all I needed was darkness and a radio.

If there were campers here, they were hidden among the trees. Occasionally a car approached, flooding the branches with light as cold and inimical as mercury; but they hardly even slowed down as they took the bend south and away.

I was alone.

I turned on the radio and fell asleep to the breakfast news.

The Americans had bombed a pharmaceuticals factory in Libya. Geri had left The Spice Girls.

Nobody mentioned Zoe.

I woke, about a couple of hours later, to the sound of Frank Dobson and the sight of my own breath. I turned off the radio. It was light out: a grey, felty, February morning. I was so cold I could barely turn the key in the ignition. I ran the engine a while to warm myself up, and then, because I had nothing better to do, I got out and took a look in the boot.

Loh wasn't small for a Chinese: I was surprised Zoe had got the lid down over him. As it was his face carried the impress of the lid. He looked a lot different without his spectacles, never mind the mess she had made of his neck.

It must have been messy. No wonder she had changed her clothes.

I wondered what to do with him, and when nothing sprang to mind I shut the boot again.

I got back in the car and ran the engine a second time but there was a chill in me now no amount of petrol would thaw away.

I wondered where Eva and Justin were. Were they landing already? No, they'd still be in the air. What would happen to them in Tokyo, when they landed without the device?

Then I remembered. I reached behind me, and felt behind my seat. There, under the crook-lock; there it was. I placed it on my lap. I looked at it.

Zhenshu's toy.

For those who cannot feel – feeling. For those who can already feel – what?

A growing bluntness to things. A creeping blindness, of the sort that comes from staring too long at the sun. The little death that comes from tastes too tart, sounds too high and pure and loud, sights too vivid; tremors in the skin.

I rubbed my thumb across the weal where I'd cut my hand, nearly a year before. I could not feel it any more: that piece of silver like the moon, buried in my flesh: it was gone.

I too had my scars. I too could not feel them.

Where is the point of equilibrium, between drunkenness and hangover, between passion and contempt, between brightening the light to see, and brightening it to blind? I didn't know. Nabeshima didn't know. And however careful they were, the bottom line was they wanted to use Justin to find out.

Loh had been right, of course. It wasn't my fight any more.

But if I really believed that, then I might as well have climbed in the boot with him.

The box shattered easily. The aged bakelite, long past its best, practically exploded on the first touch of the tyre. I ran the back wheel over Zhenshu's invention maybe twenty times more, but some of the more durable-looking metal components still retained their shape. An MX5 is just not that heavy, even with a dead solicitor in the boot. So I smashed the bigger pieces up a little with the crook-lock and then I ran over them some more.

By the time I finished the box looked like it had melted into the tarmac. You couldn't have prised a crumb of it up with a key. I tried. I made sure.

42

Sometimes you lose the thread of your life so totally, all you can do is shrug and laugh.

I shrugged.

Brockenhurst was the first town I came to. It was about nine in the morning, nothing was open, and I was still drunk. But I had my bearings now, at least. On the A337 towards Lyndhurst there was a petrol station open, and I managed to buy a pint of milk and a Scotch egg. The milk settled my stomach. The egg smelled and tasted so bad it made me think, maybe my mission of self-destruction had simply shifted up a gear.

But then, as I reached the outskirts of Portsmouth, the aliens woke. They stretched, and yawned, and scented sea air. Lazily they reached out with their old, tender talons, and started to pull on my guts like bell ropes, and my brain, salt-shrivelled, air-hardened, began swinging and clanging, swinging and clanging, swinging and clanging, like the clapper of a great bony bell.

BRINGING NEWS
FROM OUR WORLDS
TO YOURS . . .

Want your news daily?

The Gollancz blog has instant updates
on the hottest SF and Fantasy books.

Prefer your updates monthly?

Sign up for our
in-depth newsletter.

www.gollancz.co.uk

Follow us  @gollancz
Find us ￼ facebook.com/GollanczPublishing

Classic SF as you've never read it before.
Visit the SF Gateway to find out more!
www.sfgateway.com